A RUSE REVEALED

Those lips!

Marquand covered the distance between them in a few quick strides. As his hand closed around the slender arm and his head bent closer to the dazed face, it occurred to him that if he was wrong, what he was about to do was quite likely illegal as well as insane.

It took only an instant to know he was not about to be committed to Newgate—or Bedlam. The lips parting under his were most definitely not those of a lad, nor did the rounded swell of curves pressing up against his chest resemble any part of the male anatomy. The mere touch of them against his own taut form drove him to deepen his kiss, his tongue stealing inside her mouth to taste the faint tang of salt air and an indescribable sweetness. For one long moment, she seemed unsure of how to react, but then her mouth softened in response to his embrace, a bit hesitantly but with an undercurrent of the same hot passion he felt flaring up inside him. . . .

A
Diamond
in the
Rough

Andrea Pickens

A SIGNET BOOK

SIGNET
Published by New American Library, a division of
Penguin Putnam Inc., 375 Hudson Street,
New York, New York 10014, U.S.A.
Penguin Books Ltd, 27 Wrights Lane,
London W8 5TZ, England
Penguin Books Australia Ltd, Ringwood,
Victoria, Australia
Penguin Books Canada Ltd, 10 Alcorn Avenue,
Toronto, Ontario, Canada M4V 3B2
Penguin Books (N.Z.) Ltd, 182–190 Wairau Road,
Auckland 10, New Zealand

Penguin Books Ltd, Registered Offices:
Harmondsworth, Middlesex, England

First published by Signet, an imprint of New American Library,
a division of Penguin Putnam Inc.

First Printing, June 2001
10 9 8 7 6 5 4 3 2 1

Printed in the United States of America

PUBLISHER'S NOTE
This is a work of fiction. Names, characters, places, and incidents either are
the product of the author's imagination or are used fictitiously, and any
resemblance to actual persons, living or dead, business establishments, events,
or locales is entirely coincidental.

BOOKS ARE AVAILABLE AT QUANTITY DISCOUNTS WHEN USED TO PROMOTE
PRODUCTS OR SERVICES. FOR INFORMATION PLEASE WRITE TO PREMIUM
MARKETING DIVISION, PENGUIN PUTNAM INC., 375 HUDSON STREET, NEW YORK,
NEW YORK 10014.

Chapter One

Torchlight glimmered off the artfully arranged wheaten curls, setting them alight with the glow of burnished gold.

"You look a veritable treasure, my dear," murmured a deep baritone voice.

A whisper of evening breeze had disturbed one of them just enough so that it fell across the young lady's alabaster cheek. Before she could reach up to brush it back in place, a gloved hand stayed her slender fingers.

"No, leave it," continued the gentleman close by her side. "Have you any idea how many hours one of the Tulips of the Ton would spend before the mirror, trying to achieve such casual perfection?"

She permitted herself a ghost of a smile. "Indeed, sir, I am not sure whether I have just been complimented or castigated. I should hope I am not as vain or shallow as one of those insufferable gentlemen who sport canary yellow waistcoats and insist on spouting that awful Lord Byron's poetry in a lady's ear."

Her companion gave a dry chuckle. "I am greatly relieved to hear that you have not succumbed to the fellow's idiotic notions of romance and that I shall not be expected to memorize such drivel in order to win your regard."

"I should hope I have more sense than that."

"Much, much more. And as to the nature of my comment . . ." His words trailed off as his hand touched lightly at the small of her back to guide her around a jutting branch heavy with tuber roses. The music drifting from the open French doors grew fainter with each step along the graveled path and after one more turn he drew them to a stop beside a large fountain decorated with two marble nymphs astride a dolphin. For a moment his attention remained riveted on the polished sculpture. "All wrong," he muttered to himself. "The style is much too formal, the scale too big—"

"What was that, my lord?"

"Er, nothing." The gentleman wrenched his eyes back to the perfectly proportioned porcelain beauty at his side and cleared his throat. "Er, as I was saying, I would hope you know exactly which sentiment I intended," he continued, his voice taking on a husky intensity.

The lady blushed very prettily.

"I would also hope that you will begin to call me Adrian rather than sir, my dear, given the reason I have asked you to accompany me on this stroll in the garden."

The tinge of color on her cheeks deepened to a most becoming shade of rose.

Adrian Linsley, Viscount Marquand, watched her head turn slightly and her long lashes drop in demure response to his words, a flutter or two betraying just the barest hint of maidenly nerves. A faint smile played on his lips. It was exactly the sort of reaction to be expected from a properly schooled young lady and he was gratified that he had not been mistaken in his choice. "Honoria, I have already spoken to your father and received his permission to pay my addresses to you."

"Yes, he told me." Lady Honoria Dunster's reply was hardly more than a whisper.

"I trust that such a proposal meets with your approval as well?"

"You do me a great honor, sir—Adrian, that is. To be singled out as the future Countess of Chittenden is beyond all expectation." She drew a deep breath. "Father is delighted, of course."

The corners of Marquand's lips twitched upward. "Is that a yes?"

There was enough of a hesitation to cause the trace of humor to disappear from his countenance and the chiseled mouth to draw into a tight line. "You must forgive me if such a declaration is unwelcome to you. I had thought—"

"No!" Her head jerked up, though her eyes did not quite make contact with his. "Th—that is, I do not . . . I mean, I only wish to assure myself that you . . ." Her words trailed off in a whisper of confusion.

The Viscount's face remained impassive. "Assure yourself that I am not prone to drinking myself into a stupor each night? Or likely to squander your dowry in one night of deep play? Or flaunt one scandalous affair after another before the entire *ton*?"

Her face was now scarlet. "Oh, sir—A—Adrian—"

"No, no, you are quite right to ask. Given my family's rackety reputation, you have every reason to be concerned. But as I have told your father, I am of quite a different breed from my parents. You need not fear any excess of emotions from me. I will be nothing but an exemplary husband."

"I did not doubt it." A flicker of embarrassment and perhaps some deeper emotion lit in Lady Dunster's sapphire eyes as they finally locked with his gaze, but it was gone in an instant, replaced by their usual cool hue. "I—I just wanted to hear from your own lips an assurance that our marriage will be all it should be."

"Well, you have it. A paragon of perfection deserves no less." He raised her hand and those same lips grazed over the delicate kidskin covering her wrist. "So will you be my wife, Honoria?"

"Y—yes. Of course."

Marquand felt a frisson of . . . satisfaction. As he drew his betrothed a fraction closer, it occurred to him that perhaps he should feel more than just that, but he quickly pushed such silly thoughts away. No, this was exactly the sort of match he wanted, one that was based on a rational approach to the matter rather than raw need. And Honoria was exactly the sort of lady who suited his plans—one whose cool composure and polished behavior were as flawless as her striking looks. One whose good breeding and strict adherence to every pro-

priety made it unthinkable that even the slightest whisper
of gossip would ever sully her name.

Passion between two people be damned.

He'd seen quite enough of what havoc raw emotion
could wreak between two people. No, he had room for
only one passion in his life and it most certainly did not
have anything to do with a wife.

The kiss was over in a matter of seconds. Her mouth
remained firm, unyielding to the pressure of his embrace.
The rigid set of her shoulders had not relaxed enough
to allow his body to touch hers. He straightened, a faint
smile returning to his face. Though several years past her
comeout from the schoolroom, Miss Dunster was obviously still untutored in any sort of intimacies with a gentleman. Her stilted reaction was perfectly correct. After
all, what more could be expected from a gently bred
young lady who had never experienced any physical contact with a member of the opposite sex other than the
occasional waltz?

A voice in the back of his head answered back that it
might be nice if, in time, she might learn to unbend
enough to make the begetting of an heir a more pleasur-
able chore than the other duties required of him. But he
drowned out such mutinous whispers with a firm voice.

"I feel very fortunate, my dear."

And it was not a lie. He was happy that his chosen
bride showed no inclination to the sort of girlish romantic
notions that made a young lady imagine that burning
love was a requisite basis for marriage. In truth, she
seemed to prefer rational discourse over flowery sentiment, which suited him just as well—her cool demeanor
only mirrored his own carefully controlled emotions.
And that was merely a part of her attraction. Her intellect was sharp enough not to bore him, her poise was all
that one could wish for in a future Countess, and her
beauty had made him the envy of half the young bucks
about Town. What more could he want?

"I . . . I shall do my best to please you, Adrian."

"You need not worry on that. We are an excellent
match."

She essayed an answering smile, lowering her lashes so that the flicker of unhappiness was well hidden. "Yes, so we are."

He tucked her hand back under his arm and started to retrace their steps. "Let us return to the ballroom lest our prolonged absence set the tabbies to wagging their tongues, despite the forthcoming announcement. Besides, I believe a glass of champagne is in order for us both so that we may raise a toast to our future happiness. For we will both be very happy, I promise you that."

One of the gentleman's unsteady hands raised a glass of brandy to lips slack with shock while the other sought to wipe away the beads of sweat forming on his pale forehead. "The devil take it, Hertford! I was sure I had you this time," croaked the Earl of Chittenden before taking a hurried gulp. His eyes couldn't help but dart back down to the cards fanned across the green baize. "How is it you have managed to seduce even so fickle a tart as Lady Luck herself tonight?"

With a toss of her raven tresses, the buxom lady across the table gave a trill of laughter and draped herself suggestively over the other gentleman's shoulder. "Because his lordship is so very irresistible," she answered in a throaty murmur. A slender finger drew along the line of his jaw, turning his head ever so slightly so she could nuzzle at his ear. "And so very, very good at what he does."

His hand sought to unglue her curves from the front of his elegant jacket of black superfine, lingering for a moment on the swell of one nearly bare breast before traveling down to deposit several gold guineas in the *décolleté* of her gown. "Later, *ma cherie*," he growled, without so much as a glance at her pouting face. "Now, go fetch another bottle for the earl."

"No!" It was more of a cry than a statement. "I'm done for it."

Hertford's ice blue eyes narrowed for an instant before lightening in a show of contrived comraderie "Oh come now, Chit, show a little more bottom than a schoolroom miss. Let's have one more hand."

The earl wet his lips with what was left of the amber spirits. "You've won all I have to wager," he said in a hoarse whisper, as he stared at the pile of scribbled vowels lying in front of the other man.

"Not all," replied Hertford after a moment. A ghost of a smile played at the corners of his mouth. "There is still Woolsey Hall, is there not?"

"I . . . I cannot!" Chittenden tugged at the already disheveled cravat around his neck as if it were tight as a hangman's noose. "Promised 'im wouldn't ever risk that," he mumbled.

Hertford said nothing but waited for his companion to return with the brandy. He splashed a goodly amount in the other man's glass, then refilled his own. "You know as well as I that Lady Luck is notoriously fickle," he said smoothly. "It wouldn't surprise me in the least if she soon chooses you to cozen up to."

Hope swam to the surface of Chittenden's watery eyes. "Yer right, it's about bloody time the bitch embraced me for a change."

Hertford shuffled the deck.

"But I cannot," continued the Earl, trying to remain deaf to the siren song of the crackling cards. "I cannot, I cannot . . ." He repeated the words with increasing desperation as desire struggled against what little common sense had not been drowned by the amber spirits. The glass came once again to his lips and returned to the table empty.

Without a word, Hertford filled it near to the brim. After adding a bit to his own drink, he looked up. "What say you to the chance to win everything back in one fell swoop?"

Chittenden's jaw went slack. "How?"

"Woolsey Hall against everything else." He gestured at the mound of crumpled paper before him. "The lands in Northumbria, the matched team of bays, the yacht, the . . ."

"Stop," groaned the Earl. "All of that? Hell's teeth,

have I really lost all of that tonight?" His palms came up to press at his temples. "May Lucifer be buggered! He'll have my guts for garters."

"Really?" murmured Hertford with a show of sympathy. "Wouldn't have thought a fine fellow like yourself would allow himself to be harried by his family." He paused to toy with the gold stud at his starched cuff. "After all, it's yours to do with as you see fit. You *are* the Earl." Another pause. "And as every real gamester knows, Lady Luck always returns to toss up her skirts and give you a ride."

Chittenden's jaw jutted out. "S'right." He stared longingly at the lithe fingers tapping the cards into a neat stack. "I . . ."

The rest of the words seemed to stick in his throat as a cry of dismay pierced the smoky air. A gentleman at one of the other tables buried his head in his arms as the small crowd gathered around gasped at the pile of papers changing hands. Glasses clinked, punctuating the rattle of dice over scarred pine. Someone staggered into the shadows and retched. From the recesses of another corner came the sounds of muffled laughter and a female squeak. Guttering candles, dripping with the rancid smell of cheap tallow, cast vague shadows on the crumpled clothing and drunken thrustings. A low moan spewed forth.

The Earl covered his face with his hands as if the gesture itself could afford some measure of defense against the rampant temptation. "I cannot!" he said again, this time with a bit more conviction. "Not on the turn of a card."

Hertford's lips tightened at the unexpected resistance to his plan. He took a moment to think, then the blue of his eyes took on an even icier coldness. "Yes, perhaps you are right not to trust to chance," he said slowly, knocking the deck askew with a nonchalant flick of his fingers. "A shame. It seems I am to go home with a goodly amount of your worldly possessions in my pocket."

The Earl stifled a groan.

"That is, unless you might care to engage in a game of skill rather than luck, in order to win it all back?"

Chittenden raised the brandy once again to his trembling lips. "W—w—what do you mean? I am no match for a younger man such as you . . ."

"No, but your son would be."

The Earl's hand shook as he swallowed the entire contents of his glass. A murmur ran through the cluster of figures gathered behind Hertford's chair. Word of an interesting wager quickly spread, like blood from a fresh wound, and a number of scavengers hurried over, scenting a kill.

"S'true," slurred a voice. "Yer always bragging 'bout how yer only spawn's a bloody Corinthian."

"A fair bet!" encouraged someone else.

"Woolsey Hall against everything else," repeated Hertford. "I'm merely trying to be gentlemanly and offer you a fair chance to recoup your considerable losses, but if you'd rather not . . ." He shrugged and reached for the pile of vowels.

"Wait!"

Hertford's hand hovered in midair.

"W—what do you have in mind?"

"Oh, a match of sporting skills."

The Earl bit his lip.

"What are you hesitating for, Chittenden?" cajoled a drunken gentleman at his elbow. "The Viscount's the best damn shot at Manton's, drives like a banshee, and ain't been downed yet at Gentleman Jackson's. You've windmills in yer head if ye don't have the bollocks to accept."

A number of voices seconded the sentiment, and a few jeers from the crowd questioned his manhood along with his nerve if he backed away from such a generous offer.

The sweat on the Earl's forehead was now trickling down to his twisted collar. More seconds passed, and with mutterings of disgust, several figures drifted away in search of better entertainment. Hertford let out a sigh and made to rake in his winnings.

"Done!" croaked Chittenden.

The other man's mouth quirked up ever so slightly. "Ah, it appears we have a wager, gentlemen," he announced to the remaining crowd. "The Earl of Chittenden pledges Woolsey Hall against my winnings here"— he gestured at the stack of promissory notes—"in a match of sporting skills between myself and his son, Viscount Marquand. Agreed?"

The Earl's head jerked in assent. After a moment he managed a hoarse whisper. "Shooting? Handling the ribbons? Riding? Boxing? What sort of match do you have in mind?"

Hertford's smile became more pronounced. "Oh, nothing so banal as those common pursuits," he answered. Reaching out for the bottle, he poured another stiff drink for the other man and clinked glasses. "No, my dear Chittenden, in order to decide the fate of Woolsey Hall, the Viscount and I are not going to culp wafers, race curricles, take fences, or trade left jabs. We are going to play a round of golf."

Another two glasses came together, these with the clear ring of crystal rather than the dull chink of ordinary stuff.

"So, she has accepted your suit." Anthony Ellington regarded his friend from over the rim of his champagne flute. There was a hint of hesitation before he forced a smile to his lips. "I wish you happy." His tone, however, lacked any of the effervescence of the wine he brought to his lips. "You must be in alt."

"What man wouldn't be, on becoming engaged to the Season's Incomparable?" Marquand drank as well, then set his glass down and stretched his long legs out toward the roaring fire. The chiseled features, smooth and pale as marble, gave little hint of any emotion, joy or otherwise, as he contemplated the dancing flames. His eyes, a gray-green akin to the sea in winter, were equally unfathomable, though the look of keen intelligence lurking in their depths could not be completely drowned by the show of studied aloofness.

Ellington squirmed in the face of such sangfroid. "Of

course, of course," he muttered. "Once again, my best wishes."

A faint smile finally cracked through. "Go ahead and spit it out, Tony. Much as it is amusing to see you wiggling around like a trout with a hook in its mouth, I'd rather cut line and have you say what you really mean. We have known each other far too long for you to keep your true thoughts submerged."

Ellington's mouth opened and closed several times, looking for the moment exactly like a fish out of water—and every bit as uncomfortable. "I, er, that is . . ."

"Spit it out, man."

"It's no joking matter—this is deucedly hard," he grumbled. "I *do* wish you happy, Adrian . . ."

"Yes?"

"It's just that . . . I fear you won't be."

One of Marquand's dark brows rose in question.

"Miss Dunster is beautiful, charming, accomplished in all things a proper young lady should be and, well, altogether perfect."

The brow rose a fraction higher.

"That's the damn trouble, Adrian! There's not a hair out of place, if you take my meaning. Everything about her is buttoned up and stitched down tight—I fear there is not a loose thread among all the finery."

Marquand's mouth tightened ever so slightly. "I've had quite enough of loose threads—and loose screws—in my life. Believe me, I shall welcome the sort of order and predictability you allude to. Furthermore, it shall be a pleasure to become part of a family that is a pattern card of propriety."

"Hylton is a pompous ass! If he is a stickler for propriety, it is not out of principle but because he lacks the imagination to act in any other way."

"Trust me, Tony, the last thing I desire in my future family is imagination or uniqueness."

His friend muttered something unintelligible under his breath. He, too, gazed moodily into the flames for a bit before tossing back the contents of his glass. "I know how difficult it has been for you over the years. Your father and mother possess a certain, er, exuberant charm, but—"

"Charm is not exactly the adjective that comes to mind," said Marquand, with some bitterness. "Oh, of course they could be charming. And witty. And gay. But as a child I did not find it charming in the least when my parents would fly into one of their raging fits of temper, hurling the Staffordshire figurines at each other—or at me. Nor was it charming when the fires could not be lit and every bloody room was as cold as a witch's tit because Father had gambled away all his ready blunt." He ran his hand through his thick dark locks in the first overt show of emotion. "I was no doubt one of the few boys who found life at Eton a respite from home. Whatever the hardships and rigors, at least one knew what to expect there."

"I know," said Ellington softly. "I haven't forgotten the time you returned for Michaelmas term with your arm in a sling and a bad cut on your brow. It is a wonder you ever bothered to go back to the Hall after that."

"I didn't hate him, you know. I knew he didn't mean it. The drinking actually stopped for quite some time after that unfortunate accident." The Viscount shrugged, as if the memory did not cause his insides to constrict in a tight knot. "Besides, my parents might have destroyed each other, but they didn't destroy my love for Woolsey Hall. I love every stone and bit of mortar, every creak in its floors, every layer of beeswax and lemon oil on the patinaed woodwork, every quirky mark left by generations of Linsleys. And most of all, I love the lands, the undulations of the meadows, the stately trees lining the drive, the woods thick with oak and elm. Long ago, I made a promise to myself that I would restore it to the glory it deserves. I mean to keep that promise."

Ellington blinked at the sudden show of passion in the Viscount's voice. He shifted in his chair and took another sip of his champagne. "Do you love Miss Dunster as well?" he asked abruptly.

The Viscount's face became stony again. "What has that to do with it?"

"Quite a bit, I should think. If you wish to avoid the pyrotechnics of your father and mother's match, perhaps it would do well to choose someone for whom you can have a real regard. Not to speak of someone who might share your same . . . interests."

There was a short, mirthless laugh. "Good Lord, don't tell me you are turning into a blathering romantic! One would almost think you've been stealing a peek at those ridiculous offerings your sister buys from Minerva Press."

Ellington flushed slightly, but refused to be lured into a discussion of a different sort. "You haven't answered my question, Adrian."

Marquand was silent long enough that his friend thought he didn't mean to give a reply. Indeed, the Viscount settled deeper into the leather wing chair and appeared to forget the other man's very existence, so engrossed was he in watching the myriad of tiny bubbles burst in a series of tiny explosions on the surface of his drink. Finally he set the glass aside without a taste. "We both know that marriage is a practical alliance, one that can work quite well if the parties involved act with discretion and abide by the rules. Miss Dunster and I shall each get what we desire. She shall be a countess, gaining one of the oldest and most respected titles in the land, while I shall have a polished wife of impeccable breeding and flawless manners, one who will never give cause for any scandal to attach itself to the Linsley name." He drew in a deep breath. "Indeed, we are both agreed. We are an ideal match."

"How admirable, Adrian." A tinge of sarcasm colored his friend's words. "I can see you have given perhaps the most important decision in your life the sort of rational, dispassionate consideration it deserves." There was a brief pause as he reached for the bottle to refill his glass. "Remind me to take you with me next time I need to choose a new style of coat at Weston's or purchase a hunter at Tattersall's."

A slight tightening of the jaw was the only reaction from Marquand.

"Sorry," mumbled Ellington after a moment. "That was uncalled for. It's just that, as you said, we have been in each other's pocket since we were in leading strings. So although you choose to appear as cool and immovable as one of those Greek statues you place in your designs, I know that beneath the façade you present to the rest of the world beats a real heart, one that feels flesh and blood emotion. One has only to look at your . . . work to see that." He cleared his throat. "Hell's teeth, Adrian, you deserve more than a block of stone for a wife, no matter how flawless the exterior appears. I cannot believe you will be happy with such a spiritless match."

"Flesh and blood emotion?" A mocking smile twisted Marquand's lips. "Oh, I have seen just what that can result in. The Linsley coffers are nigh empty, the lands—what are left of them—have been stripped bare, and my estimable parents vie with each other as to who can engage in the most scandalous affairs. You would have me risk my own future on something as ephemeral as love?" If anything, his tone had become even more sardonic. "Believing in love is equally as dangerous as trusting in luck." His voice hardened into a steely growl. "I have seen quite enough to know that both those ladies are nothing but fickle temptresses, waiting to destroy any man who thinks he can win at their game."

"Both entail chance, if that is what you mean, but perhaps you must be willing to hazard some risks in life to reap the rewards."

"That sounds just like one of my father's platitudes! However, when it comes to *my* life, I don't intend to leave *anything* to chance." There was a brief ripple of emotion in the Viscount's eyes before a flat calm returned. "You see, despite all that my father has frittered away, I have made him swear by all that is holy that no matter how pressed, he would never stake Woolsey Hall on the turn of a card or roll of dice." His fingers twisted at the gold signet ring on his pinkie and a smile of grim satisfaction played on his lips. "And such precaution on my part is about to pay off. In spades. Not because of luck, but because of meticulous planning and disciplined perseverance." He paused to take up his glass once again. "Actually, I have another reason to raise a toast. You know that for the past six months I have been working devilishly hard on securing a certain job—well, I've just found out that my proposal has been chosen over all the others."

For the first time that evening, Ellington's eyes lit with real enthusiasm. "By Jove, that's wonderful news! Such an important commission will almost certainly guarantee a successful future in the field. Why, with Devonshire's backing, you may even be able, in due time, to let the truth come out."

"Let us not celebrate too soon—I must still come up with the actual plan," warned Marquand, but he could not hide the note of satisfaction in his voice. "But if all goes as designed, the Hall will soon belong to me outright, for I have a proposal for my father as well. And when it does, I mean for it to have the Countess it deserves." His gaze once again strayed to the crackling fire. "So you see, you have no need to feel concern for my happiness, Tony. Believe me, I have considered everything very carefully and have taken into account all contingencies. I am well satisfied with my plans for the future."

"And your intended? I take it she is aware of what you do and has no objection to it? After all, she will be allying herself with a husband whose activities can hardly be deemed . . . conventional."

For the first time, the Viscount betrayed a crack in his composure. A hint of color rose to his lean cheeks and he shifted uncomfortably in his chair. "Er, well, not yet. I shall, of course, make everything known to her in good time. But I assure you, it will not be an issue. I have taken a good deal of care to protect my true identity and there is no reason to think the *ton* will ever learn the truth unless I choose to reveal it."

"Hmmph." His friend looked at him askance. "Subterfuge and secrets between the two of you? Hardly an auspicious beginning to a lifetime together."

Marquand's color deepened. "I assure you, I am keeping nothing meaningful from Miss Dunster. And as for her"—he paused to give a short laugh—"why, you cannot seriously think that she is harboring any dark secrets."

There was a long pause before Ellington raised his glass in slow salute. "Well then, let us cry friends and say no more on the subject. You know that as your closest friend I only wish the best for you, Adrian, but it seems you have everything worked out, down to the last nail . . ." A sigh, eloquent in its skepticism, sounded, followed by a further mutter. "I just hope it isn't sealing your own coffin." He swirled what remained of his champagne, then downed it in one gulp. "I shall forbear saying that I wish you luck, knowing your sentiments on that subject, and merely repeat that I wish you happy." Under his breath, he couldn't help but add, "However, to achieve that, I fear that you are going to need more of luck's help than you think."

Chapter Two

"**Y**ou *what!*"

"I'll not have it, my own son ringing a peal over my head." The voice was querulous, its tone wound even tighter by the goodly amount of port the Earl had already consumed. He reached for the bottle as he spoke, but the Viscount knocked it from his hand. The glass shattered on hitting the floor, spreading a dark stain the color of newly spilled blood across the unswept wood. Both men watched it begin to seep toward the threadbare Aubusson carpet beneath the desk. "Now look what you've made me do. That piece was bought by your grandfather and now it will be ruined."

"Ruined? You dare talk of Linsley heritage as if it actually meant anything to you?" Marquand knelt down and removed a handkerchief from his pocket. "Shall I remind you that until six months ago this carpet graced the library of Hadley Hall, until you lost that estate to Strickley at the roulette table—or was it faro?" With a ragged sigh he set to blotting up the sticky liquid. "I am heartily sick of always having to clean up after you, Father."

To the Viscount's vague surprise, his father reacted not with the usual, voluble show of indignation at having his judgment questioned, but rather collapsed in a nearby chair, his lower lip trembling.

"I have stood by while the family fortune carefully built up by our forebears has been bled dry by your profligate habits, voicing only the most moderate of suggestions as to how to keep from utter ruin," he continued. "And on more than one occasion it has been the savings from my own prudent investments that have bailed you out of the River Tick, at no small cost to several . . . projects that meant a great deal to me.''

The Earl of Chittenden hung his head.

"In return, you made me a solemn promise.'' Marquand's voice couldn't help but rise several notches. "You *promised* never to wager the Hall on your cursed games, Father. That you chose to throw away your money and the rest of your considerable lands was not something I begrudged, as long as you left Woolsey Hall untouched. But now that you have broken that pledge and lost it all on the turn of a card—''

"But I didn't,'' whispered the Earl.

The Viscount's lips compressed in some contempt. "Ah, forgive me—was it the rattle of the dice instead?'' he said with cutting sarcasm. "You may find such nuances of some importance, but I do not—''

"Not dice either, Adrian, I . . . didn't break my promise. Not exactly.''

"I tell you, I care as little for your play with semantics as for your other games, Father. The cold fact is that Woolsey Hall is lost—''

"But it isn't! N—not yet.''

His son turned to stare at him. "What is that supposed to mean? You just were telling me how you wagered it to the Marquess of Hertford in some desperate attempt to recoup yet another round of losses.''

The Earl brought his hand to his brow. "I did, but it is not what you think. The Hall is not yet lost, it is pledged, not on a game of chance, but rather one of . . . skill.''

Marquand's eyes pressed close. "Good Lord. And what skills do you imagine you possess, other than becoming foxed in the blink of an eye or frittering away a fortune?''

"N—none.''

The answer was barely audible and the Viscount couldn't help but catch the welling of tears in his father's eyes before the Earl bent to take his head between his hands. For some reason, it shook him more than he cared to admit.

"God knows, I have been a sad failure as the head of this family, and an even worse hand at being a parent." The Earl's frail fingers raked through his graying hair. "The only thing of any real value I have done is to . . . produce you. But even for that I fear I deserve little credit, for you quite obviously did not inherit your good sense or excellent character from me."

Marquand found his anger slowly evaporating, just like the spill on the floor. Instead, his father's poignant revelations filled him with an aching sadness.

"I can hardly blame you for holding me in disgust," he went on in a shaky voice. "I've given you precious little reason to think otherwise. If you want to know the truth, I think even worse of myself than you do." He looked up, remorse etched on his still handsome features. "I've tried. God help me, I've tried to act with some restraint. I don't know why I am just not capable of behaving in a rational manner. But there it is. This time, perhaps it would be best to let me suffer the consequences of my own foolish actions. Surely I cannot be much more of a disgrace to you than I already am, no matter what the tattlemongers choose to say about me refusing to honor a bet."

The Viscount gave a harried sigh and began to pace before the meager fire. "I've managed to pull you out of the suds before, so I imagine I will be able to figure out something this time around as well." His mouth quirked upward in spite of the situation. "Indeed, there is another rather important reason I would prefer to avoid any egregious scandal at the moment. You see, I have just become betrothed and would rather not give my intended's father reason to cry off. He was skeptical enough of the connection without creating further cause for concern."

His father essayed a real smile through his guilt. "Why, I wish you happy, son. And hope that you don't make as much a hash of it as I have done. But you won't. Too much common sense in that bonebox of yours. May I ask who the lucky lady is?"

"Lady Honoria Dunster."

"Hylton's chit? A Diamond of the First Water," he said with frank approval. "Real diamonds are rare in our little world of paste and false sparkle. And all the more precious for it. No doubt she brings a plump dowry as well, though it seems to me the lady is making quite the better of the match." He cleared his throat. "Er, have you set a date?"

"Not as yet, but it is my understanding that the family wishes to wait at least until the Little Season."

The Earl looked vastly relieved. "So, ah, there is no reason why you cannot . . . travel in the next few months?"

The smile, however faint, disappeared from Marquand's face. "And why would I want to do that?"

"Well, you see, there is the matter of the, er, test of skill with Hertford. As luck would have it, it is to take place in Scotland—"

"Scotland?"

"Er, yes." Out of habit, Chittenden reached for the bottle that was no longer there, then a sheepish expression stole over his features as his hand fell back to his side. "And it's—well, it's rather important that you be there."

Marquand felt a stirring of unease. "I think you had best explain just exactly what it is you have wagered, Father."

There were several moments of silence as the Earl tugged at a corner of his waistcoat. "No doubt I was a greater idiot than usual to sit down at the gaming table with the damn fellow, who never seems to have a run of bad luck—"

"Ha! Luck indeed! An experienced gamester such as yourself should know enough to suspect such it is more than luck."

The Earl paled. "You think he . . . cheats?"

"I have no proof of it, but I have heard enough about his so-called luck that I should never be tempted to engage in any sort of dealing with the fellow."

There was a moment of awkward silence as Chittenden shifted in his chair. "Well, as to that . . ."

"Indeed, whatever possessed you to think you might best him in a physical challenge?" continued his son. "You must have been more thoroughly jug-bitten than usual to have had such windmills in your head."

"You may be sure that even in my deepest cups, I never imagined that *I* could match him in any test of skill." He swallowed hard several times before going on. "No, I'm afraid that it is *you* that are pledged to meet him in a sporting match."

"Me!"

The Earl winced at the volume of the yelp, than gave a nod.

"You must be a candidate for Bedlam, to think I would ever be a willing participant in any of your wagers!" Marquand began to pace the floor, restraining the urge to kick each piece of furniture that he passed. After a moment, his brows furrowed in consternation as he considered his father's words. "And even if I was, I cannot quite understand why Hertford would offer such a challenge. As you say, he rarely engages in any endeavor where the odds are not stacked in his favor." He drew a deep breath and went on in a low voice, as if to himself, "It doesn't make sense. Surely he must be aware that I am accorded to be more than adequate with a pistol or the ribbons or my fives."

He paused by the mantel and picked up a small miniature framed in silver. Staring at the earnest young face depicted there, it struck him that even as a child he had felt the weight of the world on his small shoulders. The only times he had felt truly carefree as a boy was romping through the stately rooms of the Hall, or running through its magnificent grounds. Aside from the solitary dreams that had flowered there, he had, for the most part, had precious little to smile about.

Well, it was certainly not going to begin now, he thought with some resignation. Though resentment and anger still welled within his breast, it was tempered by a grudging forgiveness for the past. On catching a glimpse of what lay behind the excesses and the bravado, it seemed as if the old man had suffered nearly as much from all the pain he had inflicted on the rest of his family. It was impossible to feel hate, only a pinch of sadness at a life that must, at bottom, be as empty as the glass that stood by the trembling fingers.

The Earl's gaze was focused on the small painting as well. "You were always the strong one, Adrian, even as a lad," he whispered, a tentative smile ghosting over his lips. "I have always been so proud of you, though I could rarely express it." He bowed his head. "I'm . . . sorry. I had no right to entangle you in a snare of my own making. Perhaps I can convince Hertford to reconsider and accept another hand of cards. This time, I swear I shall come to table sober and be on guard for any—"

"No!"

Chittenden fell silent.

"If Woolsey Hall is at stake, I prefer to trust to my own skills to wrest it free from Hertford's grasp. But on one condition, Father."

"Only name it."

"If I win, you will sell the Hall to me."

"Sell!" The Earl made as if to rise from his chair. "Even I am not such a dastard as to make you pay for what will rightfully be yours anyway when I shuffle off this mortal coil. Consider it yours."

Marquand shook his head. "I have no intention of helping you meet your Maker, nor of asking you to give up such an asset as Woolsey Hall without recompense. I would be as guilty of manipulation as Hertford for taking it from you in such a manner. So I am making you a business proposition, Father. It is the only way I can, in good conscience, permit it to be done."

The Earl thought for several moments. "Very well, if it must be as you say, I imagine that you need for me to name a price."

Marquand's fingers tightened around the small frame.

"It will, naturally, have to be a goodly sum, considering the value of such a fine estate.

"Naturally."

"I cannot think of where you might get that kind of blunt," persisted his father. "I'm well aware of how paltry an inheritance was left to you by your grandfather." He hesitated for a fraction. "Just as I well know that you have never frequented the gaming establishments or other even less savory hells where money might be made. And however plump in the pocket Hylton is, I doubt his daughter's dowry will cover such a large expense."

A cynical smile played on the Viscount's lips. "Not gaming, no. But I'm afraid I have been engaged in another pursuit that would be considered by many a far worse vice for a gentleman, though I've been quite discreet about it. Suffice it to say that I think I shall manage to meet your terms, so long as they are not unduly high."

The Earl looked as if to say more, then bit off the words and began to drum his fingers on the table. "Well, then if you insist, here is what I propose," he said after a lengthy pause. "If you win at Hertford's game, you will redeem not only Woolsey Hall but all the other vowels in his possession. They are, I regret to say, considerable. And by all rights, they will belong to you for the victory—"

"I don't want them—"

It was Chittenden's turn to interrupt. "I have a modicum of pride too," he said with some emotion. "If you will not accept Woolsey Hall from me outright, than I certainly won't allow you to wipe the slate clean of my debts. And since I will never take a farthing from you to buy your own birthright, we are at a stalemate. Unless you agree to the terms I suggest."

"Which are?"

"You may return my vowels to me in exchange for the Hall."

"An even trade?" Marquand's hand came up to rub at his jaw as he considered his father's suggestion.

"Think of it as the business proposal you wish it to be. You will be paid for your efforts, that's all. It is a reasonable solution."

The Viscount replaced the picture on the mantel and resumed his pacing.

"And fair, more than fair. To me, at least," continued his father. "Perhaps I might find the sense to take better care of my holdings," he added softly. "You would be doing me a great favor, Adrian, though I have little right to expect it. What say you? Do we have a deal?"

Marquand's breath came out in a harried sigh. "I suppose we do."

"Well, at least I feel I have made one good bargain in my life."

"That has yet to be decided," cautioned the Viscount. He made another turn, then stopped to take up the poker and give the dying embers a good jab. "So what is it to be?" he asked dryly. "Sabers at dawn? Pistols at twenty paces? You still have not told me just what I must do to win this damn wager."

"Oh, nothing so dangerous as that," replied the Earl with forced heartiness.

"Well then, what? And why in the name of Hades must I travel to Scotland to do it?"

Chittenden toyed with the loose ends of his cravat. "Well, er, it *is* a tad out of the ordinary . . ."

"Are we to test our prowess on the grouse moor? Stalk roe deer in the Highlands? Race curricles along Hadrian's wall?"

"Actually you are to play a round of golf. At St. Andrews."

"*Golf!* Hell's teeth, I've never played golf!" exclaimed Marquand. "And what the devil is a 'round' of it?"

"Dunno. But it's a game that involves hitting a ball with a stick—how difficult can *that* be?" reasoned his father. "You're a dab hand at cricket. You'll master it in a trice."

Marquand muttered something under his breath.

Chittenden couldn't repress a twitch of his lips. "Did my high stickler of a son just say what I thought he said?"

"Never mind." He had a mind to take a swat at the nearest object with the poker, regardless of whether it was round or not. "When, may I ask, is this event scheduled to take place?"

"In little more than a month's time."

The oath that followed was even more scathing than the first.

"Er, St. Andrews is accorded to be a very civilized sort of town. University and all that, you know."

The Viscount stalked to the sideboard to retrieve his hat and gloves. "Ah, well, then I should have no trouble finding a book on the bloody rules."

"Where are you rushing off to?"

"To check myself into Bedlam. Where no doubt I belong."

"Adrian, if you wish to reconsider—"

"Just a little gallows humor, Father, though it appears I may well be strung up before this is over. Hertford has spent most every summer of his life in Scotland. I imagine he is an expert at whatever this game of golf entails, else he wouldn't have made the wager. Still, it looks as if I shall have to give it a shot, if I am to have any chance of keeping Woolsey Hall." Tucking his walking stick under his arm, Marquand started for the door. "Hell's teeth, the timing could not be worse for certain of my other endeavors." He sighed, "However, there is nothing to be done for it now. I suppose I had better consider heading north as soon as possible if I am to entertain any hope of success. You had best wish me . . . well."

He chose to avoid the world "luck," as he felt even less in charity with the word at that moment.

"Golf!"

Marquand nodded glumly. "My sentiments exactly." He picked up a heavy, stitched leather cricket ball from his friend's desk and hefted it from palm to palm. "How difficult can *that* be?" he repeated, mimicking his father's throaty tones with some asperity. "Easy for the old fellow to say." He tossed the ball high into the air, casually catching it with one hand as it came down. "Any idea how big a golf ball is?"

"Rather smaller than that."

"Hmmph."

"And stuffed with feathers, I believe."

Another snort sounded, followed by something that sounded suspiciously like a curse. "A sport for the birds," he muttered. "What sort of bat is used?"

"Club," corrected Ellington. "And there are more than one."

Marquand pulled a face. "The devil you say. Why?"

"It depends where the ball is lying."

The Viscount's head jerked around just as the cricket ball began its descent. It caught him a glancing blow on the shoulder, then slipped through his fingers and bounced across the polished parquet. "You're joking. It's not moving? It just sits on the ground?"

"That's right."

"So you can just step up to it and give it a thwack?"

"Something like that."

Marquand stooped to retrieve the errant cricket ball. "How difficult can *that* be?" He resumed his game of catch. "So perhaps there is hope yet. After all, I have a keen eye and a steady hand."

His friend gave a dry chuckle. "Trust me, Adrian, it is not quite so simple as it may sound. There is some technique involved. And strategy."

"Oh come now, Tony, don't wax melodramatic. We are talking of striking a ball, not of Wellington maneuvering his troops on the field of battle."

"We are talking of putting a ball in a hole—a rather small hole—in the face of the same sort of hazards that can flummox the best of generals, such as wind, rain, trees, ditches, and the like. And you must do it with fewer strokes than your opponent." Ellington poured himself a glass of sherry. "Sounds suspiciously like a war to me. After a sip he added, "You know what competition is like. When the stakes are sufficiently high enough, it can turn the playing field into a real battleground."

Marquand pursed his lips and frowned. "It sounds as if you have actually played the game."

"Remember the trip I took with Bowmont last summer to visit his family in Kelso? Well, his father is an avid player. He actually has several holes laid out along an old Roman viaduct that crosses their lands along the River Teviot."

"Roxbourghe plays golf?"

"Quite well I am told, though I'm scarcely one to judge. I took my hacks at it, and felt rather foolish most of the time. Jamie, though, shares the Duke's enthusiasm and when we traveled up the coast, we stopped at St. Andrews for a few days so he could play the course there." He pulled a sour face at the memory. "Can't say I enjoyed it much. Every evening over our claret I had to listen to him either rave about a glorious shot he made or moan about some unfair twist of luck that had caused the ball to bounce askew. Lord, I'd almost rather listen to a fellow talk about his latest mistress than wax poetic about golf."

The cricket ball bounced against the wood paneling with a resounding crack. "The devil take it, Tony, what am I to do if the cursed game is truly so difficult to master? I have only a month's time before I stand to lose Woolsey Hall."

The glint of humor in Ellington's eyes died away, replaced by a flare of sympathy. He put aside his drink and rubbed at his jaw as if, like some character from an Arabian tale, he might conjure up a genie to solve his friend's dilemma by mere friction. "I think Jamie is still in Town," he said after mulling it over for a bit. "Perhaps we should pay him a visit. After all, he is well acquainted with the town and many of the locals, so he might have an idea."

Marquand looked dubious, but as he had nothing better to suggest, they took themselves off.

It took several hours to trace the Marquess of Bowmont's movements from a small dinner party with friends to the theater to one of the rooms at White's. He was seated in a comfortable chair before a roaring fire, an ironed newspaper open to an account of the recent peace talks in Vienna, a decanter of rich burgundy by his side. At Ellington's greeting, his head raised from the creased pages, a decided glimmer of relief apparent on the angular features.

"Tony, how delightful. You have saved me from having to read the rest of this interminable column. I must admit, it may as well be Greek to me for I don't understand a jot of what they are squabbling about." The Marquess tossed the paper aside and motioned for them to join him in a glass of wine. "I hope you wish to talk about something more interesting than the fine points of international diplomacy."

"Golf," replied Marquand.

Bowmont's eyes lit with a rather rapturous light. "Pull up a chair! Did I tell you about the marvelous course in Dornach, up in the Highlands, where I played in a roaring gale—"

The Viscount gave an inward wince, wondering how anyone could speak of such an experience as if it had been in the least pleasant.

Ellington cleared his throat, "Er, yes, I believe you did, Jamie. Several times, in fact. What we were hoping for, actually, was some advice . . ." He went on to outline their particular problem.

"Hmmm." Bowmont passed a speculative eye up and down Marquand's tall form for several moments. "Hmmm. Good set of shoulders. Strong legs." He steepled his fingers under his long, aristocratic nose and let his hooded lids fall to half mast. "Hmmm. I've seen you wield a racquet at Hampton Court and it appears you have balance and timing as well. Hmmm . . ."

Finding his usual reserve stretched past its limit, Marquand could bear the hemming and hawing no longer. "Well? Can you help at all?" he snapped.

At enigmatic smile came to the Marquess's full lips. "Patience, my dear Viscount. Patience is one of the first things you must learn about golf. It does not do to get in a temper on the course."

"You need not worry on that score, Bowmont," he replied through gritted teeth. "I assure you that I am more than capable of keeping my emotions under tight rein."

"Adrian is top-of-the-trees when it comes to facing down the odds," added his friend.

The Marquess darted a quick look at Ellington. "So I have heard," he replied softly. "It takes a cool fellow indeed to face a crack shot such as Darlington and put a bullet in his shoulder."

"It was what he deserved. I don't have much tolerance for liars and cheats."

"Yes, I have heard that as well. Just as I have heard that you have little tolerance for the sort of debaucheries favored by a fellow like Hertford—or your own father. Is that true?"

Marquand's jaw tightened. "I should hope my own reputation would be answer enough to that question." There was a perceptible pause. "If you are satisfied, perhaps if you could spare an hour or so, we could ride out to Houndslow Heath in the morning and you could show me a thing or two about knocking the ball—"

"No, I'm afraid that would be of little help." He held up his hand to forestall the retort he saw forming on the Viscount's lips, and went on. "First of all, I'm not so sure I would be very good at explaining all the nuances of the golf swing as I'm rather a neophyte at it myself. And most importantly, one of the keys to a good round of golf is being familiar with the course—the terrain, the prevailing winds, the position of the bunkers—"

"Bunkers?"

"Pits of sand," piped in Ellington. "Nasty. Very nasty."

"My advice to you is to head to St. Andrews as soon as possible," continued Bowmont. "I know a excellent chap up there who is not only the finest clubmaker in all of Scotland, but an excellent teacher to boot. Although he's in great demand, at my request I'm sure he'll be able to rig you out with just the right mashies, spoons, and niblicks for your size and swing."

Marquand was beginning to feel he was listening to a foreign language.

"And best of all, he is on intimate terms with all the local caddies—"

"Caddies?"

"The fellows who tote your clubs," explained Ellington.

"Aye," added Bowmont with a nod. "But a good one

is much more than a mere pack mule. In addition to simply helping find an errant ball and judge distances, he can save you several strokes a round through knowing the nuances of the course and the local conditions. That may well be the difference between victory and defeat." He grinned. "Trust me, Marquand, for a man in your position, an experienced caddie will prove more than invaluable. I daresay he'll become the best friend and ally you have. And Philp will be able to make sure that you have the most skilled one of the lot. I shall write to him tonight and see to it."

"We can't thank you enough for your help, Jamie," said Ellington. "It's more than sporting of you."

The Marquess took a long sip of his burgundy as he regarded the Viscount. "You may repay the favor by thrashing that smarmy bastard's hide," he said quietly. "Hertford's unsavory reputation extends well beyond London, and his presence at his estate near St. Andrews is about as welcome among the local folk as a storm from the North Sea blowing down the Firth of Forth." His voice dropped even lower. "There are murmurings that he's forced himself on more than one respectable girl from the town. The people there have become my friends, and if I had a shred of proof that would stand up in court, I'd see him clapped in irons just as quickly as I can swing a bottle-nosed driver." His broad mouth compressed in a tight line, squeezing away all traces of his earlier good humor. "With such despicable behavior, it is no wonder the English, especially ones of title, are not much welcome across the northern border. So make short work of him, Marquand."

"I promise you I shall do my best, Bowmont. Of that you may be sure."

"St. Andrews?" Baron Hylton set down the delicate Sevres teacup in surprise, sloshing half its contents on the damask tablecloth and turned his startled gaze upon his daughter. "St. Andrews?" he repeated, his tone becoming, if anything, even more incredulous. "In Scotland?"

"Yes, Father." Lady Honoria carefully rearranged the

napkin on her lap. "That is what Lord Marquand's note said. He has written one to you as well."

Noting how his wife's pinched face had already tightened in concern, he leaned his considerable bulk forward in his chair. "You haven't by chance already . . . quarreled with the Viscount?" His eyes narrowed. "Good Lord, I've just sent the announcement into *The Gazette*—"

"Hardly, sir. I should hope I would never give his lordship reason to quarrel with me," she responded primly. "He writes that it has something to do with a . . . a family matter."

A sigh of relief escaped the Baron's lips as he fell to slicing off a goodly chunk of the broiled kidney on his breakfast plate. "Good gel, I know we may depend on you to act with the utmost of sense, especially now that you have managed to bring the fellow up to scratch."

"Yes. Of course you may," she murmured.

Her father smiled through his chewing. "To think that you will soon be a Countess, my dear. And future mistress of one of the oldest estates in England." His expression then darkened considerably. "That is, if the old reprobate Earl doesn't manage to make a muck of things by tossing what little he has left of his fortune onto the gaming tables. Especially Woolsey Hall. The devil take him if he ever—"

"Fitzwilliam! Please reserve such vulgar language for your clubs," chided Lady Hylton, a moue of distaste on her thin lips.

"Er, sorry." He took a large swallow of tea and turned his attention back to his daughter. "But there is always the possibility that the old rakehell might squander away what is left of his fortune. In fact, I was almost of a mind to have you look to one of your other admirers for a proposal, given Marquand's recent family history."

"Don't be silly, Fitzwilliam, you know quite well that the Linsley Earldom is one of the oldest and most respected titles in the land. It cannot be gambled away," spoke up his wife in a tight voice. She shot another quick glance at her daughter and seemed to be somewhat reassured by the absence of any visible emotion. "No matter that the behavior of the Viscount's father is beyond all that is shocking, Honoria did very well by attaching him. From all that we have seen and heard, he is a true gentleman and cares a great deal for his heritage, as well he should. I cannot think he would ever allow Woolsey Hall to slip through his fingers."

Honoria broke a crust from the untouched toast on her plate. "As to that, perhaps you had better read Lord Marquand's note, Father."

The fork hung poised in midair.

With a sharp intake of breath, Lady Hylton rang for the butler and ordered the silver letter tray to be brought in without delay. The baron broke the wax wafer and scanned the short note. "Hmmph!"

His wife grew a shade paler.

"Just as I feared. Something havey-cavey is going on." His eyes came up from the thick cream parchment. "It seems Marquand is required to leave for Scotland this very morning in order to engage in some . . . sporting endeavor to save Woolsey Hall." After another moment of careful perusal, he laid the note aside and jabbed at the scrap of Yorkshire ham still left on his plate. "Well, I suppose we must consider it our duty to lend him a measure of support," he announced, spearing the morsel on the point of his knife. "I was already engaged to visit Jolliffe's estate near Kelso at the start of shooting season. It isn't that far out of the way to make a short visit to St. Andrews first. Might as well keep an eye on what is going on."

"All of us?" demanded his wife.

"Don't see why not." He pushed back from the table and signaled for the footman to remove all but his teacup, which he waved like a white flag before his daughter's nose "But if he should fail, I've a good mind to tell him he's forfeited his chance and that you are going to cry off from the engagement. No matter how old and respected his title is, it ain't nearly as valuable without a grand country estate attached to it, eh, missy? And with your looks, my dear, you can always look higher than an impoverished Earldom. Why, I could tell the Marquess of Pierson would be interested if given a little encouragement."

"But, Father—" She caught herself and fell silent.

"He'd be a fine catch, even if he is a tad older than you are."

"If that is what you want, then I shall of course abide by your wishes," replied Honoria softly. Her father seemed oblivious to the subtle note of irony in her voice, but Lady Hylton cast a searching look at her daughter and fell to twisting at the rings on her fingers.

"Well," he continued after slurping off the last bit of his tea. "I suppose it won't hurt to wait and see how Marquand fares before we make any final decisions. Time enough to cast him aside for a better prospect if things don't work out to our advantage."

Honoria ducked her head to hide her expression. Calmly folding her napkin into a neat square, she set it beside her plate and rose. "Shall I begin packing?"

Chapter Three

"Ohhh, that's a bonny hit, if I say so messell, Derry." The gray-haired man shaded his weathered face with a callused hand and watched the small sphere sail in a graceful arc over the patch of gorse. It landed not a yard away from a small flag fluttering in the gusting sea breeze. "You're getting to be a dab hand at knocking the ball up and over a tricky hazard like The Principal's Nose," he said with a nod of gruff approval. "And you've judged the wind exactly right."

The slight figure by his side tucked the hickory-shafted baffing spoon in the crook of one arm. "Well, I've had a decent-enough teacher." An impish grin stole forth. "Once I knock it in, that will give me a"—there was a slight pause for a bit of mental arithmetic—"a six." The announcement was made with a note of triumph to its tone, followed by an even wider smile. "And as you can't do better than a seven, even if you put your ball in the hole on the fly, I've won yet another hole on this second nine. Before long, Hugh, I shall be beating you at your own game, see if I won't!"

The two of them began walking along the wide expanse of close-cropped green that paralleled the road leading in from Leuchars. "Auch, is that so?" replied Hugh Philp with a mock jeer. "You may be ready to take a shilling from Jamie or old Da, but rest assured, you will be sprouting a long beard ere you'll be taking a coin from my pocket, my wee friend."

The remark elicited a peal of laughter from the older man's companion. Fingers slender yet strong came up to run over a cheek smooth as churned cream, the lightly tanned complexion unmarred by any hint of an incipient stubble. "Well, that day still appears far off, so I guess I had best not start to count my farthings." Their boots clattered over the stones of the small bridge crossing Swilkan Burn. "Still, I am at least making you work just a little to beat me, am I not?"

"Indeed you are, Derry." On regarding the eager expression of the upturned face, he felt his throat constrict and turned away to watch a solitary gull flap its way out over the foaming waves. "I daresay you've become the best of all of them that hang around the shop, for you are willing to listen, and to work hard at it. You may not be as strong as Jamie or Tom, or as talented as Angus or Gordie but you make up for it with pluck and imagination. And to my mind, that's the true mark of a good golfer." He stopped for a moment to withdraw a pipe and flint from his pocket. "Aye, I daresay you're on your way to becoming a real player."

His companion's head dipped in awkward embarrassment at the uncharacteristic direct praise. "Thank you, Hugh," came the low reply as Derry removed the flagstick from the diminutive hole in the ground and set up to tap the feathery ball into its circular depth. "But I've still much to learn." The freckled nose wrinkled in some consternation. "If only . . ." The faint words trailed off to the soft twock of wood on leather.

Philp squinted up at the slate gray clouds scudding in from the Bay. "Best we hurry if we mean to finish the last hole without a soaking, for there promises to be a spot of rain afore long." He cleared his throat and reached down to retrieve the stitched ball from its shadowed resting place. "Seeing as you are feeling on top of your game, do you care to make the finish interesting, say with a small wager on the outcome on eighteen?"

A keen twinkle came to Derry's eyes. "Just what do you have in mind, Hugh?"

"Oh, as to that, if you win, you may choose a new club from the shop." There was a momentary hesitation as he fingered the sheepskin grip of his long spoon. "And if I win, you will . . . do me a small favor."

All of the mischievous humor disappeared from his companion's features, replaced by a look of great seriousness. "You know very well you don't have to win any favors from me, sir. You have only to ask and I should be more than delighted to do anything of your bidding."

"Not this, you won't," murmured Philp under his breath. In a louder voice, he replied, "Nay, I should prefer to do it this way, fair and square." It was quite clear from his manner that he was uncomfortable having to ask anyone for aid, especially the person by his side.

"Very well. Then of course I accept." An edge had crept into Derry's voice, betraying a trace of bruised feelings at being denied the chance to help outright.

A wisp of a smile flitted over the leathery face, and he threw his arm around the smaller set of shoulders. "Don't be falling into a fit of girlish vapors—it doesn't suit you in the least, my friend. Besides, I wouldn't have thought you intended to lose."

That drew a reluctant twitch of the lips from his companion. "I don't. However, as you have seen fit to name your own prize, I should like the right to do the same."

The older man opened his mouth as if to argue, but stopped short on seeing the stubborn jut of his young friend's jaw. It was a look he recognized all too well, just as he recognized the futility of arguing the particular point. "I suppose I can guess what it is," he grumbled in grudging resignation. At the confirming nod, his breath came out in a sigh, "Well then, it looks as if the match is dormied before it starts."

Derry's head cocked in mute question at the strange word.

"It's one of our more obscure golf expressions," explained Philp. "It means, in a broad stroke, that I cannot lose. But don't say I didn't warn you. Believe me, you would have vastly preferred that new heavy iron that just arrived from Bobby Kirkaldy's forge as your prize."

"Then I shall just have to win it some other time."

A drop of rain splashed on the tip of the older man's beaked nose. With one more glance at the ominous skies, he shrugged in exasperation and decided there was little point in avoiding the other inevitable black cloud that was going to descend over his head. "If you don't mind, I'm in a bad-enough humor without these old bones getting chilled to the marrow. Why don't we forego the eighteenth and return to the shop?"

"Aye, and you can tell me what it is you wish me to do on the way."

It was well enough that the large workroom was deserted, for the oath that rent the air redolent with wood shavings and linseed oil as the two of them entered the side door was best left unremarked by any bystander.

"I should cuff both your ears for such language," muttered Philp, his fierce scowl directed as much at himself as at the figure who was glowering back with an equally disgruntled expression. He had known it was going to be difficult to explain things without causing a storm, but he hadn't anticipated quite such a clap of thunder. "Lud, your aunt is leery enough of what you are doing here, without her thinking I'm turning you into a veritable savage."

The thick tweed cap was yanked off with some impatience and Miss Derrien Edwards shook out a mass of damp curls. "I'm not such a gudgeon as to forget myself in front of her or any of proper Society, but if Willie and Fergus can say such things when they are angry, why can't I?"

"You know *exactly* why, lassie."

She made an unladylike sound but then fell silent, her fingers fiddling angrily with a length of tarred twine. After a few minutes she looked up again, her hazel eyes flashing with fresh indignation. "Why must *you* feel obliged to teach some visiting lord to play golf because of some stupid wager? And an *English* lord at that?"

"Because Bowmont asks me to."

She gave what sounded suspiciously like a snort. "Since when have you become so . . . so spineless as to be ruled by the whim of a fancy toff, no matter that he is a Marquess and his father a Duke—"

Philp's response was no less emphatic for its quietly measured tone. "I do it not because he is titled, but because he is my friend," he interrupted, crossing his arms and drawing himself up to his full height. "On the golf course, I've always held that a man earns respect not for his birth or position but for his character and skill. Bowmont has both. I am honored that he should seek my help."

A rush of color flooded Derrien's face and she ducked her head in shame. "I had no right to say such a horrible thing. Forgive me, Hugh. I fear I let myself become overset for a moment."

"I know, lassie." His tone softened considerably. "I wouldn't have even considered asking you to be involved, if there was aught else I could think of."

As he spoke, his gnarled fingers raked through his graying hair, as though some other answer might be hidden amid the wiry strands that sprung up from his wide forehead. He knew enough of her family tree to understand the roots of her aversion to any Englishman, especially one that sported a title. Her mother had been perhaps a year younger than Derrien's age, and just as full of dreams that soared far above the stone and mortared walls of her own little shire, when the dashing young officer had seduced her with lofty promises of a life rich with all manner of new experiences. Unfortunately for the impressionable auburn-haired beauty, his words were as bankrupt as his morals and purse, once the current quarterly allowance from his family had been squandered in gaming and the pursuit of the fairer sex. When the gentleman's father discovered the extent of his son's profligate habits in the north and demanded an immediate return to Town, where a closer eye could be kept on such excesses, the heir was quick to slink back to London, leaving her with only a brief note and swelling womb as the sole concrete tokens of his pledges of undying affection.

There was little sympathy from her strict Presbyterian mother, even less from a straitlaced father who declared with solemn finality that his youngest daughter had, quite simply, ceased to exist as far as he was concerned. If it hadn't been for the generosity of her oldest sister, married and living some distance away in the university town of St. Andrews, Derrien's mother might have been cast out to a life on the streets. Instead she was offered a refuge where she might have a chance to put such a calamitous mistake behind her and begin life anew.

The new mother and child were welcomed into a home of rather more progressive ideas than existed in most Scottish households. Anyone who asked about her history was simply told that the young lady had lost her husband. Her brother-in-law, a professor of semantics at Union College, had regarded that as true enough. The extended family was a close-knit one, with little Derrien becoming as doted upon by her childless relatives as by her natural mother. When a bout of influenza carried away her own parent two years later, there was no question as to who would care for the young child.

As Philp watched the gamut of emotions that washed over Derrien's expressive features, he couldn't help but wonder if he had done the right thing in broaching the matter. Though he owed a good measure of loyalty to a generous friend and patron such as Bowmont, his deep feelings for the young lady far overbalanced any sense of debt to the Marquess.

"Nay, it's I who should apologize. I can see that I was wrong to bring it up," he continued after some time. "The trouble is, I can fit the fellow with a decent set of clubs and show him a thing or two about the basic swing, but for what he needs to learn in the space of a few weeks, he must be out on the course every day with someone to offer both advice and instruction. I have lately received a number of important commissions and cannot spare the time without doing irreparable harm to my business, something I simply can't afford, no matter how much I value Bowmont's friendship." He drew in a long breath. "Willie might have been able to do a credible job, but he's broken his leg, helping his father gather mussels in Eden Estuary. Fergus has the right sort of knowledge, but he's prone to tossing back more than his share of our local whiskey. Why, he would as likely show up in a tavern in Dundee as on the first hole. Mayhap Tommy—"

Derrien bit her lip. "I'll do it, Hugh."

Philp answered with a heavy sigh. "No, no, there must be someone else, but strike me down with a long spoon if I can think of who." He began to fiddle with his silver-rimmed spectacles. "It must be a fellow who knows the course and all its nuances as well as the basics of technique. Even more importantly, it must be someone with a good head on his shoulders, for this English lord is going to need a clever caddie if he is to have any hope of besting an opponent of greater skill and experience." There was a short pause, then his face brightened considerably. "Ahh! What about Charlie Kidd?"

She gave a shake of her head. "That won't fadge at all. Though Charlie takes great pains to appear a fine fellow, I've seen enough of him to know his loyalty can be bought by the highest bidder. When he caddies for Mr. Heatherington, he will use his boot to improve the ball's lie if passed an extra penny." Her lips twisted in a grimace of distaste. "I wouldn't trust him farther than I can kick a featherie on the strand."

"Hmmm. Well, I suppose that rules him out . . ."

"I said I'll do it, Hugh."

Philp held up his hand and cleared his throat. "Er, now that I think of it, there's one other thing I hadn't properly considered. There's too great a risk that our little secret may be discovered."

Derrien dismissed the matter with a derisive snort. "Oh, come now. None of the locals has the foggiest notion that I'm not a lad, and they see me all the time. No English lord is going to suss it out in the course of a few weeks. No doubt he's so puffed up with a sense of his own consequence he'll waste no time looking at the likes of me. Besides, I take great care to wear a floppy hat and have enough smudges obscuring my face that I'm known as "Dirty Derry.""

Her friend looked torn. "People here don't notice because they have grown so used to seeing you hang around the shop since you were a wee thing, not much different than a lad—"

"People see what they wish to see." Her voice had a raw edge to it as she slowly wound the thin cord around her thumb. "Let us cease to argue about it. I'm the best one for the job and you know it. That's why you asked in the first place."

"You are, Derry," he admitted. "And I would dearly like for us to triumph in this match, but are you sure it is not asking too much? I can always write to Peter McEwan in Edinburgh to see if he might be able to suggest a good lad from up his way—"

"No!" Her voice came out in a sharp cry. "If it must be done, I'd rather it was me working with you." After a moment, a certain keen curiosity gave rise to a probing question. "Why is a victory so important, Hugh? I know you well enough to sense it is something more than a cordial acquaintance with Lord Bowmont that has stirred your competitive fires."

He gave a ghost of a smile. "Like I said, you are too sharp by half, lassie. The fact is, it matters to me because the opponent is Lord Hertford."

Derrien's face paled considerably. "Why didn't you say so in the first place?" she demanded in a near whisper. "To thwart that dastard I would be willing to caddie for Lucifer himself."

"I wished to know first if you could truly endure the idea of working with an English lord. If not, I would have found some other alternative. But I admit, I should rather have you on our team."

"Then the matter is settled." She pulled the twine tighter. "When does this gentleman arrive?"

"Any day now."

"Has he any aptitude for sport? Or is he some preening peacock, with need to resort to padding in his stockings?" She gave a grimace. "Perhaps he is someone whose most pressing concern is the cut of his coat or the color of his waistcoat. If so, then our task may prove hopeless, despite our best efforts."

"Bowmont's note states he is not some mincing dandy,

but rather a tall, handsome figure of a man, who rides, shoots, and boxes with the best. And apparently he wields a fierce bat in cricket and a skillful racket on the tennis court, so things do not look entirely bleak."

Handsome as sin, a man of leisure, and given the reason for his journey to St. Andrews, a reckless gamester. Derrien hated him already.

However, she gave a curt nod of her head. "Good. Then between us, we should be able to whip him into adequate shape." Her eyes strayed to the battered clock that rested atop one of the long workbenches. "I had best get home before Aunt Claire thinks I've been swallowed by a sand trap." She reached for her cap and began to tuck her unruly curls back under its cover. "Don't worry, Hugh," she added with a grim smile on catching sight of his furrowed brow. "You've done the right thing. We'll manage to pull this off."

As Philp watched her stride toward the door, the gently rounded outline of her slim hips mercifully hidden by the baggy pair of breeches, he wished he could feel quite as sanguine.

The rain was falling harder, but Derrien was almost grateful for the chill drops, in such marked contrast to the heat of the emotions still flaming inside her. Of course, there had never really been any question as to whether she would help her dear friend. Hugh Philp, her uncle Alistair's good friend and mentor on the links, had become nearly as much a father to the young orphaned girl as the professor, encouraging her natural physical talent for the game of golf as well as the agility of her inquisitive mind, no matter that most of Society thought both traits unacceptable for a female. When it became clear that her interest—and skill—in swinging a club had far exceeded the confines of the family garden, it was Philp who had come up with the idea of disguising her as a lad so she would have a chance to play the real course at St. Andrews.

She couldn't help but smile on recalling how she had quickly discovered the trick very useful in other ways, as it allowed her to hang around the University without

attracting undue notice, and to sneak into the odd lecture
once in a while. Even when such irregular behavior had
come to light, Philp had been just as willing as her uncle
to discuss the sorts of things that interested her, whether
it be the latest advances in botany, the aesthetics of garden design, or even so radical a topic as the ideas of Mr.
Franklin, the statesman from America who possessed a
Doctor of Law degree from St. Andrews. He had never
once scoffed at her opinions during the long conversations that accompanied their play on the course or the
meticulous shaping and sanding that took place at his
workbench. Instead he had treated the young girl as
though her thoughts were as of equal merit as his own.

Derrien's smile deepened into something more complex than amusement. Perhaps it was because he sensed
a kindred soul in her, no matter the rather obvious differences between them. Philp had a passion for what he
did. His work transcended mere craftsmanship. The perfection of his clubs, their exquisite balance and graceful
curves, had serious golfers speaking about him in the
same tones of hushed reverence that art connoisseurs
reserved for the Old Masters. Bowmont preferred to
liken his friend's creations to the work of another maker
of performance instruments, a gentleman by the name of
Stradivarius, saying both men were true artists. Philp
scoffed at such lofty sentiment, saying he was just a man
who paid attention to detail, but Derrien knew the Marquess's words were true. Philp saw things in ways other
men didn't. One of his workers might lay aside a club as
finished, only to find, hours later, the master engrossed
in carving and sanding until the minute flaw that was
apparent to only his eye was fixed.

Philp must have recognized the same dedication in her,
not only to a game such as golf, but to the other passion
that had blossomed up in her life. She must have been
not more than twelve when her uncle had brought home
the picture book on gardens. From that moment on, she
had been captivated, reading everything she could get
her hands on regarding the theory and practice of landscape design. Walls had been scaled in the dead of night

to view some rare specimen planting and agricultural tomes had been ploughed through to learn the basics of growing techniques. Her aunt and uncle had been more supportive than most guardians of a young female's interest in something other than knitting or embroidery, with only the occasional gentle reminder that there could be no future for her in such things.

But it had been Philp who had truly understood what it was to have a passion take root, how no amount of effort could weed it out of one's breast. During the countless hours she had watched him hunched at work, putting the finishing touches on his own masterpieces, they had talked of her dreams, of the marvelous gardens she could create only in her mind. He had always encouraged her to cultivate such dreams, saying that with a little luck nothing was impossible. For that she would always be grateful, and so she would never turn her back on him, no matter how onerous the challenge.

But why did it have to involve an Englishman, and a titled one at that?

She gave an inward curse, one even more fiery than the words uttered aloud earlier. Her boots rang a peal over the slick cobblestones as she passed the Tron in Market Square and turned down the narrow lane leading to her aunt's home. Well, there was nothing she could do about it, she reminded herself on catching the reflection of her scowling face in a rain-streaked shop window. It was silly to succumb to pointless anger, and indeed, she had a feeling she had better start practicing a measure of self-control. No doubt she was going to need every ounce of it during the coming weeks.

There was one other thing of which she had no doubt. Her aunt might smile wistfully and say she possessed the same delicate beauty and unquenchable spirit as her mother, but she would *never* make the same naive mistake. Miss Derrien Edwards was not going to be seduced by a titled Englishman, no matter what sort of charm or prowess he was said to possess.

Especially if he couldn't play a decent game of golf.

*　　*　　*

Marquand stared glumly at yet another field filled with sheep. A driving rain had turned the road from Edinburgh into a veritable quagmire, so that the progress of the coach had been painfully slow. The landscape had seemed one interminable pasture with only mossy drywalls or the occasional stand of forest to break the monotony of hay, thistle, and sodden wool on the hoof. He vowed if he had to endure one more greasy meal of stewed mutton he would fall on his hands and knees and begin baahing like a lost lamb.

Which is exactly what he felt like at the moment— alone and helpless. And unlikely to survive the coming few weeks.

He had come to the conclusion that his situation was even bleaker than the weather. Not only did he face having to master an entirely new discipline in a woefully inadequate amount of time, but the skills he already possessed would be sorely tested as well. Of all the devilishly bad luck, the commission he had been fervently hoping to attain for the past six months had come through just days before his forced departure from Town. The deadline for its completion was tight, so somehow he would have to manage to come up with a suitable inspiration while here in Scotland.

It would be no easy task under the best of conditions, he reminded himself morosely. As if to echo his mood, a pelting rain rattled against the carriage window, sounding for all the world like a hail of bullets. Marquand winced. The notion of standing before a firing squad seemed uncomfortably real.

He forced his attention back to the pile of papers on his knees. At least he had found plenty of time to study the sheaf of plans he had brought along, as well as begin some preliminary sketches. Still, the enormity of the task was daunting, even if he could devote his full efforts to it.

"Did you know there is a yew said to be nearly three hundred years old in one of the private gardens in St. Andrews?"

Ellington's voice jerked the Viscount from his pessimistic thoughts. "No doubt it will be the real highpoint of our visit to the city," he replied, hoping his voice did not sound quite so waspish to the other man's ear as it did to his own."

His friend merely arched one brow in mild surprise and went back to reading the book in his lap. It was some miles before he looked up again. The clouds had finally broken up, allowing a shaft of pale afternoon light to pick out the ripples and eddies on a body of fast-moving water that paralleled the muddy road. "Ahh, at last," remarked Ellington with some satisfaction. "Look, Adrian, we are about to cross the River Eden. That means we are not far from our destination."

Marquand bit back a sarcastic retort. It felt more like he was about to pass over the River Styx into Hades rather than enter any sort of Paradise. However, as Tony had chosen to accompany him north for no other reason than a bond of friendship that stretched back to the time they were both in leading strings, he decided it would be most churlish of him to continue venting his ill-humor. His friend had endured the rigors of the journey with his usual unflagging good spirits. He owed it to such a stalwart companion to try to appear less crotchety than he felt.

"How very encouraging," he replied, trying hard to keep a note of asperity out of his voice. "Now if only the Good Lord will grant us a minor miracle after such an epic journey and allow the heavens to remain unclouded for more than a passing moment. Perhaps then it might be possible to begin swinging a cursed spoon or mashie, or whatever the devil you call the clubs. That is, if I can manage to straighten my spine after this interminable confinement."

Ellington grinned. "Oh, come now, stop talking as if you wear corsets and walk with the aid of a stick. And besides, any odd cricks or spasms are no doubt due to the fact that you have spent most of the hours hunched over your books or your sketchpads. A hot bath along with a night's rest on sheets that are moderately clean and free of crawling bedfellows will put you right as rain."

"I should prefer you don't mention that particular word," he muttered, but a reluctant smile pulled at his lips. It was hard to remain blue-deviled in light of his friend's banter.

He allowed himself to be further coaxed out of his sullens by a running commentary on the sights leading into town. "Look," cried Ellington, craning his neck to peer out of the rain-streaked glass. "You can just make out St. Rule's Tower if you bend your head just so. It was partially destroyed during the Reformation of 1559—"

"Then I imagine it will survive another quarter of an hour, until I may alight from these cramped quarters and take a proper peek," he said dryly.

A chuckle sounded from his friend. "Since I have been forced by the lack of congenial conversation to immerse myself in a history—a rather thick history, I may add— of the town, you might at least indulge me for a bit and listen to my prattle about the famous landmarks and such."

"Very well. What else should I know?"

Ellington thought for a moment. "Since this is your first visit across the border, you should be aware that the Scots are a wee bit different from those of us used to the ways of London. They can be quite reserved—some may even go so far as to consider them dour. And they have little tolerance for frivolous behavior—"

"Then it sounds as if I shall have no trouble fitting in," broke in Marquand.

His friend fell tactfully silent.

The coach bounced around a bend in the road. "What do you suppose they are hunting?" asked the Viscount, indicating two men on hands and knees in the middle of a broad swath of cropped grass. From a distance, they appeared to be poking about in a thick patch of willow herb and whin with several long, thin sticks. "Surely with the amount of racket they are making, any rabbit will have long since gone to ground."

There was a hoot of laughter. "They are hunting a

golf ball. That, my dear Adrian, is the hallowed links of St. Andrews."

"Hmmph." Marquand crossed his arms. "Not much to look at. Why, there's hardly a tree in sight. What's all this nonsense about hazards and strategy? Looks to me like there's precious little to prevent you from simply standing up and giving the ball a sound whack straight ahead and straight back."

"Indeed?" murmured Ellington with a wicked grin. "I shall remind you of those words in a week's time."

"Hmmph."

A short while later they rolled through the West Port arch and down South Street, past several intersections before turning right onto a snug street lined with linden trees. On both sides were a row of pleasant town houses, their weathered granite façades still wet from a passing shower. Modest in scale, the residences looked to have a solid, if not spectacular, comfort. Ellington consulted a piece of paper he had drawn from his coat pocket, then glanced again out the window.

"There it is up ahead, Number Eighteen." He pointed to one with a large brass knocker in the shape of a thistle that distinguished it from its neighbors. "The housekeeper comes highly recommended and has already hired a staff suitable for our needs. Bowmont has also written to several of his acquaintances in town of our arrival so that we may expect to dine out several nights a week."

"Hmmph." Marquand knew he should muster more enthusiasm than that. Tony had gone to a great deal of effort to secure decent lodgings and staff for their extended stay while he had been occupied with arranging his affairs for such a long absence. But the fact of the matter was, he was feeling even less sanguine about the prospects of this whole endeavor now that they had arrived. The task which had seemed daunting enough in London now appeared, in light of countless hours of rumination on the way north, to be a fool's errand.

"Of course, August is hardly the height of the Season, and such entertainment as it is, especially here in Scotland, will hardly match the sort to which we are accustomed to in London. But Bowmont has assured me that he means to see us introduced to local Society . . ." His friend kept up a stream of pithy comments, but Marquand could not help but find his thoughts straying back to his own bleak reflections.

Fool, indeed! His lips compressed in a tight line. Nobody but a fool would imagine he could master a complicated sport in a few short weeks, much less best an opponent who had been playing the game for years. No, to have any hope of success, he would have to be extraordinarily lucky, and the thought of such dependence on serendipitous chance, rather than his own hard work, galled him no end. He had spent most of his lifetime as an unwilling thrall to the Lady of Fortune, witnessing how fickle her attentions could be. His father might have chosen to make her his mistress, but he had always sworn he would never be seduced by such promiscuous charms.

The coach creaked to a stop, and Marquand realized he hadn't heard a word of what Ellington had been chattering about for the last few minutes. Quelling the urge to order the coachman to turn right around toward London without so much as setting a foot on the slippery cobblestones, he sighed and made to follow his friend in climbing down to the street.

"Come now, Adrian, you are not usually one to shy away from a challenge. Stop looking so mutton-faced!"

The problem was, he felt just like a sheep being led to slaughter.

Chapter Four

Philp sucked in a mouthful of pungent smoke and ran a hand along the edge of his jaw. He sat for what seemed like an age, staring at the figure standing in front of him before finally speaking. "Turn around."

Marquand's eyes narrowed slightly in irritation but he did as he was told.

"Hmmm. Now face me again, if you please." When the Viscount had complied, he went on. "Bend forward slightly from the waist, sir, and let your arms hang straight down."

"What the deuce am I, an ape on display at the Tower Menagerie?" growled Marquand under his breath. He fell silent on catching a warning look from Ellington but his expression didn't hide what he thought of the proceeding so far. His misgivings were only exacerbated when Philp came over and gave his wrists a shake. "Looser, sir. You must relax." When he had complied, the older man wrapped the Viscount's unresisting hands around a tapered stick.

"I thought you were going to teach me about golf," he said with some impatience. "In case Bowmont did not make it clear, I have precious little time in which to gain any proficiency in the sport, so I would prefer not to waste even a morning of it."

Philp only gave an enigmatic smile and continued to make a number of marks on the length of hickory with a piece of chalk.

However the slender figure seated in the shadows of the workroom gave an undisguised snort of derision. "Perhaps the gentleman has no more brains than a monkey, Mr. Philp, if he has so little faith in your knowledge and expertise." The words were spoken just loudly enough for Marquand to hear them. "As you have often said, even a monkey may be taught to strike a golf ball. But to be a real player he must be willing to listen and learn. And trust that his teacher knows what he is talking about."

"Derry," warned Philp in a low voice as Ellington stifled a chuckle.

A faint flush rose to the Viscount's cheeks. "Who is the brat?"

"Don't take offense, sir," murmured Philp as he straightened and began to measure the width of Marquand's palm and the length of his fingers with a piece of narrow canvas tape. "The lad may have a sharp tongue"—he directed another pointed look at Derrien—"but he possesses a knowledge of the game that is equally well-honed. He's going to serve as your caddie these coming weeks."

"The devil he will! If you think I'm going to allow some impudent—"

"Ahem." Ellington cleared his throat with deliberate loudness, causing the Viscount to bite off the rest of his retort. "Mr. Philp *does* come highly recommended, Adrian, and we are quite fortunate to have his help. I think we may trust his judgment in matters of golf."

Marquand fixed Derrien with an icy glare but remained silent. Her look of disdain was much more obvious, however a sign from Philp to bring over a bundle of unfinished clubs forestalled any further comment from her lips as well.

"And though you may chafe at the delay, my lord, a set of clubs tailored to your stance and height will greatly add to your chances of performing well. After all, you wouldn't attempt to ride to the hounds in a pair of boots several sizes too large, or a saddle whose girth was too tight around your hunter, would you now?"

The Viscount acknowledged the sense of Philp's words with a curt nod. "Your pardon, Mr. Philp. I did not mean to imply I doubted your expertise, and I shall try to refrain from questioning your methods," he said rather stiffly.

"One of my men will finish up a number of these to your specifications by morning, sir," continued Philp, picking out a selection of scrapers, middle spoons, and cuttys from Derrien's arms. "In the meantime, if you return here this afternoon at two, I shall take you out back of the shop and we may begin working on the rudiments of the stance and swing."

Despite the assurances he had just uttered, Marquand couldn't refrain from another sharp question. "Why not out on the course? I am anxious to see what a real fairway—or whatever the deuce it is called—is like."

Philp smiled. "In good time, my lord, in good time. When you see the sort of exercises I have in mind, you will not object in the least to our first lesson taking place in a more private venue."

Marquand took his snugly tailored jacket back from Ellington and slipped it back over his fine linen shirt.

"Oh, and it would be best to wear a loose-fitting shirt, with only a Belcher neckerchief, as well as a shorter jacket, sir. You are going to be . . . exerting yourself more than you might think."

"More likely he's used to starched shirtpoints that come up past the ears and a cravat that requires half the Royal Navy to tie in a knot." Derrien snickered from behind Philp's back.

The Viscount pretended not to hear the remark, though in truth it took a concerted effort to stop himself from informing the impertinent little urchin that he had never in his life dressed as such a ridiculous poppinjay.

Ellington's hand on his shoulder quickly propelled him toward the door, ensuring that he could have no second thoughts about remaining silent. "Er, thank you, Mr. Philp. I shall have his lordship back here promptly at two."

It took a discreet elbow to Marquand's ribs to elicit a civil good-bye from him as well. Once they had reached the street, he turned and regarded his friend with a look of bemused surprise. "What has got into you lately,

Adrian? I don't believe I've seen you display your pique like that in all the years I've known you. Lord, you are usually the very picture of control, and not at all given to any show of emotion. But since we left London, I vow, you have been most unlike your regular self."

"Sorry, I—"

"No, no, don't apologize." His lips quirked upward. "Actually, I'm not sure it's a bad thing at all. You know, your work fairly blossoms with exuberance and life, and yet, if you don't mind me saying, in public you choose to appear a . . . rather dry stick, though I know you are not." Ellington hesitated for a moment and slanted a look of concern at his friend. "There is nothing wrong with allowing an occasional curse to shoot forth. A laugh or two might serve to lighten your spirits as well."

Marquand clamped his curly-brimmed beaver more firmly on his dark locks. "Hmmph! It's hardly a laughing matter. My entire future is riding on a damnable game of golf! Not to speak of the other undertaking I must finish while I am here." He shook his head. "However you're right about losing my temper back there. It's absurd to let some muddy-faced urchin with a tongue as loose as that floppy tweed cap on his head get under my skin." He walked on for a few more steps before another snort escaped his lips. "Hmmph! The notion that a pipsqueak of a lad could teach me anything . . ." His words trailed off into an unintelligible grumble that went on until they turned the corner. Suddenly the Viscount stopped in his tracks. "This Mr. Philp seems to have some decidedly odd ideas. You do not think he is truly out to make a monkey of me?" he demanded.

Ellington pursed his lips. "I cannot think Bowmont would suggest him if he was. Jamie wants to see Hertford beaten nearly as badly as you do, and it's clear he thinks very highly of Mr. Philp. No, I believe we may trust this man." He slanted a sideways glance at Marquand's frowning face. "Adrian, I also believe that you are going to have to get used to a number of odd notions here in Scotland, if you wish to have any hope of securing your future . . . happiness."

The Viscount's expression darkened to match the low clouds scudding in from the sea. "I shall do my best, you may count on it." Under his breath he added, "But that doesn't mean I shall like it in the least."

That evening a weary Marquand couldn't help but wonder if his best was going to be anywhere near good enough. Easing his lanky frame into the overstuffed chair by the banked fire in the library, he rubbed absently at his aching shoulder while contemplating the lunacy of embarking on such a cork-brained quest. Not only had he looked like a monkey for the past several hours, but he had felt like the verriest of fools. Why, he must have appeared a complete cawker, with his ungainly movements and precarious balance.

He winced on recalling his more awkward cuts at the little ball lying on the turf. Good Lord, he had actually missed it outright on several occasions, and it wasn't even moving! It was a wonder he hadn't ended up on his rump, for he had nearly lost his footing on a number of swings. How his friends would have whooped with laughter to see one of London's leading Corinthians stripped down to his shirtsleeves, flailing furiously at a perverse little sphere of stitched leather that refused to budge from the stubbly grass.

But worse than merely looking like an idiot was the disquieting feeling that perhaps he was not up to meeting the challenge, both physical and mental. Excelling at such sporting endeavors as riding, boxing, shooting, and cricket had always been easy for him, so he supposed he had taken it for granted that he would learn golf with little difficulty. The past afternoon had been a rude awakening. He had been awful. Truly awful. That the game looked so maddeningly simple only exacerbated his sense of frustration.

Hell's teeth. What was he going to do?

If things didn't improve rapidly, he might as well slink home with his proverbial tail between his legs, for ignominious defeat, and with it the loss of his beloved Woolsey Hall, seemed inevitable. With a bitter grimace, he raked a hand through his still-damp locks, then rose a bit stiffly and went to pour himself a generous glass of the local spirits. As the heat of the whiskey rolled over his tongue, he couldn't help but feel in danger of being drowned by a fear far deeper than failure.

Was he a coward as well? A number of Ellington's recent words echoed in his ears. Much as he wished to deny it, his friend's sharp observations had begun to chop away at the carefully constructed walls that guarded his true feelings. He had always prided himself on the ability to keep all emotions locked safely away, but perhaps, as Ellington hinted, he had only created a prison rather than a place of refuge. His hands came up to rub at his temples and he found the fiery brew was having little effect on the cold knot that had settled in the pit of his stomach.

With all the precision of a skilled architect, he had drafted a plan for his future, sketching in the exact measurements of its main components with an eye to making an impregnable structure. His bride-to-be could not fit in more perfectly, and yet somehow, as his friend forced him to stand back and scrutinize the whole, the proportions of what he had wrought were looking slightly out of kilter. He shook his head, as if a slight jiggling could serve to straighten everything back to its proper place. But still, he could not seem to erase the feeling that the foundations were not as sturdy as he imagined. Perhaps the uncharacteristic moodiness that had colored his behavior since their departure from London had as much to do with his own flawed choices as those of his father, and he was just too afraid to admit it.

A muscle of his jaw twitched ever so slightly. Surely his engagement had been fashioned with a steady hand? Miss Dunster was the perfect material for a wife—cool and lovely as the finest marble, and just as unlikely as that substance to display any sudden shifts from her proper place. Yet Ellington's gentle criticisms had given him pause to think.

He, of all people, knew the difference between a work where all the angles were correct, resulting in a perfect hard-edged beauty that all might admire, and a creation that stirred a more . . . passionate response. One was craft, the other art. Would he truly be satisfied with mere correctness in his personal life, something which he would never settle for in his professional affairs? He couldn't help but recall his reaction to kissing his intended. Even then, he hadn't been able to repress a vague notion that despite all his meticulous planning, some crucial element had been left out that would doom his marriage to being no more than mediocre.

The thought was chilling.

His eyes strayed to the decanter on the sideboard, and for the first time he could remember, he felt a twinge of understanding for those whose inner demons drove them to drown self-doubt in a deluge of drink. He felt a rather strong temptation himself to drain the entire contents, but a glance at the clock on the mantel reminded him that tomorrow promised to be as long—and no doubt as trying—as the past afternoon. Honor bound him to give his best effort in meeting any challenge. And as he was not quite ready to hoist the white flag over his ramparts, he put aside his glass and rose with some stiffness, then took himself off to his desk. He still had a great deal to do before he could allow himself the luxury of some sleep.

"You must remember to shift your weight to your right foot when you take the club back, sir, and then fire through, as if you were throwing a rock toward that patch of gorse." Philp took the club from Marquand's hands and dropped a ball from his pocket onto the grass. The hickory shaft came back and then forward in one fluid motion, sending the small leather orb in a soaring arc through the light fog. "Like that." He dropped another ball at the Viscount's feet. "Try again."

Jaw clenched, Marquand took up his stance.

"Lord, try not to grip the club as if you were going to smash someone over the head with it," came a low snicker from behind his back.

Marquand restrained the urge to do exactly that to the speaker.

"Ahem!" The caution from Philp was clear.

"But he doesn't seem to be attending to anything you tell him," protested Derrien, shifting the group of clubs from one arm to another.

The older man fixed her with a stern look. "That's hardly fair la—lad. You know very well golf is not something that is learned in a day. His lordship is progressing quite nicely."

She ducked her head in mute contrition. He was right, of course, she allowed to herself, but it was irritating in the extreme to watch the stiff-rumped English lord approach the ball as if it were something he could hammer into submission—no doubt that was what he was used to! Still, she must remember that much as she disliked him, his upcoming opponent was an infinitely worse sort. Her attempts at advice should, as Philp had just hinted, be couched in a more positive manner. After all, she had promised her mentor that she would do her best to help.

Philp had turned back to the Viscount. "Now, sir, go ahead."

Marquand set his feet once again, then drew the long shaft back in the sweeping motion he had been taught, goaded by Derrien's caustic reminder to keep his hands well relaxed. The club paused for a fraction at the top of the swing, then started down, gathering speed as it descended toward the ball. The head of the long spoon made clean contact, and with a sweet thwock, the featherie flew up into the damp morning air, landing in the middle of the fairway not far from Philp's drive.

"Well struck, sir!" exclaimed his teacher.

"Good shot," allowed Derrien, though she couldn't help but add under her breath, "It's about time you got the hang of it."

A slow smile lit up Marquand's face. "So that's how it's done," he murmured to himself, unable to mask the note of elation in his voice. "Lord, it seemed so effortless. I hardly felt any impact at all, and look at how far a distance the ball traveled."

Derrien had to admit with a grudging sniff that when the Viscount unbent enough to show aught but a look of icy hauteur upon his rigid features, he could appear almost attractive. That is, if one favored tall, broad-shouldered gentlemen of title with no apparent skills other than the ability to shuffle a deck of cards or knot an intricate cravat. Which, of course, she most certainly did not.

Philp also chose to indulge in an uncharacteristic show of emotion, going so far as to clap Marquand on the shoulder. "We'll make a golfer of you yet, my lord."

The Viscount's smile broadened, revealing a boyish enthusiasm Derrien wouldn't have guessed possible. He further surprised her by breaking into a most unlordly trot in his haste to reach his ball. "The middle spoon," he called, waving at her with undisguised impatience. "Stop dawdling, lad." He nearly snatched the club out from under her arm as she approached. "What say you, seventy yards to the flag?"

Derrien squinted to make out the flutter of bright cloth through the mist. "Nay, the distance is deceiving in this weather. It's more like eighty." She stood quite still for a moment, gauging the feel of the swirling breeze. "And another ten for the wind." Her hand reached out and pulled the middle spoon from his grasp. "You'll need the heavier club."

"The devil I will." Marquand ignored the proffered handle. "Give me the middle spoon."

She clamped the club in question even more firmly under her arm. "You'll hit what I tell you to hit." There was a deliberate pause before she added, "sir." Even a half-wit could not have mistaken the sneer in her tone.

Philp hastily interposed himself between the two of them to ensure that the next swing of a club was not directed at Derrien's head. "What's the trouble here?"

Marquand pointed a long elegant finger at his scowling caddie. "This impudent little wretch won't give me the deuced club I asked for."

"Of course I won't, Mr. Philp, because it isn't the right shot to attempt." Her chin jutted out with a defiant tilt.

"You said I was to try and teach him something about the game, but if he insists on being a total gudgeon . . ." Her words trailed off, but not without a decided snort of contempt.

"Hmmmm." The older man looked from lord to lad, then slowly removed the pipe from his pocket and took his time in tamping down the fragrant tobacco. Several puffs of smoke curled up into the gusting breeze before he spoke. "How far do you hit a middle spoon, my lord?"

"You just saw. It was eighty yards at least."

"Aye, and a bonny shot it was. The best you've struck so far." He paused for a fraction. "How often could you do it again, sir? Nine times in ten? Seven in ten? Or perhaps only two in ten?"

Marquand's lips compressed, and much to his chagrin he felt a tinge of color creeping to his cheeks.

"Now, do you know what lies in front of the green? Or behind it?"

"Of course he doesn't," interrupted Derrien. "He didn't know enough to ask." She turned a look of withering scorn on the Viscount. "There is a sharp gully cutting in front of the hole, while behind it, the ground rolls off in a gentle incline. If you hit your ball short, it will take several strokes to recover, while there is little penalty for hitting it long. It's quite simple, really. One way you give yourself a chance to win the hole, while the other—"

"Thank you, Derry. I believe you've made the point sufficiently clear." Philp slowly let out another ring of smoke and watched it drift toward the waves breaking upon the strand. "Golf is a mental game as well as a physical one, Lord Marquand. Especially match play. Think of it this way—you will soon be going into battle against a tough opponent. You would do well to consider yourself a Wellington of sorts. You must weigh risk, understand your own capabilities—and those of your foe—in order to devise a strategy that will give you the best chance of success."

A muscle twitched in the Viscount's jaw. He was sorely

tempted to use Philp's advice to justify an immediate retreat to his residence, and then back to London. If he could be outwitted and outmaneuvered by a mere schoolboy, surely he had no chance up against a canny veteran like Hertford. He drew in a long breath, feeling the master's appraising eyes on him. But it was the veiled look of triumph in the caddie's eyes that decided his course of action. Why, it was just what the imp expected of him, to explode in a fit of pointless pique or quit the field in a huff.

He reached out his hand. "The scraper, if you please."

Derrien gave it over without a word.

Marquand took his stance over the ball, taking care to set his feet at the proper distance. He gave the club a waggle or two, then let go with a prodigious swing, powerful, yet controlled. The ball shot off, as if fired from a cannon, and ripped through the fog to land a scant five yards past the flag. Without so much as a look at Derrien's face, he flipped the club in her direction, then stalked off toward the green.

"Well, well. So his lordship has some competitive fire beneath that icy exterior." The fine lines around Philp's eyes crinkled in humor as he gave a low chuckle. "Derry, my dear, I think our man might just have a chance."

"How did the lesson go today?"

Marquand tossed his jacket over the arm of the sofa and sat down with a sigh. "Philp seems to think I am making some progress. And it does appear that the ball is beginning to go in the vague direction that I am aiming." His lips pursed. "Though it is still up in the air as to whether I shall be able to refrain from throttling that irritating little caddie before the match with Hertford." After a moment's reflection, he gave a rueful grimace. "However, I suppose I had better keep my hands wrapped around the club, for despite his egregious manners, the damn brat does seem to know a good deal about the game."

Ellington laughed. "Well, you did imply at one time that you thought the game would be child's play." He tossed a thick vellum card onto the Viscount's lap on his way to pour himself a glass of Madeira. "Do not forget, we are invited to an evening musicale at Sir Twining's residence tonight. It is to be our introduction to local Society, so I'll not hear of you trying to cry off," he added, on seeing the look of incipient mutiny that crossed the Viscount's features. "Jamie has gone to a good deal of trouble to arrange our welcome here, and it would be most rag-mannered of us to ignore such efforts." He took a sip from his glass. "Did you not notice there was also a note on the tray downstairs for you? It arrived only an hour or two ago."

Marquand pulled a face. "I cannot imagine who it might be from. I have no acquaintance with anyone in town."

"Well, that may no longer be the case, Adrian. I saw a traveling coach pass down Market Street when I was out earlier, and if I am not mistaking the crest upon the door, it appears the lovely Miss Dunster and her parents have arrived in St. Andrews."

A muttered oath slipped from the Viscount's lips. Now what the devil was Lady Honoria and her family doing here, he wondered? A sudden vision of Lord Hylton's corpulent face came to mind, and how the man's greedy eyes had blinked in rapid succession on hearing the request for his daughter's hand, as if they were the beads of an abacus adding up the possible assets of such an alliance. His mouth tightened in a grim line. Whatever was in the note that awaited his perusal, he could already read between the lines. It was clear he was not the only one with an interest in the fate of Woolsey Hall.

It shouldn't be of any great surprise, he told himself. After all, hadn't he also voiced the opinion that a match should be based on a purely rational assessment of the benefits? Still, he found himself feeling rather like a stud being led out at Tattersall's, to be watched intently by the prospective buyers as he was put through his paces.

And he found himself chafing at the bit.

"I would have expected a slightly more, er, joyous reaction on learning that your bride-to-be and her family have journeyed such a great distance to lend support to your endeavor." Ellington toyed with the silver stopper of the decanter, his gaze ostensibly averted from Marquand's stony countenance.

"If Hylton is to lend anything, you may be sure he expects a handsome return on his investment." The words were barely audible but they caused his friend's fingers to pause on the polished top. Rising abruptly, Marquand took up his jacket, still heavy with the salt air. "If you will excuse me, Tony, I have a number of things to attend to before we must make our appearance tonight."

Chapter Five

Ellington could see that the last few hours had done little to improve his friend's disposition. The Viscount had sat in gloomy silence during the short carriage ride to North Street, and his expression as they mounted the stairs to the Baronet's drawing room might charitably be described as "mulish." Several less flattering adjectives came to Ellington's mind, and as their host stepped forward to greet them, he was forced to whisper a harsh rebuke in Marquand's ear.

"Ah, gentlemen! So nice to make your acquaintance." Sir Twining pumped each of their hands in turn. "Bowmont has written that we are to take good care of you, though I fear that after the sort of things you are used to in London, our small town and its entertainments will seem sadly flat to you."

"Not at all," demurred Ellington. "Especially seeing as we plan to take advantage of the marvelous sporting opportunities afforded here in Scotland during our stay. Isn't that right, Adrian?"

"Yes. Of course," said Marquand, the reply nudged out of him by a discreet poke to the ribs.

"Well, if you have come for golf, you have come to the right place, indeed!" With a smile, the Baron slipped his pudgy hand around Ellington's elbow. "Do you shoot as well, sir?" The affirmative nod caused the fellow to look even more pleased. "Then you must meet Sir Strathburne, whose grouse moor is unrivaled . . ."

Marquand couldn't make out the rest of the words as his friend was hauled off toward a trio of stout gentlemen near the stone fireplace. Reluctant to be drawn into what promised to be a long conversation regarding birds, as well as the relative merits of guns made by Manton versus the new upstart, James Purdey, he remained where he was, doing his best not to glower as if he were nursing a backside full of buckshot. His friend was right. It would be unforgivably rude to spurn this generous show of hospitality by the local gentry, but as his gaze swept over the assembled guests, he found both his manners and his patience close to deserting him. Spotting several large botanical prints that promised to be of more interest than any of the people present, he made his way over to the quiet nook where they hung. Though the plants were a rather obscure native variety with which he was unfamiliar, and the quality of the line and colors unusually fine, they failed to lift his spirits for more than a brief moment before his mind strayed back to what had him in such an unsettled mood.

That this unexpected wager had turned his meticulous, well-ordered life on its ear still rubbed him raw. He had worked so hard to avoid being at the mercy of chance, and yet despite all his careful planning, his future was to be decided by something just as serendipitous as the turn of a card. His mouth quirked at the bitter irony of it. The odds of emerging a winner certainly seemed stacked against him. Perhaps it would have been better had the match with Hertford been scheduled right away rather than in several weeks. That way, he thought with a tightening of his jaw, his defeat would have been mercifully swift, instead of having to endure this tortuous round of small humiliations. Why, even this afternoon, a mere lad had shown him to be hardly more than a fool, and an arrogant one at that—

"Lord Marquand?"

His head jerked around from the gilt frame.

"I fear the mere mention of winged targets makes our host fly into a description of the joys of hunting in the Highlands which even a devoted marksman might find trying." A tall, rather gaunt gentleman whose receding silver hair only accentuated his long, narrow face and beaked nose peered at the Viscount through a pair of silver-rimmed spectacles with a faintly bemused expression. "I hope he has not left you feeling too neglected?"

Marquand managed a civil reply.

The other man stole a glance at the engravings that the Viscount had been studying. "Have you an interest in botany, my lord?"

He merely shrugged.

The fellow did not seem undeterred by the lack of an answer. "I am Mr. Walter Kildare, professor of literature at the University and a cousin of our host. Since he is occupied in regaling your friend with yet another hunting story, perhaps you would permit me to introduce you to some of our other guests?"

"Of course." Marquand turned away from the pictures and tried to look as if it were not he who was feeling like a stalked creature.

Several other faculty members were brought forward, along with the rector of United College. Kildare's dark hazel eyes then took on a decided twinkle on reaching for the hand of the next person "Ah, in case you were beginning to think us a sadly misogynous group, please allow me to present Mrs. Edwards, widow of one of our esteemed colleagues and a lady whose tireless efforts on behalf of those in the local orphanage are much admired by all of us."

The Viscount expected someone of ascetic mien, without an extra ounce of good humor or joviality to her thin frame, so his eyes betrayed a flicker of surprise on being presented. The older lady's graying hair and modest attire could not dull the fact that she had been a rare beauty in her day. Even now, her porcelain skin and generous curves would have drawn a glance of admiration from many a gentleman—and from the stealthy looks cast by her surrounding company, it still did.

"Lord Marquand." She gave a playful smile as she dipped a graceful curtsy. "Let me add my voice to that of Mr. Kildare in assuring you that not all Scots are quite as bloodthirsty as our host."

Ha! Her words brought to mind his combative caddie, who had looked ready to knock his head off with a baffing spoon only hours earlier. Still, the obvious dry humor in her tone caused his own lips to twitch upward for the first time that evening. "I shall take your word for it ma'am, though from what I have witnessed on your local links, I would have to say your countrymen are not without a certain taste for blood."

"Ah, but that is golf, sir!" she replied with a twinkle. "A game, I have heard on numerous occasions from my late husband, that may drive even the mildest of men to contemplate murder."

An appreciative chuckle escaped from Marquand. "My limited experience has done nothing to gainsay such sage observation."

Mr. Kildare looked rather pleased at having finally chased the scowl from the English lord's face. Emboldened by his success, he sought to continue with his introductions. "Lord Marquand, I don't believe you have met Mrs. Edwards' niece." As he spoke, his spindly fingers reached behind a squat potted palm and reappeared wrapped firmly around the elbow of a young lady, who looked none-too happy at being dragged away from whatever it was she had been doing. "I have the honor of presenting Miss Derrien Edwards."

The Viscount saw a marked family resemblance, though the niece was shorter and more willowy than her aunt, and her cornflower blue eyes a shade lighter—but perhaps that was because they were at the moment warmed with a distinct look of displeasure. He gave a slight incline of his head. "Miss Edwards."

The candlelight glinted off the coppery highlights in her blond hair, giving her a decidedly Mars-like aura that matched the grim expression that had spread over her delicate features. Marquand stifled a wry grin at seeing a mood that so closely matched his own, wondering at the same time what could have caused such an unusual show of emotion in a girl barely out of the schoolroom. It was rare to see anything but a carefully schooled mask of bland cheerfulness on the face of a young miss, much less any hint of irritation.

"Lord Marquand." The young lady barely dropped a

curtsy and withdrew her fingers from his with what seemed to be obvious haste. He could swear she would have turned and retreated back behind the fronds of the tree had not the professor kept a tight grasp on her arm.

Puzzled by such behavior, his eyes lingered on her person as if to discover something of its source. Like her aunt, Miss Edwards was not attired in anything resembling what passed for fashion in London, yet the dark, serviceable garments could not altogether disguise what looked to be a graceful neck and lovely set of shoulders. He found himself almost wishing that the neckline of her gown was a good deal more up to date so that he might see if her skin was as creamy as . . .

He jerked his thoughts away from such ridiculous musings. It was a testament to how out of kilter his mind had become that he was taking any notice of an ill-mannered country chit. And one with a feisty attitude, a lightly tanned face, and a dusting of freckles to boot! Why, the little minx was probably hoyden enough to run around outside without a bonnet on. That gave him pause for a moment, as a vision of the sun playing over the masses of golden curls popped into his head.

His lip curled in a self-mocking grimace. One would think he had been imbibing that strong stuff the Scots seemed so fond of by the crazy meandering of his thoughts! After all, she was not in the least the type of female he was attracted to. He preferred a proper sort of lady who was cool, composed, and most of all, biddable—

A loud announcement by the butler caused the Viscount's gaze to shift abruptly and all improper reveries concerning Miss Derrien Edwards were immediately chased away by the booming words. Other heads swiveled as well, silence reigning as the local gentry took in the silky splendor of the trio ascending the stairs. The gentleman stepped forward after his eyes had completed a brief sweep of the assembled guests and gave a tug at the lapel of his claret-colored swallow-tailed evening coat.

"Well, Marquand. You have chosen a deucedly strange place in which to rusticate for a time."

Arrogant coxcomb! fumed Derrien as the Viscount walked away with only the most cursory of excuses to her aunt and Mr. Kildare.

The nerve of the odious man to rake his eyes over her person as if she were no more than a cut of lamb set out for his supper and then to walk away as if what he had seen quite robbed him of his appetite! She had not missed the slight curl of his well-chiseled lips nor his haste to quit her presence as soon as his English acquaintances had arrived. Not that she cared one whit what he thought of her, but his haughty reserve, broken only by fits of ill temper, was even more abrasive here in the drawing room than on the links. It was clear he had no desire to be mingling with the local gentry. He had been wearing an expression as black as the set of elegant evening clothes molded to his muscular frame since the moment he had mounted the stairs, and even his friend had had enough manners to demand a better face.

Did the insufferable Viscount hold all Scots to be beneath an Englishman's notice? Or was he merely a stiff-rumped prig in general? Derrien ventured a peek at the tall, flaxen-haired beauty whose hand he was bringing to his lips. The young lady was dressed in an elegant gown of pale gray watered silk, cut to accentuate the svelte curves of her feminine from. The candles danced over the shimmering material, and with her pale coloring, frozen features, and the knot of pearls at her throat she looked to Derrien's eyes exactly like an icicle—a vision of cold, sharp perfection.

Derrien couldn't repress a smirk. What a couple! The lady was undeniably beautiful, and despite her instinctive dislike for the Viscount, she could not deny that he was an extremely attractive man, with his dark curling hair, piercing gray-green eyes, and sculpted features as classic as any wrought by the Greeks. That was just it—the two of them appeared to have no more heart or soul than the works chiseled by the ancient masters from inanimate marble.

She brushed an errant curl back from her freckled cheek. The Viscount's exterior might be flawless, but she knew the faults that lay beneath the surface. He was a reprobate, a gamester, and no doubt worse. Of the young lady's shortcomings Derrien could only imagine. But judging from the beauty's rigid features, she was like all other ladies of the English *ton,* puffed up with a sense of her own consequence and concerned with naught but money and social position. Yes, the two of them were eminently suited to each other, with their polished appearance and stiff-rumped demeanor. With one last disdainful look in their direction, Derrien slipped back into the tiny alcove hidden by the leafy palm and picked up the book on gardening that she had been eagerly perusing before the professor's unwelcome interruption.

It was a work with which she was unfamiliar, and the diagrams were most intriguing, so at least the evening was not going to be a complete waste of time.

"I thought I might play along with you on your round this afternoon." Ellington speared another piece of kippered herring and poured both of them another tankard of drink. "That is, if my presence won't distract you from your lesson with Mr. Philp. I know that you have little time to spend with him these days."

Marquand looked up from the piece of paper on which he was busy scrawling some diagrams. "Er, no, you are welcome to see how I am faring." His attention immediately returned to his jottings.

His friend craned his neck to peer over the pitcher of cider. "Notes on strategy?"

"Ahhhh." The sheet was folded and hastily stuffed in his pocket. "Actually, some notes on a garden I passed this morning," he admitted with a sheepish grin. "The arrangement of rhododendrons and Norfolk pine was most interesting and I wished to remember how they were placed."

Ellington smiled in return, taking in the dark circles

under the Viscount's eyes. "Knowing you, half the night was spent filling your notebooks with such scribblings as well. Lord, you can still think of your work, even under these circumstances?"

"I hardly think of it as work, Tony. For me it is . . ." He paused, struggling to put his feelings into words.

"A passion?" suggested his friend.

"That seems a bit melodramatic. I'm not a very passionate fellow. It's just that when I pick up my sketchbook or look at a patch of dirt and begin to envision a plan, I can forget all else. My imagination can soar as high as the clouds—" His voice cut off, a look of slight embarrassment stealing over his features.

"Not passionate? Why, you've become a poet as well as an artist." Ellington gave a low chuckle. "Lord, there's hope for you yet, Adrian."

A faint tinge of color rose to the Viscount's cheeks.

Ellington took a long draft of his cider. "And what does your intended bride think of this . . . work of yours?"

"I told you, she isn't aware of it—yet."

His friend's brow shot up.

"I shall tell her, of course," he added defensively. "Not that it will make any difference to our . . . arrangement."

"No, of course not," murmured Ellington softly. "It should not matter a whit to Miss Dunster or her family that the future Earl of Chittenden is engaged in trade."

The Viscount didn't answer. Groping in his pocket for a handful of coins, he stood up abruptly and tossed them on the table to pay for their meal. "Come on, we must not be late for our game with Mr. Philp."

The master and caddie were waiting at the first hole, Philp tamping a pinch of fragrant tobacco into the bowl of his pipe, while Derrien swung one of the tapered hickory clubs in some impatience, neatly trimming a large tuft of grass down to a mere stubble with several swipes. Her eyes narrowed at the sight of the tall English lord and his friend approaching. He wore the same grim expression she had come to expect, but today, there was also a look of fatigue etched around his eyes. Out gaming all night, she thought, repressing a snort of disgust. Or indulging in one of those other activities that rakes and wastrels did.

"I hope you do not mind if I play along?" asked Ellington. "I should like to try out the new long spoon I purchased from you."

Philp gave a friendly wave of his hand. "You're more than welcome to join in, sir. Shall I send up to the shop for the rest of your clubs and another caddie?"

"Nay, no need for that. I'll make use of the Viscount's new sticks." He gave an appreciative glance at the finely tapered heads and neatly corded wrappings. "A lovely set they look to be."

"Let's get on with it," muttered Derrien under her breath as she readied a club. A sharp look from Philp pricked her conscience, reminding her she was here for a reason other than to antagonize their pupil. "Your club . . . sir," she said in a louder voice, striving for a less hostile tone.

Marquand took the proferred long spoon without so much as a look at her and waited for her to finish building the small pile of sand on which his ball was placed. Aware of three pairs of eyes on his back, he took an extra few moments in his setup. His arms finally drew back a bit stiffly, then swung forward at a rapid clip. However the timing was a touch off. The clubface lagged behind his hands, making contact with the ball at an odd angle. The leather-covered sphere sliced low through the breeze, drifted right, then came to rest in the middle of a patch of tall grass, not more than fifty yards from where it had been struck.

A low oath escaped from between the Viscount's clenched jaw.

His friend quickly averted his eyes and appeared to be studying the progress of a gull out over the strand.

"Throw down another, Lord Marquand," advised the master.

He did so and swung again. The results were nearly the same, only this time the ball arced even farther right and did not travel quite as far.

"I assure you, I have been hitting it better than that of late, Tony," growled the Viscount, his cheeks taking on a deeper shade of red than the wind might have been expected to raise.

Derrien stared pointedly at the two wayward shots. With an exaggerated sniff, she handed him a lofted iron. "You'll need this one to get out of that sort of trouble."

Marquand stalked after her without a word. Once the first ball had been located in the rough, he sought to find some sort of stable footing in the tangled grass. Despite all his efforts, he could gain no more than an awkward stance, which allowed him nothing but an off-balance hack at it. The club cut through the tall stalks with the swish of a scythe.

The ball didn't budge.

He swung again, this time even harder. It popped forward maybe three inches but still remained deeply embedded in the rough.

Derrien suppressed a grin. "Maybe you should just use your foot, sir."

The Viscount looked less than amused at the jibe. His grip tightened around the sueded sheepskin grip and it appeared as though his next swipe might do damage to more than a mere blade of grass.

Philp gave a discreet cough. "You may count that as the first of your lessons for the day, my lord. All beginners play badly when performing before their first audience. Don't fret on it. With some practice, you will soon get used to it. It's important to just relax and forget about the presence of any onlookers. Now pick up your ball and we will move on to the second hole."

From the expression on the Viscount's face, Derrien was fully ready to see him explode in a fit of pique at the blow to his pride. Instead his lips slowly curled in a rueful smile. "I take your meaning, Mr. Philp. I have seen countless green cubs at Manton's or Jackson's Boxing Saloon make a fool of themselves by trying too hard. I suppose I must have looked equally as ridiculous. It's a mistake I'll try not to repeat."

Her brow furrowed slightly at the unexpected response.

However unlikely, it appeared the starchy English lord could actually laugh at himself. Grudgingly, she found her opinion of him rising just a notch. Perhaps the gentleman was not as totally lacking in sensibility as she had thought.

The next several holes went more smoothly. With a few additional pointers from Philp, Marquand began managing quite a number of credible shots. By the ninth hole, he even bested his more experienced friend in putting the ball in the hole, drawing an appreciative whistle.

"A round of ale says you will not beat me on the back nine." Ellington grinned as they turned to start making their way back toward the town.

"Done."

The two of them began a match of teasing words as well, the bantering growing more lively as the match remained close. From beneath the brim of her floppy tweed cap, Derrien observed the animation of the Viscount's face, further surprised by the boyish enthusiasm of his grins and the flash of spirit in his gray-green eyes. Relaxed in the company of his friend, he appeared a completely different person from the one who set her hackles up. His wit was engaging, his laughter infectious. He even had the taciturn Philp grinning at some of his more pithy sallies.

Why, the fellow was proving to be human after all—and a rather interesting one at that. For some reason, she found that to be a most unsettling discovery. It was much easier to despise a block of stone.

After striking their first drives on the fifteenth hole, the two English lords strolled to where their caddie and the golfing master were standing, one hundred yards up the fairway, behind a thick copse of gorse. "Hell's teeth, I fear I had one too many glasses of that excellent cider," muttered Marquand as he stopped and began to unfasten the flap of his breeches.

"W—what are you doing?" cried Derrien with a sharp squeak.

The Viscount's fingers paused on the buttons. "What do you think I am doing, lad? I am taking a leak." Caught up in the teasing mood that had sprung up between himself and his friend, his lips curled faintly in a mocking smile as he winked at Ellington. "Or are Scotsmen built on a different jig?"

"Good Lord! Well, aren't you going to . . . t—turn around?"

Philp cleared his throat. "Ahhh, he's a rather innocent lad," he murmured to the two Englishmen. "Only females at home. Very, er, religious household. Not used to seeing, er, such—well, you know."

Marquand's brow arched up. "Are the Presbyterians so starched up they believe the Almighty has forbidden man to take a piss?" Nonetheless, he turned around to face the bushes.

Derrien's face was a vivid shade of scarlet by the time the Viscount had finished. On seeing the caddie's acute discomfort, Marquand found he could not refrain from the childish urge to pay his caddie back for some of the previous humiliations he had endured from the lad's sharp tongue. As they began to walk toward their drives, he turned to Ellington with a casual question. "No doubt you are missing the charms of that delectable little opera dancer you've tucked away in Chiswick?"

Taking the Viscount's cue without missing a step, his friend grinned. "Ah, the lovely Mademoiselle Antoinette? Indeed I am." They proceeded to discuss—in graphic detail—just exactly what those charms comprised, pointedly ignoring all of Philp's strangled coughs.

Finally, Marquand turned a quizzical eye on his teacher. "Are you Scotsmen so straitlaced as to have no interest—or appreciation—of the opposite sex? His gaze shifted to a furiously blushing Derrien, and with a wicked gleam in his eye, he inquired, "Had any luck yourself, lad?"

To her intense mortification, the color in her cheeks deepened to match the scarlet stripe in Ellington's waistcoat.

"Scottish lasses must be much shyer than the girls in the south," he went on. "I'm surprised you haven't managed a tumble in the hay as of yet. You're a good-looking youth"—he winked again at his friend—"and *big* enough, wouldn't you think, Tony? Though we'll be better able to judge when he's ready to relieve himself."

Ellington gave a peal of laughter as Derrien began to fairly sprint ahead. "Don't worry, lad," he called. "Your size may not match his lordship's yet, but it will increase as you *grow* to manhood."

Marquand's lips quirked upward. He looked back at the older man. "Bit of a prude, that lad. Why, by his age, both Tony and I had no doubt been near to bedding a willing wench or two."

Philp fixed them with a look of stony reproach. "Perhaps you gentlemen wouldn't mind if we turned our attention back to golf?" he said rather sharply. "You would do well, Lord Marquand, not to waste what little time you have with me in frivolous behavior. If you must indulge in bawdy talk, I should ask you to confine it to the taverns, not the links."

All trace of amusement disappeared from Marquand's face. "Forgive us if we have offended you. We were merely having a bit of friendly sport with the lad, as gentlemen are wont to do. Hell's teeth, the cocky little urchin has been asking to be taken down a peg or two—"

"No! I must have your word that you will leave off any further teasing of my young friend. Derry is . . . more sensitive than most lads, and I'll not have my best caddie overset for any reason. Otherwise, you may seek out a different teacher."

"Very well," replied the Viscount stiffly. "We shall refrain from any more bantering with the brat, though I must say, he's a deucedly odd lad to be so missus about the normal way of things between men."

Philp cleared his throat. "I daresay some Scots may be a tad different from the English in certain respects. Now, sir, as to the position of your left hand when you set up to drive . . ." With a deft turn of the phrase, the master steered the conversation away from any further hazards.

The round finished without further incident, and Philp congratulated his pupil on his progress. "Well played, sir. You are at the stage now where practice is more important than further instruction." He made a show of adjusting the silver spectacles perched on his nose. "For the next little while, I shall leave it up to you and Derry to work together on the course."

The Viscount and his caddie exchanged scowls.

"I trust you will find a way to make some progress." Philp regarded both of them with a meaningful look.

"I don't suppose I have any choice," growled Marquand.

"Not if you wish to have any hope of success, my lord."

Chapter Six

Derrien yanked the brush through her tangled curls. *Odious man*, she repeated yet again. If it weren't for her friendship with Hugh she would be sorely tempted to abandon the debauched London rake to the hazards of the links and Lord Hertford without a second thought. He certainly deserved as much. Her cheeks nearly colored again on recalling a few of the more spicy details exchanged by the Viscount and his friend. How dare they speak in such a vulgar and unrestrained way in the company of a . . . Her fingers paused in teasing out another snarl and she gave a rueful grimace into the cheval glass. In all fairness, he could not be accused of *that*, she admitted, just as honesty compelled her to acknowledge that his comments had not been so very different from those she had heard bandied about among the caddies on numerous occasions. Still, there were plenty of other sins to lay at his door.

Gambling, for one. He wouldn't be here unless he was a reckless gamester, stupid enough to risk a fortune on the turn of a card. And wenching. His conversation had made it quite plain that he was no stranger to the game of seduction. For a moment, a picture came to mind of piercing gray-green eyes peering out from beneath dark, windblown locks and she imagined that he had no lack of invitations from eager partners. No doubt the thought of those broad shoulders and strong, lithe hands would make any lady more than willing to offer . . . The bristles of the brush dug in deeply enough to cause her to wince.

Whatever was she doing, thinking such ridiculous thoughts—even for an instant!

Men like Viscount Marquand and the Marquess of Hertford seduced women without a care to the pain and suffering they left in their wake. The reflection in the mirror caught the hardening of Derrien's expression. Though she felt a simmering anger for the Viscount and his undoubtably rakish ways, her contempt rose to a boil on considering his coming opponent. Forced to make a choice between them, she had to admit that Lord Marquand was the lesser of two evils. She could only imagine his faults, while those of Hertford were all too real.

For the sake of the unfortunate women who had fallen victim to his practiced charm—or brute strength—as well as her dear friend Hugh Philp, she would do her best to see the dastardly Hertford beaten at this particular game, even if it meant helping . . .

"Derrien?" Her aunt poked her head into the small bedchamber. "My dear girl! The invitation is for eight and you are not near ready. I shall send Lucy in to you right away. She will be able to make short work of that unruly mop of curls."

Derrien glowered at her own reflection. "I would much rather stay home and finish the book I borrowed from Professor McAuley's library."

"That may be so, my dear, but as Baron Twining is anxious to show the visitors from London that the folk of St. Andrews may be as cultured and hospitable as any people to the south, we owe it to our friend to help make a favorable impression on the English guests."

Ha! There was little chance of that, she thought in silent retort. However, she decided to keep such things to herself. While her aunt knew of her usual masquerade on the links, she was not yet aware of her niece's involvement in training the English lord. And though in general she was the most tolerant of guardians, Derrien decided it would perhaps be prudent not to put the issue to a test.

"For his sake," continued her aunt, "I know you will do your best to be pleasant to Lord Marquand and Lord Ellington."

Derrien ducked her head, feeling slightly guilty to recall the numerous snide remarks she had flung at the

Viscount over the past little while. "Very well," she muttered, rooting in her dressing table drawer for a ribbon to match the trim of her gown. Glancing up at her reflection, she made another face. Lucy might well be able to coax her curls into some resemblance of order, but there was little anyone could do about the smattering of freckles across her nose. She couldn't help envisioning a certain creamy complexion, unmarred by any such unladylike imperfection, and for some reason her mood grew even more prickly.

As she waited in some impatience for her aunt's maid to arrive, she withdrew a small notebook and pencil from a drawer and added it to her reticule.

She had heard that Mr. Gregory had recently received several unusual specimen plantings from the West Indies for his garden, so perhaps the evening would not prove to be a total bore.

"Well now, finally a moment alone." Marquand's steps came to a halt before a wrought-iron bench and his gloved hand shifted beneath Honoria's fingers. "Would you care to sit down, my dear?"

"No, thank you. Since Mama was feeling poorly and required me to sit and read to her all afternoon, I think I should prefer to keep strolling, sir—Adrian, that is." The last vestiges of the setting sun suffused the garden with a pale wash of gold, and for an instant, the soft play of light and shadow across her profile and the folds of her ivory silk gown made her appear at one with the carved statue standing behind her. "It is a pretty garden, is it not? Only look at this charming Greek faun standing among the bower of dahlias."

He forced a weak smile. "It is a Roman satyr and the flowers are common tuber roses."

"Oh. How . . . interesting."

It was clear that it was no such thing, and the Viscount found his teeth setting on edge. Her air of cool detachment had been one of the qualities that had attracted him to her—she was no voluble schoolroom chit given to wild flights of emotion. But he suddenly found himself wishing she might show a bit more . . . life. He knew that she possessed opinions and the intelligence to express them in an interesting way, for the conversations they had shared as they became acquainted had assured him that she was by no means a vapid idiot. He would never have been able to tolerate that, not even for a lovely face and generous dowry. Yet since his intentions had become clear, it seemed that for some reason she was becoming increasingly rigid and remote in his presence, rather than the opposite. He couldn't begin to fathom why. Of late, she looked as though the prospect of their upcoming nuptials was about as palatable as a dose of castor oil.

The thought was rather disturbing.

She must have sensed the stiffening of his arm. Her head turned slightly. "Is something wrong?"

"Not at all," he lied, drawing them a few steps farther along the graveled path. There was an arrangement of rather unusual plants behind a large urn that had caught his eye. "And what of you, Honoria? You seem a trifle preoccupied of late. Is there something on your mind?"

"I—I suppose I am still a bit overwhelmed with the honor you do me in asking me to be your future Countess. I shall try to be worthy of the choice."

Were her words really as stilted as they sounded to his ears? He drew in a sharp breath, but quickly brushed aside any momentary irritation and compressed his lips in what he hoped was a semblance of a smile. "Worthy? Why there is nothing to be nervous about. You are the very model of perfection." Now it was his own phrases that sounded hopelessly contrived. At least she appeared not to notice.

"How kind of you . . . Adrian. I shall try not to give you any cause for further comment. Mama says that gentlemen dislike above all things being distracted by a fidgeting female."

His brows drew together. "I should hope you would always feel free to discuss with me anything that was bothering you."

"Yes. Of course." She bit at her lip and turned to

examine the carving along the rim of the garden ornament. "Actually, sir, there is a matter that I should—Eeeeek!" A shriek interrupted her halting words as she suddenly tripped over a figure crouched among the cascading ivy. "Good heavens! There is someone hiding here in the bushes!"

Marquand rushed to steady Honoria's trembling form. "There is no need for alarm, my dear." His gaze had already raked over Derrien's slightly disheveled gown and the bits of broken leaves that had twined themselves in among her golden curls. "It is only one of the other guests."

Honoria's hand flew to her alabaster throat on taking a second look at the figure still half hidden in the shadows of the swaying boughs. "It is hard to believe that the local young ladies have no more concept of proper behavior than to be sneaking around in the dark, spying—"

"I was *not* spying," retorted Derrien, rising to her feet and brushing a stray lock from her cheek. "As it happens, *I* was here first."

A faint gasp sounded. "But what were you doing out here if not skulking after his lordship and myself?"

Derrien's hands came to her hips. "I was having a look at the *Ananas bracteatus* that Mr. Gregory has just received from the isle of Jamaica."

Marquand edged slightly closer to the bed of plantings and stole a quick glance. "And a most unusual specimen it is," he murmured, itching to bend down as Derrien had been doing and subject the multi-colored striated leaves and cluster of spidery stamens to a more thorough examination.

Honoria's eyes widened in confusion. "What—?"

"Ahh, most unusual," he repeated gruffly. "For a lone female to be outside unaccompanied—"

Derrien interrupted him with an unladylike snort. "What fustian your silly set of Town strictures are. I'm hardly in any danger of running into trouble among people I've known all my life—or of being a threat to any sensible person. It is only a martinet such as you who would kick up a dust." She turned to Honoria, her eyes sending off more sparks than the garden torches flickering in the salty breeze. "And as for spying on you—if I was going to run the risk of being caught out in such an outrageous breech of manners, I would certainly pick a more interesting couple to eavesdrop on! I vow, the two of you appear to have ice water rather than blood running through your veins. I wish you happy with each other, for I can't imagine any person with a real pulse wishing to cultivate an acquaintance with either one of you." With a flounce of her unruly curls, she turned on her heel and stalked back toward the stone terrace.

The Viscount's lips twitched in some amusement at the whole situation, but he quickly covered such transgression with a brief cough.

Ashen-faced, Honoria drew in a sharp breath, and her hands clenched into tight fists by her side. "Everything about this odd country is quite . . . unexpected," she whispered.

"Pay the annoying little chit no mind. She's obviously naught but a sharp-tongued little hoyden, with none of your ladylike polish," said Marquand, his arm stealing around her rigid waist at the same time that his gaze couldn't help but follow the defiant tilt of the other young lady's slim shoulders and the lively swaying of her boyish hips.

He forced his eyes back to Honoria's pale face, which in the faint wash of light appeared as if it were carved from the same block of marble as the urn behind her. For an instant, he couldn't help but recall the flashing blue eyes, flushed cheeks, and expressive mouth of the other young lady's visage, and for some reason felt a tightening in his chest. He gave another cough, then tried to offer some additional soothing words to his intended, but they seemed to stick in his throat.

"Please, sir." Her eyes pressed closed. "Perhaps it would be best to go back inside, where we will not run the risk of any more . . . surprises."

He cast one more longing look at the plants, then swallowed hard and offered his arm. "Yes. Of course, my dear." Yet for a moment he didn't move. "Er, was there something you were going to tell me before we were interrupted?"

Her gloved hand tightened on his sleeve. "It can wait," she said softly.

By the time they reentered the large drawing room Honoria had composed herself so that no trace of emotion marred her lovely features. Chin held high, a faint smile upon her finely shaped lips, she caused more than a few conversations to falter in midsentence as she passed by.

"My dear Lord Marquand, you would not really be so heartless as to deprive the rest of us of the company of such a charming beauty as Lady Honoria for the entire evening," called Sir Twining from where a small group of gentlemen had assembled near the fire.

The Viscount gave an inward wince at the man's choice of adjectives.

"Especially since you are to enjoy countless more evenings of the lady's company in the years to come," he added with a jovial laugh. "We have just now learned that congratulations are in order, sir." With a broad wink, his pudgy hand came out to take Honoria's other arm. "So, my lord, I must insist that you relinquish your future bride for a bit to others less fortunate than you. I wish to introduce her to a group of our most learned professors." He inclined his head a fraction "That is, of course, if you are not averse to mingling with us rough folk, Miss Dunster."

"Indeed not, sir." She readily allowed herself to be drawn away from the Viscount's side. "I should enjoy meeting all of the people who have been so hospitable to us strangers. And I am sure Lord Marquand will not mind being abandoned for a short while."

The Viscount's eyes strayed back to the open set of French doors. "No, no, not at all. Do go on, Honoria. In fact, there is something I wish to discuss with Tony before it slips my mind." After a brief bow, he turned and made his way toward the opening to the terrace with a purposeful stride, careful to avoid any eye contact with those he passed. He paused to take a glass of punch from a passing footman, then, after giving a furtive glance left and right, he slipped out into the cool night air. Putting the glass aside without so much as a taste, he hurried down the graveled path.

It was nearly dark, but by removing the torch from its bracket and holding it carefully to one side, he was able to study the rare plants for some time. It was a shame, he thought with a silent oath, that his snug cutaway evening jacket did not allow for the addition of pencil and sketch paper to his pockets, for he would dearly have loved to make a drawing or two, and a notation on color—

"I guessed you had stepped out here to blow a cloud and thought I'd join you." Ellington stared down at his friend, who was half hidden in the drooping ivy. "But what the devil are you doing down there? Practicing how to line up your putts?"

Marquand scrambled to his feet, brushing bits of dirt from his immaculate fawn trousers. "Er, looking at a plant. Several, in fact. They are quite rare in Britain, and I don't often have occasion to look at one closely."

Ellington lit up two cheroots and handed one to the Viscount. "One might think you would have other things on your mind besides exotic plants, Adrian." He grinned. "Did you and Miss Dunster enjoy a pleasant stroll out here alone?"

The Viscount growled something unintelligible, then, dragonlike, let out a puff of smoke. It swirled in a lazy circle, then spiraled upward in the gentle breeze to disappear in the darkness. "Have you been introduced to a Miss Edwards?" he inquired abruptly after a moment of silence.

His friend's brows drew together as he sought to put a face to the name. "Ah, yes. The blond sprite who is niece to the charming widow. She has a pretty enough face. With a snip or two of the scissors and decent modiste she would be quite presentable, don't you think?"

Marquand grimaced. "Ha! She would need a good trimming of her tongue as well before her presence would be acceptable in Polite Society. The little hellion has the manners of a Highland savage." At Ellington's questioning look, he went on to explain his comments. "She was frightfully rude to Honoria earlier this evening." He exhaled another wispy ring and watched it float away. "And on our first introduction, her whole demeanor was barely civil. I cannot help wonder why she has seen fit to act in such an odd way."

His friend shrugged. "Who can comprehend the inner working of any young lady's mind? But I shouldn't think overly about some rag-mannered country chit barely out of the schoolroom."

"Don't worry. I shan't." But somehow he could not seem to banish the vision of flashing blue eyes, a pert nose, and an expressive—most expressive—mouth. Just as he could not help comparing that animated face to one displaying a good deal more composure and well-schooled control. He drew in a lungful of smoke. Control? Or, as the little minx suggested, mere lack of feeling? He threw down the cheroot and ground it out beneath the heel of his boot, angry with himself for letting yet another impudent little brat of a Scot get under his skin. "Come on, Tony. We had best return to the party before we offend our host."

As the two gentlemen made their way back toward the stone terrace and the faint trill of voices, Honoria smiled at yet another of the professors from the University, this one a burly fellow with a bristling red beard who was introduced as one of the leading experts in Reformation theology at St. Mary's. However, it was impossible to judge whether or not the man was capable of rational thought, for he was unable to utter a single coherent word in her presence, merely stuttering and turning a shade matching his whiskers when she touched her glove to his.

"I hope we are not trying your patience too much," whispered the Baronet as he shooed the poor fellow away. "There is just one more member of our faculty that I should like to make known to you. And since he has spent several years in the environs of London, I trust he will show enough polish not to find himself tongue-tied in the presence of a lovely lady."

She touched his arm lightly. "Please do not apologize in the least, sir. Everyone here has gone to great lengths to make us feel welcome and I look forward to thanking as many of them as I can."

"You are as gracious as you are lovely, Lady Honoria. The Viscount is a lucky man, indeed," murmured Twining, bringing a faint flush to her cheeks with the effusive compliment."

He steered them past the ample bulk of two dowagers grousing with each other over the shocking rise in the price of herring to where three men stood in a circle, engaged in an earnest discussion on the merits of Byron's latest epic. Without waiting for a pause in the conversation, the Baronet tapped the shoulder of the man standing with his back to the rest of the room. "Charles, you have only arrived back from your trip to Glasgow this afternoon, so I don't believe you have had the pleasure of meeting our charming visitor from the south."

The man slowly turned around.

"Lady Honoria, may I present Mr. Charles Ferguson. Though he may appear a mere babe in years compared to the rest of us old coots, I assure you that he is one of our most respected scholars here at the University." So intent was he on composing a proper introduction that he failed to note all of the color had suddenly drained from the young lady's face and that her hand was clutching at his sleeve as if to keep herself upright.

"Charles," he continued in the same jovial tone, "I have the pleasure of presenting Miss Honoria Dunster . . ."

Ferguson bowed. "Miss Dunster," he murmured.

"Mr. Ferguson," she managed to whisper.

Sir Twining smiled. "And, I might add, soon to be Lady Marquand and the future Countess of Chittenden."

It was the young man's turn to go a deathly pale.

Honoria attempted to move, but her knees buckled and she swayed against the Baron's shoulder. "Good heavens! Are you feeling ill, Miss Dunster?" His arm came around her waist. Let me see you to the settee. Vinaigrette! Does someone have a bottle of vinaigrette?"

"Please," she murmured. "There is no need to make a fuss. I am merely feeling a bit . . . faint, that is all. If you would be kind enough to help me to that chair by the door, a breath of fresh air is all that I need."

He helped her sit down and the murmur of excitement that had raced through the assembled guests quickly died away as it became evident that nothing serious was amiss. Her mother hurried over and clapped her hands to her cheeks on taking in her daughter's wan face. "Honoria!" she exclaimed with some alarm. "Oh dear, what has happened, child?"

"My fault entirely," said Twining with a baleful grimace. "She was much too polite to tell me the crush of strangers was simply too much to bear." He turned to Honoria. "Can you ever forgive me for being such a nodcock?"

"You mustn't worry about it, sir. Really." Her eyes remained locked on her lap, where her fingers were twined together in a tight knot. "I may have experienced a bout of lightheadedness for a moment, but I . . . I am quite fine now, I assure you."

Her mother straightened. "Where is Hylton? And where is Marquand?"

"I am here," said the Viscount, stepping in through the open doors. "What is the matter?" His gaze traveled from Lady Dunster to Sir Twining to the face of his intended bride, still white as a sheet. "Good Lord, Honoria," he said, hurrying to her side. "You look as if you have seen a ghost."

"Ghost!" Lord Hylton elbowed his way through the ring of people who had gathered near his daughter's chair. "Don't be absurd, man! Never heard of a ghost who dared make an appearance in a room full of flesh-and-blood people—"

"I was merely indulging in a bit of hyperbole, sir," murmured the Viscount.

"Eh?" The other man eyed him with some suspicion. "Well, see that you don't make a habit of the stuff," he muttered. "I'll not tolerate any show of dissolute behavior. Can't have you turning out like the present Earl." A frown puckered his jowly face as he turned his attention back to Honoria.

"A grim fate indeed, to end up resembling one's father." Marquand spoke so softly that Hylton took no notice of his words, but Honoria cringed, her shoulders pressing hard against the back of the slatted chair.

"Hear now, missy, what's all this sprattle about ghosts and such?"

"It's nothing, Father. I'm feeling much better now." She essayed a smile but managed only a wan twitch of her lips.

"Hmmph! Not at all the thing, to have an evening of entertainment where a proper young lady is subject to such dashedly odd happenings," he grumbled. "Your mother and I are taking you home without delay. I'll not have your delicate constitution overset with farrididdles about apparitions and spirits."

"Yes, Father," she said in a small voice. "But truly, it is just a case of the room being a trifle . . . crowded. You know very well I am not so much of a silly widgeon to be spooked by mere talk of specters from the past. Any sensible person knows there are no such things as ghosts."

Yet as she rose, her expression looked nothing short of haunted.

Chapter Seven

The lord and the lad regarded each other with thinly veiled mutual suspicion. Philp, his head bent low over his workbench, never once looked up from the delicate task of shaping the curve of the baffing spoon's head. "I must have this set of clubs finished by tomorrow for Laird McAllister, else I risk losing an important patron. So the two of you will go out alone this afternoon. Now, Lord Marquand, I want you to work on your drives for an hour, concentrating on placing the ball in the fairway. Your distance is fine, but you must try to correct your tendency to slice the ball—Derry will explain what I mean. Then on the morrow, I would have you start playing a few holes as you would in a match. You must get used to the notion of working together as a team."

Neither of them budged.

"Well?" The master put down the file and pushed the spectacles back to the bridge of his nose. "His lordship's set is stored in the same rack as usual, lad," he murmured. "A box of new balls has arrived from Mr. Robertson's shop. Grab a handful when you leave and see what you think of their performance on the course."

Derrien, the hint well taken, shuffled off to retrieve Marquand's golf clubs.

The Viscount's jaw set. "Mr. Philp, I do not mean to question"—the man had already returned to scraping the edge of the fine-grained hawthorn wood—"your expertise, but—"

"It's getting late, my lord. Are you aware that if you arrive more than five minutes past your agreed-upon starting time in a match, you will be penalized?" The file moved back and forth in methodical fashion. "While you are walking toward your ball, you might ask Derry to go over the thirteen rules of the game. They were drawn up in 1744 by the Company of Gentlemen Golfers in Edinburgh and adopted here in St. Andrews ten years later. For a beginner they can be very confusing, but the lad understands their nuances quite well." He paused to locate a small razor. "Was there anything else, my lord?"

Marquand shoved his hands in his pocket and made for the door.

A stiff breeze was blowing in from the strand as they approached the first hole and the sun dodged in and out of a low bank of clouds. Several players were visible up ahead on the third hole, but other than such distant play, the course was deserted, save for an elderly woman and two children walking along Granny Clark's Wynd, the narrow path that cut along the eighteenth and first fairway. Derry took out the new balls and carefully inspected each one, discarding several in the process. These she placed in the left pocket of her oversized jacket while the others, save for the last, went into the right pocket. This one she tossed onto the stubbled grass, then handed the Viscount his long spoon. Not a word had passed between the two of them since leaving the shop, and as she stepped back and tucked the rest of the set under the crook of one arm, she showed no inclination for breaking the awkward silence.

Marquand took several practice swings, well aware of the pair of eyes boring into his back, then stepped up to the small featherie and let it fly. It started off in a nice arc, but then began tailing badly to the right, coming to land in one of the cart ruts that skirted the edge of the strand. Hand on his hip, he watched its flight, muttering a low oath under his breath as it bounced along the rocky ground.

"Your wrists, sir. Too stiff by half."

His head jerked around. "But Philp said the grip must be firm—"

"Aye, firm, but not as if they were made of iron. They

must release at the moment of impact." She dropped all the clubs but one and took an easy swing. "Like so."

"Again, if you please."

Derrien swung once more. "Here," she said as the sole of the spoon brushed along the grass. "See how the wrists turn over? It squares the clubface and thus allows the ball to fly in a straight line."

His brow furrowed slightly.

She tossed another ball on the ground. "Try again."

He took up the proper position, but as he drew the club back, it was clear that her explanation had only served to confuse his efforts. His movements became jerky and rather than catch the ball with a clean blow, the long spoon merely grazed the top of the stitched leather, causing it to dribble no more than a few yards from his feet.

Derrien choked back a guffaw and threw down yet another.

On the next try, the head of the club missed the ball entirely, gouging out a large piece of sod several inches behind it.

This time the bark of laughter was unrestrained.

He retrieved the divot and put it carefully back in place, pressing around the edges with the toe of his boot. With the tip of his club, he moved the ball to an unscarred patch of grass, but rather than set up for another swing, he suddenly turned on his heel and walked over to where Derrien was standing, coming to a halt squarely in front of her nose.

"Is it me in particular, Master Derry? Or are you merely an ill-mannered brat in general, childish enough to find another man's honest efforts a source of cruel amusement?"

The curl of contempt disappeared from Derrien's lips.

"I am heartily sick of your attitude, lad. If you have a quarrel with me, give voice to it, rather than snort in derision and mutter snide gibes. That is how *real* gentlemen behave." Marquand's eyes had become as stormy as the chop kicking up out in the bay, flecks of green awash in a sea of slate. "Now, I am going to try again, and if you don't care to make a constructive comment you may simply drop the clubs and take yourself off. Philp seems to have nothing but praise for you, but of yet, I've seen naught but a snotty-nosed brat too full of misplaced arrogance to share whatever knowledge he is supposed to possess."

He stalked back to his place, leaving Derrien mute with shock, not just from the force of his words but from the realization of how richly she deserved them. When she had promised to help Philp, she had made a commitment to do her best, and of yet, she had failed miserably in keeping her word. She had allowed her own personal prejudices to interfere with the task at hand, something she had assured Philp would not happen. The English lord was right—her attitude had been inexcusable. Philp had been dropping gentle reminders but it appeared that what she had needed was a good kick in the tail.

Well, she had certainly gotten it, so surely and swiftly delivered that she could almost feel the physical sting of it.

She ventured a peek at Marquand's tall form taking a stance over the ball. The wind had blown his long hair in disarray, and it tumbled over his forehead and around his ears as his head came forward. The tangle of dark locks could not, however, obscure the intensity of his eyes as they locked onto the small leather orb at his feet. Even at a distance she could sense the determination there, mirrored in the tilt of his broad shoulders, the set of his lean hips, the grip of his strong hands around the slender shaft of hickory.

For a moment her breath was quite taken away by the sight of such raw masculine power. Good Lord, had she really called him bloodless?

In the next moment, the club cut a swath through the salt air, and with a dull *thwock,* the ball lofted into the breeze. Again, it started off straight, only to take a turn to the right. The slice was not quite so bad as the first but the ball still landed well off the fairway.

"It's still in the wrists," she said softly while his back

was still toward her. Her voice still had an edge, but not nearly as sharp as before.

He turned halfway around. "Show me what you mean."

Derrien stepped forward. "Look here." She took one club between her slender fingers and held it out in front of her. "If I keep my wrists locked as straight as a piece of iron, they are wont to drop the head of the club behind them. See what that does to the clubface?"

He regarded her hands, then ran his eyes along the length of the shaft to where the head of the club angled off to the right. "Ahhh," he murmured. "Now I begin to understand. The ball cannot help but go in that direction since that is where the clubface is pointing when it is struck."

"Precisely, sir." She relaxed her grip and flicked the club back and forth. "See how if I let my right wrist turn over my left, the clubface becomes square?"

"Yes."

She propped the club on her shoulder. "Now you try it."

He held out his hand for a ball.

"No. First take several swings without trying to hit anything, just to get the feel of what you are trying to do."

Marquand looked as if to argue, but then pursed his lips in a rueful grimace and did as he was told. After a couple of tries, he stopped and with a muttered oath removed his jacket, pausing to roll the sleeves of his white linen shirt back to the middle of his forearms. It took a bit more practice before she was satisfied. At last, however, she removed a ball from her pocket and tossed it at his feet.

He set his stance. "One more thing," he said, his head coming up slightly. "Why were you inspecting the balls so carefully? And why are some in your right pocket and some in your left one?"

"I was looking at the seams and the stitching. Just as the angle of the club can impart a spin to the ball, causing it to move left or right, so, too, can any unevenness or raised welt affect its flight. Mr. Philp is a stickler for such detail. He says attention to such little things can mean the difference between winning and losing just one hole. And that can decide a match. So, although Mr. Robertson is by far the best maker of featheries, he knows to expect a return of those that don't meet our standards." She patted her left pocket. "These have enough flaws so that they must go back."

The Viscount's mouth quirked up at the use of the word "our," but it was evident that the master trusted his young caddie's expertise in such things. He quickly ducked his head to hide the smile, unwilling to break their tentative truce by appearing to laugh at the lad. His next drive landed just on the fringe of the green, not perfect but a decided improvement over the others.

"That's getting better, but you need more snap."

"Snap?"

"Yes." She pantomimed a movement. "Snap."

He tried it himself, drawing a shake of her head. "Not quite. Your right wrist must not jerk through the motion, but roll more naturally."

"Snap but not jerk," he repeated under his breath, setting up for another swing.

His next effort still did not meet with her approval. "You must try to relax the"—Derrien heaved an exasperated sigh—"oh, the deuce take it! Here, let me show you what I mean." She came over to him and took hold of his wrists. The heat from his bare skin fairly singed her fingertips and she felt her own pulse suddenly quicken in tandem with the steady beat that had been raised by his own physical efforts. She drew in a sharp breath, only to feel slightly light-headed at the faint scent of bay rum and male exertion that wafted from his person.

Good Lord, she thought, what was wrong with her this afternoon that her senses were bouncing hither and yon like an errant drive knocked out onto the rocky strand? She must get control of her emotions and keep them aimed straight down the fairway, away from all hazards. She was here simply to teach the dratted man golf. Alignment, aim, angles—those were the only sorts of things she should be thinking about.

With a tad more force than necessary, she gave his arms a shake. "Let them loose! You are not about to plant someone a facer—"

"Ouch! I might be forced to, if you do not loosen your nails from my flesh." His lips gave a slight quirk upward. "I am aware that you would like to spill my blood, but I would prefer not being clawed to ribbons by a feisty little alley cat."

She dropped his arms as if they were hot coals, her face flushing scarlet with embarrassment.

"Don't fly into the boughs, I was merely teasing," said Marquand, his face twisting in a quizzical expression. "I vow, you are the oddest lad—one would think you've never been subject to the normal teasing and taunts that boys are wont to give each other." He rubbed absently at the red marks above his thumbs. "However, that is none of my affair. May we try again if I forbear from further comment? I would like to understand exactly what it is you are trying to show me."

With a deep breath, Derrien gingerly took hold of his wrists once more. This time, she guided them slowly through the full motion. "Do you feel the way the right one should roll?" She made him go through it again, then a third time.

A slow smile spread over his face. "Aye, I do." He repeated the swing, then added a bit more pace to it. His smile deepened in a broad grin. "Snap."

Derrien couldn't help but allow a faint smile to steal over her own lips. "Snap."

Their eyes locked for an instant, sharing the moment of enlightenment. Then, suddenly aware that the beat of her heart had quickened considerably at the sight of his lean features alight with a rakish grin, she ducked her head and began to fumble in one of her pockets to mask her momentary confusion. Her odd reaction wasn't making any sense at all! Hadn't she remarked just the night before that no person with a pulse could possibly find the stiff-rumped English lord of any interest?

Well, she most definitely had a pulse. And one that

was now racing fast enough that surely he must hear the thumping of her chest.

She stepped away abruptly. It was one thing to decide to tolerate the man's presence in order to fulfill her promise to Hugh, but it was quite another to find that he had a number of admirable qualities to him—not the least of which were a dazzling smile and penetrating gaze that seemed to do all manner of strange things to her insides. Even worse was the realization that she might actually come to . . . like him! Her right hand jerked out of the rough wool and threw down the rest of the balls that remained in her pocket.

"See if you can manage to keep these on the fairway while I go fetch the others," she snapped curtly.

Marquand's brows drew together as he watched her jog off in a stiff trot. The young caddie's moods seemed even more unpredictable than the flight of the golf ball. For a brief while, it had seemed that the tension between them had eased, yet then, for no apparent reason, the mood had taken another sudden veer, and seemed to have landed back in the rough. He shrugged and after another moment of reflection turned his attention to collecting the balls lying scattered at his feet. He had enough important matters to occupy his thoughts without becoming overly concerned over the quixotic character of a mere lad.

The next hour passed with the steady thwock of leather on wood uninterrupted by any conversation, save an occasional curt pointer or correction from Derrien answered by a nod or brief question from the Viscount. When finally she acknowledged that enough had been accomplished for the day, Marquand was not sorry to toss the club down from his chafed fingers. However as they trudged back to the shop, he couldn't help but puzzle at the silence—nearly as thick as the fog drifting down from Eden Estuary—that shrouded their steps. Once a time was set for the morrow's lesson, he watched with further consternation as without so much as a glance in his direction, she stowed the clubs in their allotted rack and, cap pulled low over her face, hurried off down the cobbled street to fast disappear in the swirling mist.

The dense grayness had managed to shroud his own thoughts by the time he arrived back at his town house, leaving him with barely enough energy to peel off his damp garments and order up a hot bath. A sigh escaped his lips as he sunk beneath the steaming suds. It was not the physical exertions of the day that was wearing heavily on his shoulders. If anything, the ache of his muscles felt satisfying, as if tangible testament to the fact that he had actually achieved some measure of progress in reward for his efforts.

He wished he could say the same for the other concerns that weighed on his mind. As he took up a pitcher and let a stream of hot water wash through his locks, he had to admit that rather than engender any sort of enthusiasm in his breast, the arrival of his intended bride had left him feeling strangely flat. Was it his imagination or had Honoria's smile become more brittle during their time apart, her manner even more measured than before? Or was it that Ellington's careful criticisms had sown some seeds of doubt in his mind as to the wisdom of his choice?

His jaw set. Damn Tony—there was no kernel of truth to his words. It was merely that he was experiencing a bout of low spirits.

Marquand ran the sponge over his weary shoulders. And damn the impudent brat! For some reason it bothered him more than he cared to admit that, despite his progress in physical skills on the golf course, he had made little headway in breaking through the young caddie's obvious aversion to his person. Oh, for a moment there had been a camaraderie of sorts between them. He had sensed it for an instant in the lad's touch as he made to show the nuances of the wrist snap, but the feeling had disappeared just as quickly as the odd, wistful smile on the smudged face of—what was the moniker he had overheard one of the other boys whisper? Dirty Derry?

The Viscount's mouth pursed in a rueful grimace. A strange lad indeed. Though why it should irk him that a ragged, sharp-tongued imp held him in dislike was just as puzzling as the caddie's undisguised attitude. He knew he should simply dismiss Master Derry's surly scowls, but he couldn't shake the feeling that the fleeting expressions he had managed to glimpse beneath the oversized tweed cap were caused by something more complex than mere bad manners. But as of yet, he had no inkling as to what it was.

It seemed that an understanding of people was proving just as elusive as the intricacies of the golf swing.

With a snort of frustration, Marquand rose and reached for the towel. No doubt a good part of the reason for his depressed state of mind was due to the fact that he had not made nearly enough progress on the design for his latest commission. Ignoring the twinge in his back, he tugged on his dressing gown and resolved to spend a few hours at the desk in the library before retiring for the night.

It was sometime later that the heavy oak door opened a crack and Ellington ventured a glance at the figure of his friend hunched over a sketchpad. "Do you mean to starve yourself of sustenance as well as company?"

Marquand's head came up with a jerk. "What? Oh, er . . ." His eyes darted to the clock on the mantel. "Lord, I hadn't realized it was so late."

Ellington slowly walked over to the banked fire and stirred the embers to life. "I told McTavish to bring a cold collation up here for you. Had you forgotten that you—as well as Miss Dunster and her parents—were invited to the Playfair's musical recital this evening?"

A sharp oath cut through the air.

"I thought as much," he replied dryly. "I made your abject apologies, explaining that your efforts on the links had left you rather exhausted." His gaze lingered on the dark smudges under the Viscount's eyes. "In truth, Adrian, I am becoming concerned for you. Are you sure you are not trying to tackle too much?"

It was just the question that he had been asking himself of late.

*   *   *

"Oh, Hugh! Of all the cursed luck!" Derrien kicked at a pile of wood shavings on the floor of the workshop. "To think that Jock MacKenzie has actually asked me to help him design a plan for a series of lochside gardens at Rossdhu House and . . ." Her voice trailed off as the toe of her boot scuffed along the rough planks.

Philp looked up from the laborious task of tapering a hickory shaft by hand. "And?" His shaggy brows arched in question above the silver rims of his spectacles. "I should think you'd be elated, lassie."

She ducked her head in some contrition, suddenly aware of the import of her complaint. "I—I am. It's just that, well, I won't have quite as much time as I might wish to work on my ideas."

"Ah. Because of Lord Marquand's lessons." He went back to work with the fine blade. "If you wish to give up this endeavor, I would well understand it. This whole masquerade will have to come to an end soon in any case. It may as well be now."

"Why, what do you mean?" she cried.

A ghost of a smile played on his lips. "My dear Derrien, a small child has grown into a lad without attracting undue notice, but what is to happen to the lad? Lads eventually grow up. You cannot remain a downy-faced boy forever, my dear."

Her eyes betrayed the sudden shock of awareness his gentle words had caused. "I—I hadn't thought of that, Hugh, but . . . but I suppose you are right."

"As I said, I can write to Peter McEwan for—"

"No! I gave my promise. I'll see it carried out before 'Dirty Derry' disappears, and that's all there is to it."

The razor-sharp blade shaved away another thin curl of wood. "Very well, I know better than to argue with you when you have made up your mind like this, lassie." He slowly and methodically turned the shaft around to the other end and began the same meticulous process. "Tell me, how do you think his lordship is doing? Have we any hope?"

"Aye," she muttered. "He's not half bad. If he continues to improve as he has been, we should have a sporting chance at besting Hertford."

"I'm glad to hear it." He looked up for a moment, his gaze sharper than she would have liked. "And you are sure the task is not proving too odious?"

Derrien couldn't help but think of the chiseled strength of the broad shoulders as they whipped through a golf swing, and the rather dazzling smile those finely molded lips were capable of when the ball was well struck. She swallowed hard, hoping Philp would not notice the faint stain of color creeping to her cheeks. "It doesn't matter what I feel. I told you, I mean to see it through."

"So you did." He reached for his pipe and a flint. "Well, then you had best fetch Lord Marquand's baffing spoon and rewrap the underlisting. I noticed that the grip has shifted somewhat. Oh, and take some of the new cord in back and replace the whipping of his putter."

"Yes, sir."

"The next time you two go out, you had best begin work on his short game." A puff of smoke drifted up among the racks of unfinished clubs. "Word has it that Lord Hertford arrived in town last night."

Chapter Eight

Marquand swore under his breath, something he found he was doing with increasing frequency these days. The sketch failed to capture the exact perspective he was looking for, and so he tucked it away in the back of the small leather portfolio at his side and withdrew a fresh sheet of paper. This time his pencil moved over the surface with a surer hand, the crisp lines and delicate shading rendering a picture much more to his liking. Brow furrowed in concentration, he started to fill in the details. It was only when the clock in the nearby church tower began to chime the hour that his head shot up in consternation.

"The devil take it," he muttered with some force. He was promised for a nuncheon with Honoria and her parents. Given his egregious lack of manners in not making an appearance at the last evening's musicale, it would be unforgivable to let this engagement slip his mind as well. And he was already in danger of being late.

Several more choice words slipped out as he quickly gathered the rest of his papers that were strewn over the weathered bench and crammed the pile inside the stiff Moroccan covers. With a last, lingering look of regret at the unusual gazebo and circular plantings behind it, he forced himself to his feet. He would simply have to ask Mr. Davies if he might return another morning to finish making his sketches. Why, he hadn't even had time to take more than a cursory look at the formal herb garden set off to the right of the main house.

The sound of the bells faded away, giving further warning that he must make haste. Tucking his work under his arm, he set off down the path at a rapid clip. He had nearly reached the wrought-iron gate that led out to the quiet side street when the graveled walk took a sharp bend around a high hedge of clipped boxwood. His own hurried steps had masked the sound of anyone else approaching, and so as he rushed through the turn, his momentum made it impossible to avoid colliding with the figure who was approaching from the opposite direction.

Marquand managed to keep the other person from being knocked to the ground, but his portfolio went flying, the papers scattering across the neatly trimmed grass.

"Hell and damnation," he exclaimed, unable to contain his dismay at seeing all his precious work and reference drawings in danger of being ruined. He took an involuntary step toward the fluttering sheets before realizing he still had hold of the other person's arm. "I beg your pardon"—his irritation only increased at seeing it was a young lady he had in his grip—"Miss Edwards. For both my unseemly haste and language." His gaze remained locked on the sketches rather than on her face. Of all the deuced luck, he couldn't help but fume, to make a cake of himself by bumping into *this* particular young lady. "I'm afraid I was in a bit of a hurry."

"So it would seem," answered Derrien rather coldly, wrenching her elbow from the Viscount's fingers. "I should have been more on guard if I had any notion that another person would be prowling around in Mr. Davies's gardens at this hour—especially you, my lord, though it does seem you are partial to strolls in gardens. However, I would not have expected that a fine London gentleman rose before noon."

Marquand was already on his knees, regardless of the effect the damp earth was having on his immaculate dove gray breeches, and starting to gather up his work. "I imagine there is a great deal that you wouldn't expect about me," he muttered, his ill humor further piqued by her barbs as well as his uncharacteristic clumsiness.

Her own gaze strayed to the papers on the ground and she could not help but notice that they were drawings.

"What are those?" she added, after a moment, curiosity winning out over reserve.

When he didn't answer, she bent down as well and began to pick up some of the sheets that were threatening to fly off into the row of rosebushes. "Why, this is a sketch of one of the temples at Stourhead!" she blurted out, on regarding the first image to come to hand. She looked at the ones beneath it. "And this is from Payne Knight's design for Downton Castle. And this . . ." Her freckled nose crinkled in thought. "It looks to be the work of Chitley, but I don't recognize the commission."

Marquand's hands had frozen in their task at her first words, then his head came up with a jerk, "Y—you are familiar with garden designs and their creators?" he exclaimed in undisguised amazement.

"Yes," she replied with some defensiveness. "Does that strike you as so . . . odd?"

"It's not that. It's just, well, I suppose it's just that I wouldn't have expected such extensive knowledge from a . . ." His words trailed off as he grabbed at another piece of paper about to be carried off by a gust of wind.

"A female, and a mere provincial, uneducated one at that," she finished quickly. Her chin came up a fraction. "Well, sir, there is no doubt a great deal *you* don't expect about *me* either."

His brow furrowed slightly. What he didn't expect was to find himself thinking that her pert nose looked rather pretty, if unconventional, with its lightly tanned coloring and dusting of freckles. And that her rosy lips, slightly parted as they were at the moment, looked eminently kissable.

She captured several other sketches and ran a quick eye over them. "One of Robert Adam's picturesque castles and a plan by Repton," she announced. "And rendered very nicely at that. The question is, sir, what are *you* doing with such a collection of drawings?"

"Er, a hobby," he mumbled. He held out his hand for the papers she had collected. "And you—you certainly seem familiar with the names you have just mentioned," he went on, in order to deflect further questions. However he couldn't resist tossing out one of his own. "Whose work do you prefer?"

He noted the lively gleam of humor that came to her eyes, and wondered why he hadn't noticed before what an unusual shade of blue they were—somewhere between a smoky cerulean and sky at twilight.

"Ah, sir, that is like asking which sweetmeat does one prefer. They have all designed works that make one positively drool with delight." She paused as if to consider the question further. "But I suppose that I must say I favor the less well-known Chitley."

Marquand suppressed a strangled cough. "Why is that?"

"His imagination," she replied without hesitation. "I think he has done the best job of synthesizing the core ideas espoused in Archibald Alison and Payne Knight's essays into a coherent design philosophy, don't you think?"

He made a strange sound in the back of his throat and sat back on his haunches.

"I find his attitude on formality, color, and texture most intriguing," she went on, ignoring the lack of a reply.

"Indeed," he managed to sputter. "Well, I imagine he has been influenced by Uvedale Price as well. After all, it is Price who proposed that the Picturesque rank as an aesthetic category along with the Sublime and the Beautiful."

Derrien regarded him intently. "Now that might be a matter of debate, sir, on how similar their views are on—"

"Ha! No debate at all," he said under his breath.

"What was that?"

"Er, nothing. What I meant was, I should like to hear more of your opinions on the subject."

"Well, as I said, I find Chitley perhaps a bit more unorthodox than his predecessors." There was a slight pause. "But I am sure he is not to your taste."

"No?"

Her eyes took on a martial gleam. "You do not strike

me as having a great deal of imagination." She plucked
up another sketch from the grass.

"Ah, yes. Bloodless, aren't I? Well, perhaps that is
why my passing interest in gardens is not to be wondered
at." He snatched the paper from her fingers. "They, too,
are bloodless so we suit each other—though of course
they do have a life to them which I obviously do not."

Derrien ducked her head. "I'm sorry—my comment of
the other evening was quite uncalled for," she muttered.
"I have a bad habit of letting my tongue run away
with me."

"I hadn't noticed," he said dryly.

She made a lunge for the last piece of paper floating
in the wind. "If you truly have an interest in gardens, I
imagine you have already heard of Sir Hugh Playfair's
creation," she said in a conciliatory tone. "Of all the
private designs here in St. Andrews, it would, of course,
be the one that shouldn't be missed."

He shook his head. "Playfair? I believe I was introduced to the gentleman at some point, but have not
heard mention of his garden."

"No? But you *must* see it." Her mouth crooked in a
tentative smile. "If only to remark on what happens
when imagination runs amuck."

A faint grin tweaked at the molded curves of his lips.
"With such an interesting recommendation, I shall have
to be sure to wangle an invitation."

"Sir Hugh has invited me to make use of the grounds
whenever I care to. I had planned to make a visit tomorrow morning at this time, if"—the last words came out
in a rush, before she quite realized what she was saying—
"if you would care to go along."

It was a moment before an answer came. "Yes," he
said slowly. "I should like that." He reached out to take
the last sketch from her hand and his glove brushed
against hers, sending a frisson of heat through his blood.
Good Lord, he thought with some consternation, what
was he thinking, to let the merest physical brush with a
prickly country miss affect him like that? After all, he
was engaged to a beauty, and one whose manners—

Honoria!

Hell's teeth, he had forgotten all about the nuncheon! He was going to be frightfully late. He scrambled to his feet, clumps of mud and bits of grass clinging to his knees. "Egad, Honoria and her parents will no doubt be furious with me," he muttered under his breath. In a louder voice, he added, "Forgive me, Miss Edwards, but I must be off." His fingers were fumbling awkwardly, trying to give her a hand up at the same time as attempting to stuff the sketches into his portfolio. "If you will give me your address, I shall bring my carriage around—"

"No, no, that's hardly necessary. Just be here by this gate at ten. It's only a short distance and I . . . like to walk." She reached out to tuck an errant corner of paper back within the leather case and couldn't resist adding, "I should think an engagement with your future bride would not bring such a scowl to your face, Lord Marquand."

He finally finished tying the ribbons. "You must be mistaking my expression, Miss Edwards," he said softly. "We bloodless fellows have none to speak of, remember? Now, if you will excuse me, I really must hurry, for even people without a pulse can be roused to anger in the face of deliberate rudeness."

Derrien felt her face grow rather hot as she watched him hurry toward the gate. It was outside of enough that in some strange moment of delusion she had actually invited the English lord to accompany her to Sir Hugh's garden. But even worse was that he remembered, to the letter, her childish remarks of the other night. She might not like either the gentleman or his intended bride, but it had been horribly rude of her to snap out such nasty comments simply because she had been embarrassed herself—as the Viscount's retorts had not failed to point out. The elegant lady must think her a veritable hoyden, and no doubt Lord Marquand did as well. Certainly, her additional gibe concerning his imagination hadn't helped her cause. She bit her lip. Loath as she was to admit it, even to herself, she found she didn't like the idea of him thinking of her as, well, an ill-mannered brat.

She let out a harried sigh and then continued on to the bench facing the painted gazebo. Taking a seat, she withdrew a small sketchbook and pencil from her reticule, but on opening its pages she found her hand strangely reluctant to begin its work. Instead her gaze lifted to survey the formal row of shrubs in the foreground, which turned at right angles and led the eye back to a more natural and irregular display of foliage and flowering plants. The contrast created a certain tension, making for a more interesting scene whose complexities drew one back again and again. It was a concept the notable designers she had mentioned earlier understood intuitively, and now, as she sat and studied the view before her, she slowly realized it applied to people as well.

Lord Marquand was nothing if not a study in contrasts, and despite her firm resolve to dislike the man, she found that with each new glimpse, he was becoming increasingly . . . intriguing. Yes, he could be impossibly stiff-rumped and formal at times, yet his reaction to such an appearance was quite at odds with the raw athleticism and vibrant masculinity he displayed on the golf links. His bearing bespoke of an icy hauteur, and yet his reaction to her harsh comments had shown him to be vulnerable, to have feelings that could hurt. And while his own words could seem stilted in the extreme, the exuberant skill of his hand at rendering the subtlest of nuances could not be hidden—though most of the works had been copies, several of the scattered sketches had been his own, depicting the exact gazebo she was now gazing upon.

Her eyes dropped down to the blank sheet of paper. And that he possessed an expertise in gardens, of all things! She bit her lip. Why, oh why, had she let her cursed, impetuous tongue run so loose as to not only insult him, but then to render that crazy invitation? She was spending quite enough time with the gentleman without cultivating any additional contact. That she was coming to respect his determination and fighting spirit was bad enough. She wasn't sure she wanted to discover that he, too, was interested in the same subject she longed to discuss with another knowledgeable person. Or that he might actually listen to her and solicit her opinion. It was simply too . . . hazardous.

She might have made up her mind to tolerate him, but she wasn't about to start liking him as well.

Her rueful grimace twisted into a mocking smile as she recalled yet another facet of his character. How could she forget, even for an instant? He was also a hardened gamester, she reminded herself. One who apparently ran with the likes of Lord Hertford and thought nothing of risking a fortune on the turn of a card. While she didn't know the particulars of his wager, it must have been quite high indeed to have necessitated an arduous journey from London to Scotland. And it was only natural that a gentleman like that was also a practiced rake. She swallowed hard. That would account for the ease with which he had caused her defenses to bend, as if they were no more substantial than the fragile wildflowers that were clustered around the distant stone fountain.

No!

Derrien's hand drew the pencil over the paper, leaving a firm dark line. Then she relaxed slightly, knowing she was in no danger of succumbing to his charm, now that there had been a moment to reflect on his baser nature. In the future she'd not forget what sort of man he really was. Another few shadings were scratched on the page. That being the case, she mused, it couldn't hurt to talk about gardens with him. She was dying to know what Nash's latest essays, just recently published in London, had to say on the subject of aesthetics, just as she was curious to know more about the fellow Chitley. It appeared the bold new talent was somewhat of a recluse, and little more was known about him other than the wonderful sketches that had made their way past the northern border. She was most curious as to what sort of fellow he was, and whether any of his writings had yet been published. With the bold creativity and ingenious way of thinking that was revealed by his plans, she couldn't imagine that he was an older man, but—

A glance down at her book caused a sharp intake of breath. Rather than a quick rendering of the gazebo, her hand had somehow of its own accord sketched a rugged profile, with straight nose, lean jaw, and longish curling locks falling in boyish disarray. She snapped the pages closed with some muttered words that would have brought an instant rebuke from Philp and stood up.

Men! They seemed to be plaguing her thoughts this morning.

The dull chimes of the clock served as a reminder that she, too, had best be off to seek sustenance for the coming afternoon. As she draped the strings of her reticule around her wrist, an impish grin slowly spread to her lips. Men, indeed! Well, if she couldn't beat them, she might as well join them.

"I *said*, have you made any progress in this golfing endeavor, Marquand?" Baron Hylton had stopped chewing long enough to repeat his question in an even louder tone than before.

"What—er, that is, were you speaking to me, sir?"

"I'm not speaking to the deuced epergne though it seems I might as well be," he growled under his breath, cutting off another thick slab from his lamb chop.

"Language, Fitzwilliam!" warned his wife with a whispered rebuke.

"Father, I'm sure his lordship is preoccupied with his upcoming lessons. Just as I am sure he will do his best when the time comes," murmured Honoria, not quite able to look the Viscount's way as she offered some measure of support.

Marquand squirmed in his chair. Why was it that she couldn't seem to get comfortable speaking his name? he wondered with some irritation. A glance around the table only served to increase his ill humor. Everything seemed to be rubbing him the wrong way this afternoon, from the Baron's thinly veiled questions as to the future of Woolsey Hall, to the perpetually sour expression on Lady Hylton's thin face to Honoria's perplexing lack of vitality. It was as if all the charm and wit he knew she possessed had been drained from her veins.

He frowned slightly. *Bloodless*. That was what the little minx had called her, and on stealing another surreptitious look at his intended bride's pale face, it was hard to argue with the rather harsh assessment. His lips twitched for an instant. Miss Edwards. Now there was a young lady who could hardly be described as bloodless—bloodthirsty, maybe, given the sharpness of her claws when she was angry. He found himself wondering why she seemed bothered by his very presence—

". . . will take place in another week?" Hylton's voice once again cut through the air as surely as his knife through the rare meat.

Marquand's mouth tightened in a grim line. "Ten days to be exact," he answered curtly. "Until then, at least, Woolsey Hall is safe." His expression curled into a faintly mocking smile. "I'm touched by your concern, sir."

"Harrumph." Sensing he had perhaps pressed too far, the Baron took a long swallow of claret and changed the subject. "Well, then, I think I may pay a short visit to Preston's hunting box. He's assured me that his moors are particularly rich with grouse this year and I should like to avail myself of such a fine shooting opportunity." He motioned for his glass to be filled. "The ladies will naturally want to stay here in a more civilized setting—that is, as civilized as any Scottish place may be."

His wife grimaced. "I shall be well pleased when we may quit this savage land."

The Viscount couldn't refrain from shooting her a stony look. "Do you truly think it so, Lady Hylton? For my part, I have found the local folk to be most hospitable. What of you, Honoria?"

The Baron's wife looked too nonplussed to answer while her daughter stared at her plate and murmured something inaudible.

"More wine, Marquand?" inquired Hylton, seeking to break the awkward silence that descended over the meal.

He waved away the decanter. "I must go on to the

links, where it is imperative to keep a clear head." Making a show of consulting the clock on the sideboard, he placed the damask napkin on the table and pushed his chair back from the table. "In fact, if you will excuse me, I must take my leave now, else be late for the appointed meeting with my caddie." He cleared his throat. "And that august personage is, I assure you, not someone whose ire I wish to incur."

The Baron gave a knowing nod. "Quite right. A good, seasoned man can be a queer fellow, as temperamental as the worst French chef. Why, I had a ghilly on our trout stream . . ." He began a long-winded story which Marquand interrupted by getting to his feet.

"Good day, sir." He inclined a frosty bow in Lady Hylton's direction. "And to you, too, Honoria," he murmured. "I believe you are also invited to dine at Sir Humphrey's tonight?"

"Yes." She finally looked up, but her expression was so shuttered Marquand was hard-pressed to make out exactly what she was thinking. "And apparently there is an outing arranged for the day after tomorrow in order to view the ruins of an abbey up the coast, and a picnic as well. I . . . I trust you and Lord Ellington will be able to come along, even though it may conflict with your lessons."

"I imagine I can spare an afternoon. And I'm sure Tony will be delighted to be part of the group."

She made an appropriate response and he took his leave.

The gusty salt breeze was like a breath of fresh air, and despite its damp edge, it felt decidedly less chilly than the atmosphere of the Baron's dining room. Marquand quickened his steps, as if wanting to distance himself from the imposing gray granite edifice. His hand came up to tug at his cravat. *Lord, was he in danger of putting a noose round his neck as well as a ring on his finger?* What had, just a short time ago, appeared as a desirable match now seemed . . .

All of that didn't matter, he reminded himself with a slight clenching of his jaw. The proposal had been made and that was that. He would simply have to learn to live with it. After all, he had learned to survive a good deal worse than mere shallowness.

It was fortunate that his caddie's thoughts also appeared to be elsewhere throughout the afternoon, for Marquand had a difficult time concentrating on the task at hand. After a number of desultory drives, in which he at least contrived to keep the ball in the vicinity of the fairway, if not advancing it any great distance, they moved on to a bunker in order to practice getting the ball out of the heavy sand. After a few pointers from the lad, he spent a good part of an hour whacking at the small leather orb, sending up a spray of sand—and occasionally the ball—with each swing. However unsuccessful many of the flailing attempts were, Marquand found it a most satisfactory way to vent his pent-up frustrations. Even Master Derry, with an uncharacteristic show of restraint, refrained from more than one or two barbed criticisms and allowed him to hack away in undisturbed silence.

By the time a spitting rain caused them to curtail their efforts for the day, he found his spirits had revived enough that not even the prospect of another meal with Honoria and her parents could dampen his mood. It was not until he turned up the collar of his coat and started to make his way over the slick cobblestones, that he realized with a start that his thoughts had not been dwelling on the coming evening at all. Rather they had strayed to the engagement of the following morning.

His brow furrowed.

How was it that the idea of squabbling in the dirt with a sharp-tongued little hellion was what brought a smile to his lips?

"I see you are punctual, my lord."

Marquand turned from his perusal of the wrought-iron gate's intricate design and gave a slight bow. "I wish to exhibit some redeeming qualities, Miss Edwards," he murmured, offering her his arm. "After all, I have been made all too aware of my numerous shortcomings."

There was a fraction of a pause before Derrien accepted it. "You are teasing me, my lord."

"Just a little," he admitted. His mouth crooked into a slight smile as his free hand slipped into his coat pocket. "But perhaps we might cease our brangling long enough for you to have a glance at this?" He withdrew a slim leather-bound volume and held it out to her.

Her gaze flew to the gold-tooled title. "Chatsworth's plans for the Duke of Devonshire!" she cried. "I thought they hadn't—"

"Just published," he murmured. "I thought you might be interested in taking a look at them." His lips twitched. "Perhaps not quite as unorthodox as Chitley, but fascinating nonetheless."

"Oh, how very kind of you, sir!" She lifted her eyes to meet his and the Viscount was surprised by what the sight of such an intense color of blue did to his pulse. Ha! bloodless, indeed, he thought, feeling it course through his veins with a rising heat. "I—I can't thank you enough. I have been looking forward to seeing these particular drawings for an age." She took the proffered book and ran a gloved finger along its spine with something akin to reverence. "I promise I shall return it quickly."

The wistful note in her voice was not lost on the Viscount. "You may keep it. I have another copy."

"I—that is, you—"

"Is this the place?" He interrupted her stammerings by drawing them to a halt by an imposing set of oak doors set in a stone arch.

"Er yes, but—"

Marquand smiled at how her expression so clearly betrayed the warring of pride versus longing. "Put the book in your reticule, Miss Edwards. I give you permission to continue to cut up at me with that sharp tongue of yours without having to feel any guilt, if that is what's worrying you."

Her mouth opened, but before she could speak, he took a step toward the gate. "Might we enter now? I'm afraid I have a limited amount of time and you've quite piqued my curiosity. I wouldn't want to miss anything."

Without further argument, Derrien slipped the book into her bag and put her shoulder to the weathered wood. The doors swung open, revealing a large expanse of clipped grass, in the center of which sat a massive pagoda, towering nearly ninety feet in the air. Marquand stared at it in mute amazement for several moments, then his eyes strayed off to one side where a strange construction of wooden posts, rods, and thick hemp ropes appeared to be spinning in a slow concentric circle within a small pond.

"A water-driven . . . contrivance," she explained.

He merely nodded, then glanced in the other direction, where several large statues dominated a formal bed of multi-colored roses. Suddenly, his shoulders began to shake, and a low rumble sounded in his throat. In another moment, he could contain his laughter no longer. Its rich baritone sound echoed loudly off the weathered stone of the massive retaining wall. "Good Lord," he said when he finally managed to speak. "It's truly, truly . . ."

"Hideous?" she suggested, unable to suppress a grin.

"I am in awe." They stepped inside and pulled the gate shut. "Had I not seen it with my own eyes, I wouldn't have believed such a creation possible."

Derrien giggled. "Actually, sir, there are some sections which are rather nice."

His brows shot up. "Lead the way."

As they strolled along the winding path, their conversation quite naturally turned to a discussion on the principles of garden design. Marquand knew she had some acquaintance with the subject from their brief encounter of the day before, but still, he was surprised by the breadth of her knowledge and the keenness of her insight. Why, even with a number of males who accorded themselves to be experts in the field, he hadn't enjoyed such a stimulating exchange of ideas. Not only did the young lady grasp a number of complex concepts but she appeared to have a distinct vision of her own as to what made a good design. He found himself wondering what she would think of his preliminary plans for his new commission. It was deucedly frustrating at times, for he was not able to show them to his peers for fear of revealing his secret. Tony was supportive, but hadn't a clue as far as aesthetics were concerned. And Honoria didn't know a dahlia from a begonia—

". . . the perspective created by the row of espaliered pear trees, don't you think?"

"Er—"

Derrien laughed, though not unkindly. "Just as I suspected, sir. You haven't heard a word I have been saying, have you?"

"Sorry. I fear my mind wandered for a moment."

She cocked her head. "Somewhere interesting, judging by your expression." Her inflection made it more of a question than a statement.

He stopped to inspect an unusual type of geranium. "Tell me," he said while bent over the variegated leaves. "What do you think of that latest essay from Knight?"

A sigh escaped Derrien's lips. "I'm afraid it has not yet made its way north, though I have read in the journals that it has stirred up a good deal of debate."

"I happen to have that particular work in my possession as well. Are you one of the party making up the excursion to the ruins on the morrow?"

She nodded slowly.

"Then I shall bring it along and let you decide on its merits. However I must warn you it is merely a loan since I haven't yet finished it myself."

Another sigh sounded. "You are fortunate to have access to such marvelous things. At times I feel so . . . isolated up here. Why, I don't even know whether Chitley has published any writings." She slanted a hopeful look at him. "Has he? I would so like to read anything he has to say."

"Well, er, no. But I believe a volume is planned for the end of the year."

"Then I suppose I shall have to be content with waiting for that."

Marquand knew he should keep his mouth shut, but he simply couldn't resist the expression of longing on her face. "I shall make sure he sends you a copy as soon as it is printed. He, is, er, an acquaintance."

Derrien's eyes widened. "You actually know Chitley? But it is said that for some strange reason he chooses to be an utter recluse—no one has met him."

"Oh, he has a few friends."

"What is he like?" she demanded eagerly.

"Well, he is about my height—" As he spoke, Marquand was aware he was treading on treacherous ground and should stop before going too far.

"And?" she prompted.

"And . . ." He stopped as if to consider the question. "And I'm not sure you would like him very much."

"Oh fie on you, sir! You are teasing me again!"

Marquand chuckled but realized he should steer the conversation back to safer footing. "I'm not, I swear it. It's Price you would find yourself swooning over. He is tall, with the sort of artfully tousled golden curls and sensitive mien that cause females to fall at his feet in droves."

She gave a snort. "But his ideas are not nearly as interesting . . ."

Just as the Viscount hoped, the talk turned to concepts and another lively discussion ensued.

Derrien was only listening with half an ear to the Viscount's pithy comments, for try as she might, she couldn't help but be distracted by the closeness of his person. They had taken a seat on one of the benches overlooking the lake and the light pressure from his thigh was palpable even through the heavy folds of her gown. She ventured a quick glance at his profile, then jerked her gaze back to the geese drifting across the rippled surface of the water. Lord, she thought, had the man any idea how attractive he looked when his eyes twinkled with such humor and when his lips quirked upward into such a devastating smile?

Of course he did, she chided herself. He probably had

it down to a fine art. His current smile—or smirk—was no doubt prompted in part by how easy the game of charming a country miss must be appearing to him. Perhaps in the next minute he would think he could lower his head and capture her mouth in a long embrace without so much as a squeak of protest.

Her jaw clenched in anger, but it was directed just as much at herself as at him, for she couldn't deny that for the last little while she had been wondering just what it would feel like to have those chiseled lips pressed hard against hers.

". . . I'd be willing to wager a monkey that's what he means."

"Yes, I'm sure you would," she said in a tight voice, her eyes darkening to a stormy slate color with the same quixotic abruptness as the weather out on the links. "Wager on it, that is." One hand yanked the skirts of her gown away from his knee while the other searched for her reticule. "Good day, sir. I must be going—I am expected home."

All the humor drained from Marquand's face, replaced by a look of puzzled surprise. "Have I said something wrong, Miss Edwards?"

"Not at all. You have merely reminded me that you are a profligate gamester, and no doubt a . . . rake as well, sir, and not a person I care to spend time with."

His mouth compressed in a grim line. "I suppose it is not to be wondered at that in a small town such as this, the arrival of any stranger will prompt a number of scurrilous rumors to make the rounds."

"Do not deny that you are in St. Andrews as the result of some wager! Hugh Philp says—" She colored slightly. "That is, Mr. Philp is a friend of my aunt's, and it is from him that I heard you must play golf against Lord Hertford because of some large loss at the gaming table."

"Yes, it's true that I am bound to compete against the Marquess, but—oh, the devil take it, why bother trying to explain! It appears you are just as willfully opinionated as that hot-tempered brat of a caddie I have been saddled with by Mr. Philp. Both of you think that, with the arrogance of untried youth, you understand everything at first blush." He rose brusquely and held out his hand. "Come, let me see you home."

Derrien stared at him in shock, rendered speechless by the raw hurt in his voice rather than the anger. When she made no move to get to her feet, his expression hardened into a stony mask and his arm dropped to his side. "As a gentleman, I am beholden to offer my company, but as it is clear you consider me no such thing, I will assume you are capable of making your own way out." He fumbled in his pocket to withdraw a gold watch and took a quick glance at the enameled dial. "Besides, I must be off if I am not to be late for a noon engagement." His lips curled in a mocking smile. "And then, of course, I must head to the links to practice my gaming skills. Perhaps after that, I might consider deflowering a virgin or two before supper." With a curt bow, he turned on his heel and stalked off.

She watched his tall form quickly disappear around a bend in the path, then dropped her eyes to her lap, suddenly aware that the strings of her reticule were knotted so tightly around her fingers that they were in danger of cutting off all circulation. The pain, however, was not nearly as sharp as the stab in her chest as she tried to draw a breath. Her accusations had been justified, she assured herself. Why, he had admitted as much! And as to explanations—what possible explanation could there be for such behavior?

Her reticule shifted in the folds of her skirts, and the corner of the slim book inside caught against her leg. Yet how could a dissolute wastrel also possess, of all things, such a keen understanding of gardens? There was no denying his extensive knowledge of both their history and theory. Nor was it possible to question his obvious sensitivity and insight. A lump formed in her throat as her hand move to touch the leather spine. She imagined that the principles of garden design was hardly a subject that would interest most rakes and scoundrels.

It made no sense!

To her dismay, a single tear spilled down her cheek.

With an angry brush of her sleeve, she blotted it away, then forced herself to take out her own sketchbook and pencil. She had work to do, she reminded herself. Her plans for the laird's garden were much more important than dwelling on the complexities of a certain English lord. Yet somehow, as she flipped through the pages, it took her more than a few moments to turn past the quick rendering of a certain profile that was most definitely not that of a begonia or tulip.

Chapter Nine

Philp took one look at her face and put his file down. "Tommy, run along to Robertson's shop and pick up the box of featheries he has ready for me." As soon as the lad had scampered off, he turned back to Derrien. "What's wrong, lassie?" he asked in a low voice.

She took a seat on the corner of his work bench and ran a finger along the hickory shaft he was shaping. "N—nothing—"

"Don't try to gammon me, Derry." A callused finger tilted her chin up so that he was able to peer under the brim of the heavy tweed cap at her reddened eyes.

A lock of hair fell across her cheek and she reached up to brush it away. "I'm sorry, Hugh. I didn't mean—it's just that things have gotten . . . so confusing."

"Hmmm." He took up his pipe and, without a word, slowly tamped down the fragrant tobacco, patiently waiting for her to go on.

She toyed with a small pile of wood shavings, reducing it to mere dust. "He likes gardens!" she finally blurted out.

Philp didn't have to ask whom she meant. "Ah." The flint struck up a spark. "I should have thought that would not be a mark against him." A puff of smoke obscured his expression. "Indeed, I would have expected you to like him better for it."

"But I don't *want* to like him!"

"Hmmm. Well, I suppose that is perfectly understandable." He bent down to sight along the length of wood. "But the problem is that you do, don't you?"

Derrien jammed her hands into her pockets, suddenly

aware of how childish her outburst must have sounded—
and how hollow. With the unerring accuracy of one of
his golf shots, her friend had hit on the very essence of
her dilemma. A slight flush spread across her features
and for the second time that day she had the unsettling
notion that perhaps her own feelings were not quite as
sure as she might have liked.

"You have only to say the word, you know." Philp
didn't look up. "If you wish to quit—"

"I gave you my word, Hugh! I won't go back on it,
no matter what."

"No matter what?" He picked up the file and began
to smooth out a miniscule bump in the straight grain. "I
should think about that very carefully, Derry. Maybe you
should go home today and let me take his lordship out
for his lesson." He sighed as he regarded the unfinished
club. "I imagine McAllister can wait until the morrow
for his new putter."

"That isn't necessary," she muttered. She got up and
went to get the Viscount's set of clubs.

Philp pushed the silver spectacles back up to the bridge
of his nose. "I take it that it is Miss Derrien Edwards
who has been discussing gardens with Lord Marquand."
When she nodded, he took another deep mouthful of
smoke and slowly let it out. "Auch, be careful, lassie.
Whatever else you think, he is no fool."

She tugged at the front of her cap. "Don't worry, Hugh.
I keep myself pretty well hidden, and what with the
smudges on my face, he'll not notice any resemblance."
Her voice dropped considerably in timbre. "And you yourself say I've become a dab hand at disguising my voice. So
there's little to fear on that score." Hefting the clubs to
her shoulder, she turned and started for the door.

"Is there?" he whispered softly, his lined face crinkling
in concern as he wondered whether he had made a serious mistake in involving her with the English lord. " 'Tis
a dangerous game you're playing, lassie."

The ball rolled nearly four feet past the hole. With a
rather loud expletive, Marquand turned and held out his

hand for another one. "And I warn you, brat, keep any snide comments to yourself—I'm in no mood for them this afternoon," he growled, throwing down the new ball with enough force to put a noticeable indentation in the closely cropped turf.

She shoved her hands in her pockets and moved to the fringe of the green. His next putt came up at least a yard short. Another curse followed. Without waiting for the order, she tossed another ball at his feet.

"You might want to consider loosening the tension in your shoulders, sir. And your hands. Try to, well, feel the ball going into the hole," she murmured as he set up again in his putting stance.

He shot her a black look. "What I *feel* is like heaving this damnable club—and all the rest of them—into the Bay."

Derrien avoided meeting his eyes. "Aye, golf is a hard game. What Mr. Philp advises is that one must learn to deal with the anger and frustration that inevitably occur over the hours of play. He who can do that best has a leg up on winning. If something is upsetting you, try to put it from your mind. Focus on the task at hand." She kicked at a loose clod of dirt. "At least, that is what Mr. Philp says. But if you wish we can quit for the day."

The Viscount bit back another snarled retort as he realized how badly he was behaving. No matter that his mood matched the gray choppy waters crashing onto the rocky strand, the lad had done nothing to deserve having to endure several hours of his foul humor. He stepped back from the ball for a moment and took a few deep breaths, then once more took up his stance, carefully aligning his feet toward the hole. His whole body did seem more relaxed and his shoulders initiated a motion that swung the club back and then forward with a fluid precision, much like the pendulum of a longcase clock. With equal precision, the ball rolled in a straight line, its momentum dying just as it reached the lip of the hole, and dropped inside.

Derrien didn't say a word as she took several more balls from her coat pocket and tossed them on the green.

With exactly the right combination of speed and aim, Marquand proceeded to sink each of them.

He stood straight up after the last one and rubbed at his jaw, his face betraying a mixture of emotions. "May Lucifer's wings be singed," he muttered, feeling as juvenile as the lad before him. "So *that's* how it's done."

Eyes still averted, she went to retrieve all the stitched featheries. "Do you wish to keep putting, sir, or would you prefer to move on to something else?"

"Shall we play a few holes?"

A slight shrug of her shoulders, indicating the choice was up to him, was her only reply. She replaced the flagstick, gathered up the rest of the clubs, and looked to him for an indication of where to proceed.

"Let us play seventeen and eighteen."

With another wordless shrug, she turned and began to walk off toward the left.

Marquand caught up with her after several strides. He slanted a puzzled look at the top of her tweed cap as they skirted a large clump of gorse and veered around a deep pot bunker. "Oh, go ahead and say it," he finally growled with a harried sigh.

Her head twitched though her gaze remained locked on the tops of her boots. "Say what . . . sir?"

The Viscount gave a rueful grimace. "Whatever cutting set-down you wish to make over my last display of stubborn pique." When she didn't answer, his expression turned to one of faint bemusement. "I should hope I'm not too much of an ass not to be able to admit when I've acted in a stupid manner. Once again, you've proved yourself the wiser of us two, lad. My thanks for the advice."

Derrien shifted the clubs on her shoulder and quickened her stride.

Marquand couldn't help but wonder at his caddie's uncharacteristic reticence. "Is something amiss with you today, Master Derry? You are unusually silent—and unusually tactful. I have come to expect a more barbed assessment of my shortcomings rather than such measured restraint." A low chuckle escaped his lips. "Could it be that you are feeling ill?"

"There is getting less and less to criticize, sir," she mumbled. "You are making quite a bit of progress." They had reached the start of the penultimate hole and she held out his long spoon, then bent down to build a small mound of sand for his ball. "Aim at that patch of tall grass in front of the fence post," she said quickly, as if anxious to change the subject.

He glanced at the proposed target, then back at her. "But that is way off the fairway! If I hit it there, it will take me several extra strokes to reach the hole."

"Feel the wind—your ball won't go there. If you aim straight ahead, you'll end up in that thicket of gorse and will have to take a penalty for it."

His eyes swept over the course. For a moment he looked ready to mutiny, but despite his expression of grave doubt, he put his head down and drove the ball toward the spot she had indicated. It flew up in a high arc, looking at first to be headed straight for the stubbly rough on the right. A gust caught it in midflight and its direction veered sharply, curving down and sideways until it fell to earth in the center of the fairway. A bounce and a hop brought it to a near perfect angle from which to take aim at the fluttering flag.

Marquand shook his head in amazement. "How the devil can you know exactly where to hit it?"

Derrien shrugged. "Through experience." She slanted a look at his furrowed brow. "Don't be too hard on yourself, sir. It's not something you can learn in a week or two. It's the sort of knowledge that can only be gained by playing the course over countless rounds." They started walking toward his drive. "Don't worry. As long as you can hit it where I say, you have a decent chance of beating Lord Hertford. Actually, a more than decent chance, as long as you keep putting as you did back there." There was a brief hesitation before she added, "The stakes must be very . . . high for you to have journeyed here from London."

"High?" He gave a harsh laugh. "Aye, you might say

that, as the Linsley ancestral home is riding on my ability
to put the deuced ball where you tell me to."

"Lord, how can anyone be so stupid as to risk such a
thing on the turn of a card!" she blurted out. "You . . .
you must have been truly jug-bitten."

His jaw set. "No, I—" he started to say, somehow
caring more than he knew he should what his young
companion might think of him. In an instant, however,
he caught himself and his words cut off abruptly. "Oh,
damnation—never mind. You may possess a modicum of
experience out here on the golf links, lad, but you have
precious little understanding of the real world. Things are
not quite so black and white as you seem to imagine."

"W—what do you mean?"

Marquand had come up alongside his ball and merely
held out his hand for a club. "The middle spoon or the
long iron?" he demanded, his tone making clear that he
had no intention of answering her question.

She took a second to gauge the wind and the distance.
"Definitely the spoon."

"Would that all of life's choices could be made with
such surety, brat," he muttered. "Mayhap one day you
will have some idea of what I mean."

Choices, choices, he thought to himself later that evening.
They were still bedeviling him. Should he add a low
stone wall on either side of the graveled path in order
to accentuate the perspective, or use a more natural bed
of perennials to soften the straight line? His pencil hovered over the sketch of the classical summer house as he
sought another sheet of paper.

"Still at work? It's nearly midnight." Ellington placed
a glass of brandy on the edge of the desk, then took a
long sip from the one that remained in his hand.

Marquand looked up and rubbed at his temples. "Is
it?" He leaned back in his chair and took up the spirits
with a nod of thanks. "Well, there's little choice on it,
Tony. I really must have these preliminary ideas finished
by the time we return to Town."

Ellington regarded the dark circles under his friend's

eyes. "Can't your assistant take care of some of the work?"

"The fellow is fine when it comes to overseeing one of my designs, but as to any real creativity, well . . ." His words trailed off. "No, I'm afraid I have no one to look to but myself."

"Have a care, Adrian. It is a Herculean task you are setting for yourself."

He smiled grimly. "Not at all. I am only attempting two impossible tasks. I would have to accomplish five more in order to match the heroics of that mythical figure." His hand threaded through his dark locks. "Besides, I have no choice, Tony. I simply cannot afford to lose either Woolsey Hall or my business."

Ellington stirred up some flames in the banked fire, then took a seat in the oversized chair by the hearth. "How goes the golf?"

"I believe I am making some progress." The Viscount's lips twitched upward. "No less formidable a critic than my young caddie has informed me that my skills have improved enough that there is a ghost of a chance of victory—if I can manage to do as he says."

"Well, I hope for your sake that he is right." Ellington drained his glass while surreptitiously regarding the fine lines of strain etched on his friend's tired face. "At least tomorrow you shall be forced to take a break from both your concerns. Don't forget we are promised to be part of a picnic to view the old abbey near Anstruther. Perhaps a pleasant day spent in the company of the lovely Miss Dunster will help smooth the worry from your brow."

It was odd, thought Marquand, but the picture that came to mind was of a pair of flashing blue eyes and a pert, freckled nose rather than the pale visage of his intended. He made some noncommittal sound in his throat in answer to the other man before polishing off the rest of his brandy in one gulp. Somehow he doubted that any outing which included the feisty Miss Edwards was going to be very helpful in improving his state of mind, especially after this morning.

So why did he find himself looking forward to it?

His eyes fell on the slim volume of essays he had already dug out of his trunk of books. Along with a sharp tongue and prickly personality, she possessed an admirable intellect, all the more so because of the censure and ridicule she must have faced in developing it. He knew all too well what it was like to persevere in the teeth of adversity, so despite her opinion of him he meant to see she received the promised writings. He knew she would respond to the ideas with the passion and intensity that they deserved.

He wondered what else might stir such feelings in her. Would her eyes flare with heat if his lips pressed down upon—

". . . indulge in such dreaming?"

His head jerked up in some embarrassment and a hot flush rose to his cheeks. "Er, what was that?"

"I said, how long are you going to stay up trying to dream up some new design for a Greek Temple or whatever else you are envisioning for the Duke's gardens?" Ellington eyed the sheepish expression and schoolgirl blush for a moment then his brows stole up. "If I were you, I should get some sleep, Adrian. You are acting deucedly strange."

"I shall be along shortly," he mumbled.

Strange? That didn't begin to explain the half of what he was feeling.

Derrien tugged at the ribbons of her bonnet, thinking not for the first time how much she preferred men's clothing to the constraining garb required of females.

"That's a most attractive color on you, my dear," said Mrs. Kildare, smiling at her from the facing seat of the Baronet's carriage. "It brings out the blue of your eyes, does it not, Mr. Ferguson?"

The young professor regarded her scowling face with a show of great deliberation. "Indeed." He gave a sly wink that only she could see. "Though right now I believe I see a hint of some other, warmer hue in them."

She restrained the urge to stick her tongue out at him.

The older lady fell back into conversation with the portly gentleman at her other elbow, a fellow colleague of her husband's in the Classics, giving Ferguson a chance to pursue a more private talk with Derrien. "What has put the proverbial bee in that lovely bonnet?" he inquired with a smile.

"Oh, do give off, Charlie," she muttered. She squirmed yet again against the squabs. "Whoever invented these horrid things must have a great dislike of females. As if we don't wish to see what's around us! Why, I can hardly look out the window without forever bumping the cursed brim against the glass."

He chuckled. "Nevertheless, you look enchanting."

"Ha!" She brushed impatiently at an errant ringlet on her cheek. "More likely I look ready to bite someone's head off at being forced by my aunt to be a part of this little excursion."

"Not mine, I hope!" He gave a mock sigh. "Alas, I should have thought the prospect of my scintillating wit and charming company would have sparked a greater enthusiasm in your breast."

She grinned in spite of her sour mood. Over the past several years, the two of them had become good friends through their mutual acquaintances at the University. He was one of the few men who actually seemed interested in the opinion of a mere female, encouraging her to speak her mind. As it happened, they agreed on more than a few things, and those on which they differed gave rise to any number of lively discussions. A closeness had developed between them, but one akin to the camaraderie of siblings rather than one of any romantic overtones. Each had seemed comfortable with that, and indeed, Derrien thought of him more in the light of an older brother than anything else.

"If it were just you and the rest of our friends, I should find it a most pleasant diversion," she replied to his light teasing. "But the presence of the visitors from London . . ." Her voice trailed off as she attempted to turn her eyes to the passing countryside. However a corner of the chipped straw caught on the gathered curtain,

drawing some further expression, whispered under her
breath.

Ferguson stifled a laugh. "Derry, my dear, have a care
or our English guests will think that we are the wild
heathens they have been taught to expect."

"I don't give a fig what they think," she muttered.

An odd look flashed over his face, then his brow rose
in mild surprise. "Have you truly taken such a dislike
to them?"

The brim of her bonnet hid her face. "Surely you have
to admit there is precious little to like—Miss Dunster
appears as cold and haughty as she is beautiful, while
Lord Marquand . . . is said to be a drunken gamester."
Her voice took on a brittle edge. "But what else would
you expect from titled English aristocrats? No doubt they
will spend the afternoon peering down their noses at us
country bumpkins. Given my druthers, the outing is one
I would avoid like the plague, if not for Aunt Claire."

It was Ferguson's turn to stare out the window.
Though his features were not shaded by any poke of
straw, his expression was equally unreadable, though she
was surprised to catch a flare of emotion in his eye she
had never seen before. "Perhaps you are being a bit
unfair in making such a harsh judgment, Derry? You
cannot have exchanged more than a few words with either of them."

She colored slightly and began to finger the book in
her lap. "Perhaps." Under her breath she added, "But I
doubt it."

"From you, at least, I should expect a more open
mind," he continued. "Not one colored by mere preju-
dice or hearsay."

Her cheeks burned a bit hotter. Close as they were,
Ferguson knew nothing of her real background, and his
words had unwittingly struck closer to the truth than
Derrien cared to admit. "Very well, Charlie, I shall try."

The carriage rolled to a halt and Ferguson assisted the
ladies in dismounting. Up ahead, the three other vehicles
that made up the excursion were emptying of their pas-
sengers. In all there were ten men and nine ladies, the

wife of Mr. Strathyeum having taken ill with a bad cough at the last minute. Ferguson quickly slipped his arm around Derrien's elbow and drew her to one side as the rest of the party began to pair off for the stroll out to the ruins of the abbey.

"I have a great favor to ask of you," he murmured in her ear after they had fallen in toward the back of the group.

"You know you may count on me for anything."

He cleared his throat while checking that no one else was close enough to overhear. "I should be eternally grateful if you would contrive to engage Lord Marquand's attention for some reason—any reason—so that he might be obliged to walk with you for a bit." Another short cough. "And so I might be paired with Miss Dunster."

It was only with great difficulty that Derrien kept from mouthing a most unladylike word. "Oh, Charlie, not you too! Don't tell me you are going to make a cake of yourself by swooning around the lovely lady like some lovesick mooncalf! Only look up ahead at how every man, even those half blind with age, is ogling—"

A warning look from Ferguson caused her words to cut off abruptly. But as soon as the approaching couple passed them she fixed him with a black scowl. "Besides, have you forgotten she is engaged to Lord Marquand? Do you wish to end up facing a pistol at twenty paces?"

His hand tightened on her arm. "Forget it then, I shall find another way—"

"You will not," she snapped. "Of course I shall do it, but that doesn't mean I shall like it." On seeing how pale his sensitive face had become, her brow furrowed in sudden concern. "What's going on there?" she demanded in a near whisper. "I know you well enough to know this is no mere—"

"Please." His expression took on a haunted look. "Don't ask. I shall explain . . . when I can."

She bit her lip. "Very well."

Several other couples caught up to them, forestalling any further conversation on the matter. Derrien managed to make the requisite small talk, but her mind was really on her friend and his strange request. What possible reason could Ferguson have for wanting to spend some time alone with the rigid Miss Dunster? Even if he had been suddenly smitten by an unaccountable infatuation with the icy young lady, he could not be so much of a fool as to think she would pay him the least attention. If anything, he would only end up embarrassing himself—and perhaps worse. She was well-enough acquainted with the Viscount's physical prowess to imagine he would be a crack shot.

Her chin took on the stubborn tilt that her intimate friends would have recognized all too well as a sign that her mind had set upon a certain course. She was simply going to have to keep a close eye on her friend to see he didn't get himself into real trouble.

The weathered stone remains of the abbey were set on a high promontory overlooking the sea. The view from the crumbling walls was magnificent now that the early morning clouds had blown through, leaving the sky a crisp cerulean blue whose rich color was also reflected in the gentle waves breaking upon the rocky shore. It was warm enough that even the most delicate of the ladies had no objection to exploring the grounds before partaking of the repast, and with such an impressive array of scholars among them, there was no risk of anyone being left unenlightened as to the abbey's significance in Scottish history.

Even now, Derrien could make out the tall form of the Viscount, standing beside his intended bride, head bent slightly as if spellbound by Professor Kildare's detailed account of some minor skirmish from the sixteenth century. Though the words were barely audible at that distance, he appeared to be speaking with some relish of the punishments exacted by the victors—which apparently included a goodly number of severed limbs and grotesque tortures. She jerked on Ferguson's arm, drawing their steps in the direction of the trio, and as they got closer, she had to repress a grin at the look in Marquand's eyes. He looked ready to cut off Kildare's tongue, along with any other appendage within reach, if a broadsword had been handy. Derrien could almost feel a dash of sympathy for Miss Dunster, whose face had taken on a more deathly pallor than usual at the graphic descriptions.

Ferguson tried to detour around one of the massive arches, but she held firm. "We must stay close to them," she whispered. "Once Walter has finished, I have no doubt that his lordship will want to slip off for a private stroll with his lady. Then we can follow and—"

"P—perhaps we should wait until after the picnic," he stammered. His own visage had turned nearly as pale as Miss Dunster's and he appeared more nervous than Derrien had ever seen him.

"No," she said firmly. "Buck up your courage, Charlie. If you insist on doing this, best get it over with."

He swallowed hard but let himself be led on.

Sure enough, the moment Kildare wound up his narrative, Marquand left no room for another long-winded story to begin. With a civil but unmistakable indication that the history lesson was at an end, he drew both himself and Miss Dunster away from the professor and headed toward some of the smaller outbuildings, whose position on the crest of a small rise afforded a clear view out over the bay to the distant spires of St. Andrews. Derrien had to all but drag Ferguson in the other couple's wake, but in a matter of minutes they came abreast of them behind the oldest section of the original church.

Taking note of her friend's locked jaw, Derrien realized there was no choice but to take matters into her own hands.

Chapter Ten

"Good day, Lord Marquand," she said with a forced brightness. Having never been formally introduced to the Viscount's companion, Derrien knew he would be obliged to stop and fulfill the required social niceties.

He turned slowly and she thought she noted a flicker of some emotion in his gray-green eyes, though what it was she couldn't really make out. Most likely it was annoyance, if not real anger, she thought with an inward grimace. She could hardly blame him if her countenance wasn't exactly a welcome one, but for the sake of her friend she plunged ahead. "A delightful day for a stroll, is it not?" Without waiting for a reply, she held out her hand. "I don't believe I have had the pleasure of being introduced to your charming companion, sir—not formally, that is."

Whatever previous emotion had flashed across Marquand's features was now replaced by an expression of faint amusement. "Then allow me," he replied with exaggerated politeness. "Honoria, may I present Miss Edwards." There was a fraction of a pause. "Miss Edwards, Lady Honoria Dunster."

Honoria's glove grazed against Derrien's. "Delighted, Miss Edwards," she murmured.

"I believe you have met my companion, Mr. Ferguson?"

That the lady's eyes studiously avoided any contact with those of Ferguson as she managed a quick nod was not lost on Derrien, though she also noted that the Viscount seemed not to notice anything amiss.

There was some deep mystery here, she was sure of

it, and the thought of her good friend falling into some abyss from which he could not extricate himself caused her throat to constrict with concern. Yet she had given her promise to help, and until Ferguson had a chance to explain, she felt she had no choice but to proceed as planned.

"And you, Lord Marquand," she continued in the same overbrittle voice, "have the two of you gentlemen—"

"No, we have not." The Viscount interrupted her speech by inclining a slight bow in Ferguson's direction. "Marquand."

"Charles Ferguson, my lord."

Derrien was glad to note that his voice was firm, and that his return bow was no more pronounced than that of the English lord."

Having performed the necessary chore of introductions, Marquand looked impatient to be on his way, but Derrien sidled forward to effectively block his path. "I was wondering, my lord, if I might a brief word with you . . ."

His brows arched up in mild surprise.

"Ah, Charles, I'm sure Miss Dunster has not seen the view of the sea from the walkway in front of the transept," she added quickly, shooting him a pointed glance. "You know it is considered the best vantage point for, er, spotting the rare white kestrel that, er, nests in the nearby cliffs."

"Yes, the white kestrel," he repeated faintly. "Er, quite right. I should be delighted, that is, if the lady would care to accompany me, and his lordship has no objection." He cleared his throat and offered his arm to Honoria.

If possible, her color became even paler, but she placed her hand on his sleeve without a perceptible hesitation.

Marquand raised no objection. He stepped aside, and with a slight gesture of his hand, indicated that the couple should pass. Once they had disappeared around the corner of the ancient church, he turned back to Derrien and, with some nonchalance, folded his arms across his chest and fixed her with a penetrating stare.

"Well, Miss Edwards? I must admit, I am waiting with bated breath to hear whatever it is you wish to tell me. It must be of great importance, indeed, for you to seek out my company of your own accord."

Ferguson made no attempt to speak until they were well away from the others, and even then, he had to clear his throat several times before any words would come out.

"You have grown even more beautiful over the years, Nora." His mouth quirked into a tentative smile. "I think of you . . . often. More often than I care to admit, as I'm sure that you hardly remember a poor tutor who—"

Her eyes flew up to meet his, alight with a spark of emotion that the Viscount would not have recognized. Although her answering words came out in barely more than a whisper, they were no less intense. "How can you think that I have forgotten you, even for a day!"

Glancing around to make sure they were unobserved, Ferguson pulled her into the shadows of an archway and brought his lips down upon hers in a passionate embrace. Honoria returned his kisses with equal ardor, until finally, regaining some measure of discretion, she pushed away gently from his chest. "Ch—Charles, we must not allow this to happen—"

"The devil we mustn't!" He tipped her chin up so that she could not hide her face from him beneath the cover of her bonnet. "Just tell me one thing—do you love him?"

The answer was more than evident in her expression of longing. "You need ask?" she asked, the corners of her mouth trembling. After a moment she added, "But my feelings have nothing to do with it. You know I have precious little choice in the matter." An edge of bitter cynicism cut into her tone. "My father expects a handsome return on his investment of raising a daughter—I am expected to do my duty and procure a prominent title in return for his blunt, no matter that I am . . . d— damaged goods."

Ferguson's hands tightened on her shoulders.

"Lord Marquand is . . . a decent man," she continued in a near whisper. "It . . . it could be much worse."

A savage oath exploded from his lips. "I'm not a callow youth anymore, Nora! When your maid gave away our plans to elope and your father caught up with us on the Great Northern Road, I should never have let him convince me that I was too raw, too poor to ever make you happy. I realize now what a fool I was to slink away and let you go without a fight." His fingers came up to caress her cheek. "Now that chance has brought us together again, I don't intend to make the same mistake." He hesitated, a hint of doubt creeping into his voice. "That is, if you would still have me. I cannot offer you a fortune or a title, but neither am I a penniless tutor anymore. I have a good position at the University and have some prospects for further advancement. There would be no endless rounds of balls nor closets full of expensive gowns nor a houseful of servants, but we would have a comfortable life together."

She made a sound somewhere between a sigh and a sob. "None of those things matter a whit to me! All I wish is to be with you, Charles! But what can we do? My engagement to the Viscount was announced before we left London, and Mama has already picked out a date."

"When?"

"The fourth of December."

His mouth compressed in a grim line. "That is quite a long way off—much may happen to change things."

"B—but we are supposed to leave here to return to London in little more than a week."

"Don't worry, my love, I shall come up with something by then." He essayed a tight smile. "After all, this time we are already in Scotland."

Honoria answered him with her own brave imitation of his expression.

The faint echo of footsteps warned them that others were approaching. "I had best take you back." He straightened his cravat and placed her hand back on his sleeve, not before giving it a quick squeeze. "You must try to act as though nothing is amiss. I shall contrive to be included in all the entertainments to which you are invited over the next little while, and we shall manage to steal a few moments to speak privately and decide on a plan. Do you think you can do that, Nora?"

They had begun to walk at a leisurely pace back toward the other path, taking great care to appear as no more than two casual acquaintances making polite conversation. Honoria's chin came up and when she turned her head slightly to glance at the young professor, all trace of emotion had been wiped from her face. "Of course I can pretend as if nothing is wrong, Charles. After all, I have been doing it for the last four years, so another little while will hardly signify."

"Brave girl," he murmured. "My only fear is that your parents might recognize my face, despite—"

"Father is off at a friend's shooting box and Mama— I don't think Mama ever bothered to take a proper look at her son's tutor."

He gave a mirthless chuckle. "Quite right. Well then, our little secret should be safe enough for a while." He drew in a deep breath as they came to the crest of the hill. "Keep that lovely chin up, my dear. I promise you I will find some way out of this bumblebroth."

"Well, as to that, sir . . ." Derrien bit her lip, frantically searching for some plausible reason as to why she had interrupted the Viscount's stroll with his intended bride. Now that he stood there in front of her, foot tapping in some impatience, she felt totally foolish. To her mortification, her cheeks began to burn as hot as a flame, and the thought of how silly she must look caused her jaw to clench. "I . . . wish to apologize for my rudeness of the other day. I have an unfortunate knack for letting my tongue run away with me."

For an instant he looked surprised, then his expression quickly changed into one of amusement. "Somehow, Miss Edwards, such contrition is not overly convincing."

"Why—"

A quirk of a smile appeared on his lips. "Because you are scowling as though that tongue of yours would rather run all the way to China than be forced to give an apology to me."

"T—that's not true. Not entirely." Her head ducked. "I *am* sorry for what I said. I am aware that I have no right to comment on your . . . personal affairs."

"No, you do not. Especially when you don't understand that of which you speak," he said softly.

Derrien was taken aback by the raw emotion in his voice, so at odds with his cool demeanor. "But you have admitted you are here in St. Andrews because of a wager. If I am wrong in what I said, I should like to . . . to understand why."

"Understand, Miss Edwards?" He turned his head to stare out over the sea, where a rising breeze had kicked up a froth of whitecaps, and his expression twisted into one of weary cynicism. "Understand what—that my father is a wastrel and has risked the family estate on the turn of a card, leaving me with the task of salvaging the whole sordid affair? I doubt a young miss like you, raised in a warm and loving family, would understand that sort of obsession, just as you wouldn't have any idea what it is like to live with the uncertainty of whether there was enough blunt for food or whether your father was going to beat you while in a drunken stupor. Or your mother abandon you for months on end in a cold, drafty house with naught but an elderly—" He caught himself and a dull flush spread over his cheeks. His eyes pressed closed for a moment, accentuating the fine line of worry etched at their corners, before he spoke again. "Now it is I who have let my tongue run where it should not," he said quietly. One hand came up to rub at his temple and he went on in a near whisper, as if speaking only to himself. "I don't know what has come over me of late—I am not usually prone to behaving as if I were an hysterical schoolgirl. I've never spoken to anyone but Tony about such things."

For the second time in as many days, Derrien was forced to hang her head in shame. If the Viscount's reve-

lations had even a grain of truth to them, she was guilty
of a gross injustice in judging him so harshly. Not that
she doubted any of it—she had seen a glimpse of his
inner pain in the depth of those gray-green eyes before
he regained his usual icy composure. She opened her
mouth to speak but words seemed to elude her. No explanation seemed adequate to express the tangle of her
confused emotions.

He slowly forced his gaze back to meet hers. "I pray
you will do me the favor of forgetting this little scene.
Your apology, though unnecessary, is accepted." He
reached out his arm. "Shall I escort you back to your
friend—"

His gesture caused her to step forward and lay a hand
on his arm. "I—I always imagined a titled gentleman
would have a . . . a perfect life."

Marquand gave a grimace of self-mockery. "No, Miss
Edwards. More likely it is you who have had the perfect
upbringing, with doting mother and father, and now an
aunt who—"

"I never knew my father," she blurted out, not quite
sure why she was moved to make such an intimate revelation to him, of all people, when she had never been
able to discuss such painful truths with even her closest
friends.

"I'm sorry." There was a slight hesitation. "I take it
he passed away when you were very young?"

She shook her head. "No, that's not what I meant, sir.
I . . . never knew who he was. Other than that he was
a titled English gentleman, an officer posted for a short
time in Edinburgh." The toe of her half boot scuffed at
the ground. "And one who felt free to indulge in the
sorts of amusements that men of his rank and fortune
feel they are entitled to . . ." She paused to control the
tremor in her voice.

"Like gambling, carousing, and seducing innocent
young ladies." There was a flicker of sympathy in the
Viscount's eyes. "I see."

Derrien somehow knew that he did.

"Well, that certainly explains your aversion to my person."

"No!" Her glove tightened on the sleeve of his fine melton wool coat. "That is, I admit I wanted to feel that way at first. But the more I have come to know you, sir, the more I see it is not always right to make such sweeping assumptions—"

He interrupted with a short chuckle. "That's quite generous of you, Miss Edwards, but I would hardly say that you have come to know me all that well. After all, we have not spent very much time in each other's company."

Ha, she thought with an inward grimace. *More than you imagine!* However, she kept that particular revelation to herself.

"I'm afraid you would soon discover I have more than my share of faults," he continued. "I can be all the things you dislike—arrogant, short-tempered, moody—"

"Oh, I'm well are of that."

His brows drew together in question.

"I—I mean, all of us have the sort of faults you speak of." She swallowed hard, then went on in a halting voice. "But in truth, it is *I* who deserve *your* scorn, not the other way around." Her chin rose just a bit. "After all, you now know my dirty little secret. One born on the wrong side of the blanket is hardly fit to pass judgment on anyone else."

"We all have our dirty little secrets, Miss Edwards." He tucked her hand under his arm and started their steps toward the high granite walls of the old church. "Rest assured that yours is quite safe with me. And you may also be sure I think no less of you for it. I have come to realize over the years that the only people deserving of scorn are the individuals who, through their own selfishness, have caused pain and suffering for others." He drew in a deep breath. "Though perhaps what they really deserve is pity."

They walked for a bit without speaking, but it was more a thoughtful silence than an awkward one. As they approached the first of the crumbling arches, Derrien finally ventured to break it. "Lord Marquand?"

"Yes, Miss Edwards?"

"Do you think we might . . . continue to converse about gardens?"

He smiled. "Ah, gardens. There is something very magical about them, isn't there? They are all about life and growth. Cold and drought may cause them to lie fallow for a time, but there is always a rebirth of beauty, of color, of vibrancy. Such constant renewal in the face of the elements gives one cause for hope, I suppose. In any case, they rather lift the spirits." His free hand stole into his coat pocket. "Yes, I should like to continue our discussions." He withdrew the slim volume of essays and held it out to her. "Perhaps next time we meet, you would care to give me your opinion on these latest ideas from Payne Knight."

"Oh!" Her jaw dropped open in amazement that not only had he remembered his promise but that he felt obligated to keep it, despite her nasty accusations. Her confusion was made even worse by his obvious sensitivity and eloquence. As she now knew it was not he who was the inveterate gambler, it also struck her that perhaps neither was he a dissolute rake.

But just what was he?

The book was still in his outstretched hand. "Have you decided that Knight is not to your taste after all?"

"Oh no! It's just that—I—I don't know what to say . . ."

He gave a low chuckle. "Something that does not occur very often, I imagine. Why not say 'thank you' and put it away in your reticule."

She did, though her fingers seemed to move with disconcerting awkwardness. He appeared to ignore her fumblings and began a pithy commentary on how well the surrounding ruins would suit the tastes of a certain landscape designer currently much in vogue. By the time they met up with the other couple, Derrien had forgotten her embarrassment in the spirited exchange of opinions. It was with a pinch of disappointment—and perhaps some other emotion—that she relinquished the Viscount's arm to his intended bride. On stealing another glance at the cool, composed face of the young lady, her polished features unmarred by any crease or dimple of emotion, Derrien couldn't help but puzzle on what Ferguson could possibly have wanted to discuss with the regal English beauty, and why it had demanded such urgency.

Her friend's hand came firmly around her elbow. "I believe I saw that the Baronet's servants are laying out the picnic. Allow me to escort you down to a spot where we may be afforded a good view of the sea." Without waiting for a reply, he took his leave of Marquand and hastened their steps away from the slanting shadows of the crumbling nave. Derrien had no choice but to follow along, however it took a good measure of self-control to refrain from darting one last look over her shoulder at the Viscount's tall form.

Marquand forced his gaze away from the lively step of the retreating figure and the way several errant blond curls danced in the breeze, once free of the confining bonnet. "I trust it was not too great an ordeal to endure the learned professor's company? It is to be hoped that he would exhibit some common sense and limit the topic of his conversation to a trifle less bloodcurdling subject than that of his colleague."

Honoria stumbled slightly. "No, not at all. That is, I mean yes, he seems . . . a very sensible young man."

"Sensible—now that has a rather dry ring to it." He gave a low chuckle. "Was the fellow truly an insufferable bore? If so, I shall try to make sure you are not trapped in his presence—"

"N—no!" Quickly recovering her poise, she hastened to add, "That is, he was perfectly pleasant company. You needn't pay it any mind." She kept her eyes averted from his face. "And you, sir? I hope Miss Edwards was not a nuisance? She looks to be a very headstrong young lady."

"She wished to . . . inquire about a matter concerning gardens." He wondered why it was that a slight flush was creeping to his cheeks.

"How odd."

He bit back a sharp retort. "I have a passing interest in the subject, you know. In fact, one might say I have a modicum of knowledge concerning such things."

"Oh, yes. I suppose you have mentioned it on occasion," she replied absently. Her tone was distant, as if her thoughts were as far away as the gulls winging out to follow a distant fishing boat. "I imagine that most gentlemen of property do."

"Woolsey Hall has some of the most beautiful gardens in England," he continued, seeing if he might raise a spark of interest in her. "I mean to see what improvements I might add to such magnificent designs."

"Mmmm."

The sound failed to convey even a hint of enthusiasm, causing the Viscount's brow to knit in some consternation. Had she always exhibited such a flatness of emotion, or was it only the comparison with a certain other young lady that was making the lovely Miss Dunster appear to have been cut out of pasteboard? His own boot slipped on the rocky path, as if to warn him that such thoughts were in danger of treading on dangerous ground. With a reluctant sigh, he looked searchingly at her half-turned profile. "You are sure something is not amiss, my dear, and that your earlier encounters with these scholarly Scots haven't in some way overset you?"

She started. "Oh, no," she repeated, with some force. "I fear I was thinking on . . . on why the young lady would feel the need to request a private audience with you to discuss gardens."

Marquand gave a wry grimace. "I have long since abandoned any hope of understanding the working of the female mind." His light tone was designed to elicit at least an answering smile, but she remained staring straight ahead, her only reaction to his attempt at humor a slight tremor of her jaw. He gave up trying to probe any further into her state of mind and lapsed into his own moody silence.

It was with some gratitude that he saw Ellington disengage himself from a heated discussion on the merits of salmon fishing on the River Tay and make his way

toward them. His friend fell in at Honoria's other side
and the three of them proceeded to where several tables
had been set up with a veritable groaning board of food.

"I had best rejoin Mama now," said Honoria in a low
voice, glancing nervously at where Lady Dunster sat off
to one side of several couples. "She is not as yet comfortable with the local ladies."

Was it has imagination, wondered Marquand, or did
he detect a note of relief in her tone at finding an excuse
to quit his company? "Of course," he murmured politely.
"Shall Tony and I fix a selection for the two of you or do
you wish to sit for a bit before partaking in the repast?"

"I . . . I shall ask Mama what she prefers."

As they strolled away from the two ladies, Ellington
fixed his friend with a quizzing look. "Enjoying yourself?
At least you managed to grab a bit of time alone with
your intended."

The Viscount's gaze flitted from where Honoria sat in
rigid correctness next to her mother, hands folded de-
murely in her lap, to where Derrien was sprawled—none
too ladylike—on a blanket laid out on the grass, engaged
in what looked to be an animated debate with Ferguson.
He drew in a sharp breath, wondering why it was he
found himself wishing—

Wishing what?

Marquand frowned slightly. Honesty compelled him to
admit that after he fetched a glass of the local ale from
a cask set up near the platters of roast pheasant and
smoked trout, he would have vastly preferred taking a
seat on the ground by the maddening Miss Edwards to
heading to the chairs set up for the comfort of the English visitors. He found himself wondering what topic of
conversation was bringing such a spark to those flashing
eyes. He paused, his hand tightening around the glass
that Ellington had just passed to him, and found the
sudden trill of laughter from her lips was far more intoxicating than any amount of spirits. The young lady might
be outspoken, hot-tempered, and given to decidedly hoydenish behavior—in short, all the things he did not wish

for in a female. But she was also intelligent, sensitive, and undeniably passionate in her opinions.

Damnation, he thought with some vehemence, raising the glass and draining half its contents in one gulp. She was intriguing!

Ellington cleared his throat while taking up an ale of his own. "You might want to essay to wipe the scowl from your face. You are supposed to be putting aside your troubles for the afternoon, remember?" He slanted a sideways glance at Lady Hylton's pinched countenance, and added, "Though I vow, the prospect of such a mother-in-law might drive me to strong drink."

Marquand growled something unintelligible in reply, but managed to clear the dark expression from his features. His friend hadn't the slightest notion just which lady it was that was having such an effect on his thoughts, and he intended it to remain that way. "Come," he said gruffly. "I suppose we had better see which delicacies Honoria and mother would care to sample."

Plates were fixed for the ladies, and the two gentlemen dutifully took their places next to them. The buzz of voices punctuated the clink of silverware and the rustle of leaves in the gentle breeze as everyone settled down to the sumptuous array of food provided by the Baronet. The meal was well under way when the sound of an approaching horse caused a lull in the conversation. An elegantly dressed gentleman appeared at the far end of the ruins and, with a wave of greeting to the group, dismounted from his glossy stallion and began to approach. Removing his curly brimmed beaver hat, he ran his hand through his cropped chestnut locks and inclined an elegant bow in the direction of the host.

"Ah, Lord Hertford! Glad you could join us. I thought I had heard that you had recently arrived in town," called the Baronet. "Though it seems you have come north a tad earlier than you are usually wont to do."

The gentleman brushed a bit of dust from the sleeve of his immaculately tailored hacking jacket and surveyed the assembled group, his eyes lingering for a second on the Viscount before sweeping by with nary a flicker of acknowledgment. "Yes," he replied nonchalantly, his lips pulling into an sardonic half smile as he tapped his crop against the polished leather of his Hessians. "I must say, St. Andrews suddenly seemed a much more rewarding place to be than London." He smoothed at a fold in his starched cravat. "After all, Scotland affords such a wealth of pleasures for a keen sportsman, don't you think?"

Chapter Eleven

"No, no, my lord. You mustn't set that foot as if it were stuck in a bowl of porridge." Philp took up a stance and demonstrated what he meant. "Still, your swing is looking greatly improved." He placed another ball upon the ground. "Now, seeing as we are ready to make the turn, we will play the inward nine as if it were a real match. Your honors, sir."

Marquand stepped up and knocked a credible drive considerably past where Derry was standing to keep an eye on where the shot fell.

"A bit over one hundred sixty yards," remarked Philp with gruff approval as they caught up to her. "Excellent, sir, excellent. If your caddie has helped you make the same improvements in your short game, I, for one, should not care to bet against you."

"I believe Master Derry has done his best to whip me into shape," replied the Viscount dryly.

Philp gave a short chuckle. "What say you, Derry. Are you satisfied with your man's progress?"

"Aye, Mr. Philp," she muttered, ducking her head even lower to hide her reaction to the master's comment. "He has a chance." Why was she blushing like a schoolgirl at his unintended reference to the Viscount as 'her man'? she asked herself as she shifted the clubs on her shoulder. He was nothing of the sort!

Oh, it was true that she no longer held him in such low regard as before. The Viscount had shown himself to be quite different from the picture she had created in her mind of a privileged English lord—except that he was as sinfully handsome as she had imagined that sort of gentleman would be. That he was intelligent, compassionate, and not afraid of hard work to achieve his goals were qualities that had forced her to reevaluate her initial dislike. And of course, his interest in gardens alone would have been able to sway even the most hardened of prejudices against him. After all, any man who knew the difference between *hydrangea macrophylla* and *hydrangea aspera* couldn't be all bad!

"An iron or the baffing spoon?"

Derrien's head jerked around at Marquand's question. She took her time in eyeing the distance and the slight swell of hill in order to force her attention back to the game. "The spoon," she announced and handed him the club.

"Hmmm. I would have chosen the iron," he murmured, but took it without dissent.

"And then you would have risked not clearing that patch of tall grass at the crest. Once caught up in that tangle, you could lose two strokes, and maybe more. Better to be long than short."

Marquand studied the terrain for a moment before nodding in agreement. "Ah. I see what you mean."

Philip watched the brief interchange and chewed thoughtfully on the stem of his pipe. The Viscount set up, and after Derrien had murmured a reminder to keep his wrists firm but not stiff, his next shot rolled within several yards of the flag. Taking the proferred putter, he stepped to the ball and knocked it in the hole for his par.

"Well done, indeed, sir. We'll make a Scot of you yet."

Marquand grinned. "I fear I'd make a rather poor one, for I've not acquired any taste for your local spirits."

"No taste for our whiskey!" The other man pretended to be shocked. "Auch, you'll nay be a real golfer until ye can quaff yer shares of rounds with the laddies after eighteen."

"If it will help save a few strokes, I shall learn to down a barrel of the stuff." He paused in readying for his next drive as a foursome crossed the fairway up ahead, then stopped to one side of a patch of gorse.

"You may hit away. The outgoing group must stand

aside for those of us coming in," said Philp. "Now just aim down the center of the fairway, for on this hole The Elysian Fields gives you plenty of room."

Marquand hesitated, his gaze wavering between the other players in the distance and the ball at his feet. His club went back slowly, but a bit indecisively. The downswing was equally lacking in confidence, and at the last minute he yanked his hand through in order to compensate for the lack of head speed. The ball arced up in a weak hook, landing in one of "The Beardies," a group of pot bunkers off to the left. "Hell and damnation," he said through gritted teeth. "I don't know what happened—I've been hitting so much better than that of late."

The master exchanged a knowing look with Derrien, then turned to counsel his pupil, taking great care to repress the smile that threatened to crease his leathery face. "Thought you had it mastered, did you? Well, be assured that as soon as you begin to brim with such hubris, the golfing gods will take great pains to humble such pretensions. That is the one surety in the game." He paused, allowing his lips to twitch upward. "The second surety is that the first time you must hit with a group standing by, waiting for you to pass through, you will duff the shot."

At the Viscount's sheepish expression, he laughed outright. "Everyone does. Now, I should like to see you marshal your thoughts and get out of that hazard. If you can learn to recover from a lapse of concentration, it will be a lesson of more value than any of the others you have learned so far." Philp fell in beside the Viscount and after they had walked a few paces, he added, "I believe you are beginning to see that golf is quite a bit like life itself."

Marquand pulled a face. "Come now, Philp, it's just a bloody game."

"Yes, but one in which you must learn to face both triumph and disaster without letting either affect you too greatly. You must be willing to weather adversity and not let a bad bounce or serendipitous gust distract you from your long-term goals. Just as you must not let a few good shots convince you that you will sail through the rest of the round without mishap. Golf requires patience, imagination, resolve, and above all a sense of humor." He stopped for a moment to fiddle with his pipe. "Sounds rather like life to me."

"Hmmph." The Viscount made a noncommittal grunt, but his expression was rather thoughtful.

They reached the bunker and as Marquand stepped gingerly into the shifting sand, he couldn't help but note that the other golfers had hit their own shots and were moving to their balls, all of which had landed not far from where he was stuck. He set his jaw, intent on following Philp's advice to ignore any outside distraction. His hand shot out for a lofted iron, then he studied the height of the bunker's lip and the lie of his ball, trying to determine with just how much force and angle he had to swing in order to get clear of the steep sod.

"This should be rather amusing," said the gentleman nearest to him, in a voice quite clearly meant to be heard over the short distance.

The Viscount couldn't help but look up.

Lord Hertford was leaning casually on the hickory shaft of his long-nosed club. "Oh, sorry, Marquand. Didn't mean to disturb you," he murmured in mock contrition, then directed a sly grin toward his caddie. The fellow was a lad several years older than Derry, much broader in the shoulders, and possessed of a squinty gaze that even now had locked on her figure. "Hey there, Dirty Derry! Care to make our own wager on the outcome of the coming match—my gentleman against yours?" He gave a pointed look at the Viscount's predicament and tittered.

"I'll gladly take your bet, for whatever stakes you care to name! Now shut your gob, Jimmy, and let his lordship play."

Seething with anger despite all his resolve to stay focused on the task at hand, Marquand took a vicious swing at his ball. The club bit deep into the sand several inches behind the stitched featherie, sending up an explo-

sion of grains, but having little effect on the intended
target.

"The mines at Newcastle could use a man of your
talents, Marquand," joked the Marquess. "You seem
rather adept at digging holes." His other companions
gave a bark of laughter. "But don't be too discouraged.
Golf is an extremely difficult skill to master and I imagine that if you keep working on it, in a few years you
shall be able to play a decent round." Another chorus
of chuckles followed the veiled taught.

"Perhaps you might show a bit of courtesy and stay
quiet for a moment so we can continue our play, my
lord," interrupted Philp.

"Of course." Hertford bowed his head in deference to
the golf master, but not before allowing a smug snicker
to play at his lips.

The Viscount took a deep breath and swung again.
This time the ball popped straight up. It looked at least
to clear the bunker, if not advance much farther, but at
the last second it caught the edge of the lip and rolled
back down the steep pitch, coming to rest not a foot
from its original spot.

"Open the face of the club, sir, by shifting your grip
to the right," murmured Derry.

With that advice, he made yet a third try, and this
time the ball sailed out and onto the fairway.

"That's a good out," said Philp quietly. "From there
you can get home in one."

The Viscount struggled out of the soft sand, well aware
of how foolish he looked with his coat and hair dusted
with a shower of fine grains.

"Five guineas," called Hertford's caddie after the Marquess had lofted a perfectly struck drive that traveled
nearly to the fringe of the distant green. "What say you
to *those* stakes?"

It was a staggering amount for the like of two lads,
but Derrien showed not a whit of hesitation. "Done,"
she called. "And bring it in coin, for I'll not accept any
promises from the likes of you."

The other caddie gave a jeering whistle as he turned to follow his man.

"That's a very brave wager, lad. Or a very foolish one. I can't imagine you have five shillings let alone five guineas to your name."

"Hmmph." She lifted the clubs to her shoulder. "I don't intend to lose to that smarmy weasel. Do you?"

He chuckled. "It seems as if we are a well-matched team, Master Derry—indeed I do not!"

"Good. Then let's get back to work."

The fiddles sang out a lively country tune and the dancers capered through the steps with laughing abandon, faces flushed with exertion and good cheer. Marquand stood off to one side, amazed that Honoria had agreed to partake in anything quite so rustic. He had to admit that with Ferguson's arm to guide her, her steps never seemed to falter. In fact, she appeared to be enjoying herself more than he would ever have guessed possible.

"Miss Dunster seems to show a real knack for the Scottish reel," murmured Ellington as he placed a glass of champagne in his friend's hand.

Would that she would show any such spirited interest in any concern of his, thought the Viscount glumly as he watched her spin by yet again, smiling up at the young professor with an animation that nearly caused him to choke on a mouthful of the bubbly spirits.

"If you will excuse me, Tony, I think I shall steal a look at the botanical prints Mr. Cheape has in his library. He is said to possess an excellent collection of the local flora, including a number of rare species."

Ellington looked faintly puzzled by the unaccountable edge to the Viscount's words, but merely shrugged. "Suit yourself. However, I think I shall try my luck in asking that pretty redhead for the next dance."

Marquand made his way down the corridor, wondering himself exactly why his mood had taken a turn for the worse. Well, a bit of time spent perusing the delicately colored engravings would no doubt serve as a tonic to his spirits. Though the heavy oak door was open, the paneled room appeared to be deserted, just as he had hoped. However as he stepped inside and drew near to the carved bookcases, he caught sight of a figure seated on the sofa, head bent in earnest study of a large leather-bound volume. He bit back an oath, then realized it was Miss Edwards who was engaged in looking at the book.

Her head came up with a jerk, the abrupt movement sending a small sketchbook sliding from her lap to the floor. "Oh!"

He bent down to retrieve it, just beating her own outstretched fingers in scooping it up. "Most young ladies would prefer to spend an evening partnered by a young gentleman rather than an old book," he remarked dryly.

"I—I was just making a few notations in between sets," she stammered defensively. "Besides, I am not at all like most young ladies."

"I shall not argue with you on that account," he said with a smile. As he spoke, he stole a look through several of the smudged pages and his eyes widened slightly in surprise. The drawings were a mixture of skillful plant renderings along with schematic plans for their use. Even a cursory glance revealed a marked talent for detail and a bold sense of design. "Why, these are quite good," he murmured.

Derrien tried to snatch the book from his hands. "Please, sir, give it back. Those drawings are not meant for anyone but me."

He ignored her plea and flipped to a double-page plan. "Is this for something specific?"

"I—"

Her answer was interrupted by the arrival of another person. "Well, well, forgive me if I am intruding on some private meeting." Lord Hertford paused to light up a thin cheroot. "Though I must say, Marquand, if I were engaged to such a paragon of beauty as the lovely Miss Dunster I should keep my breeches tightly buttoned until after the wedding. Innocents can be quite unreasonable about such things, until they are taught the way of it."

Derrien's cheeks turned red, whether from anger or embarrassment, Marquand wasn't sure. But before he could make a reply, she snapped her own quick retort. "It is obvious where your thoughts tend to dwell, sir, but Lord Marquand and I were simply discussing gardens."

"Really?" The marquess's lip curled up at one corner as he let out a lazy puff of smoke. "Have you an interest in such things as sowing seeds, Miss Edwards?"

"That's quite enough, Hertford. I suggest you finish blowing a cloud out on the terrace before I am forced to demand an apology to the young lady."

He feigned a look of innocence. "Apology? My dear Marquand, I was merely asking Miss Edwards about her interest in gardens." He turned to Derrien and made an exaggerated bow. "Forgive me, Miss Edwards, if you have misunderstood my words. I have heard from some of the locals that you have a talent for creating some very pretty designs. In fact, why not stop by Gravely Manor sometime to discuss what flowers might be added to my collection. Naturally, I would be willing to pay for your services."

She choked down a snort. "Hell will freeze over before I set foot anywhere near your estate," she said under her breath. In a louder voice she answered, "I doubt our tastes would suit."

"Oh, my tastes are very eclectic, Miss Edwards."

Her face twisted into an expression of disgust. "Your tastes are of no interest to any civilized person."

Hertford's brows arched up. "Dear me, these Scottish lasses may have a certain prettiness but their manners do tend to be a bit rough on the edges, don't you think, Marquand?"

Marquand took a step toward the other man, one hand curling in an involuntary fist. The Marquess gave a negligent flick of his cheroot, letting the ash fall onto the thick Oriental carpet. "Oh, no need for you to work yourself into a lather. I would have thought you had done quite enough of that out on the links this afternoon." Before the Viscount could make an answer, Hertford turned and strolled from the room.

"Odious beast," she muttered.

"I'm sorry you had to endure such vile remarks, but

it would only have caused an unpleasant scene all around had I planted him a facer."

Derrien flashed a brief smile. "No doubt you would have enjoyed knocking the smirk off his face for his behavior on the golf course—"

Marquand spun around, wondering how in the devil she could possibly know about that. "How do you know aught of that?" he demanded, fixing her with a searching look.

"Ahhh . . ." She swallowed hard. "Well, Mr. Philp stopped by my aunt's house . . . on his way home and mentioned something of the matter." Quickly changing the subject, she held out her hand once again. "My drawings, if you please, sir. I would really prefer that you give them back immediately."

"Why?" Instead of returning the sketchbook, he thumbed back to the design that covered two facing pages. "This is quite wonderful. Is it for somewhere real or simply a place that you see in your mind's eye?"

"It is a part of a plan for Rossdhu House, on Loch Lomand. A good friend—a male friend, naturally—has garnered a commission from the laird of the Calhoun Clan to design a garden along the water's edge. One of his assistants has been taken ill, so he asked me to lend a hand with part of the project. These are some sketches for a section that is to incorporate the ruins of a sixteenth century stone tower."

"And this?" His finger pointed to an irregular shaded area that appeared in several places on the plan.

"Rhododendron bushes. The laird has a fancy for them and wishes to have as many as possible incorporated into the final design."

"Ah yes, we all must—" He gave a slight cough to cover up the slip of the tongue. Damnation, he must be careful, but it was remarkably easy to talk freely with Miss Edwards. "That is, all designers must learn to accede to the requests of their patrons." He took a seat beside her on the sofa. "What is that line?"

Derrien laid aside the heavy leather-bound volume of prints. "Oh, that." Her nose scrunched up in a certain way that caused the Viscount to search his thoughts for where he had seen such an expression before. It was awfully familiar, and yet he couldn't quite place it. "I'm afraid I'm having a bit of difficulty deciding how to deal with the path along the loch. I had thought of a low yew hedge, but it feels too . . . heavy."

Marquand grabbed up her pencil and without thinking turned to a blank page. "Had you considered . . ." His hand flew in a few deft strokes, sketching in a rough outline of what he had in mind.

She stared at the bold squiggles and delicate shadings and drew in a sharp breath. "Good Lord," she whispered. Her eyes slowly rose to meet his. "You are . . . *him,* aren't you."

With a silent oath, he dropped his gaze and snapped the sketchpad closed. How could he have been such a gudgeon as to let his childish enthusiasm sweep aside all common sense! In an instant, he had put all of his hard work at risk, for he couldn't afford to have his identity revealed quite yet, at least not until his commission for the Duke was completed. "I don't know what you are talking about," he said coolly, handing the book back to her.

"Oh yes, you do." Her eyes remained locked on his rigid features. "You are Chitley. I would recognize that style anywhere."

He swore again, this time out loud, as he realized the futility of further denial. She was too sharp by half to be taken in by any Banbury Tale he might try to spin. "Well, now you know *my* dirty little secret, Miss Edwards. I should appreciate it greatly if you would not mention it to anyone else."

"But why on earth would you wish to hide the fact that you are one of the most gifted garden designers in all the realm?" she blurted out.

"Because, my dear Miss Edwards, a *gentleman* does not dirty his hands in trade. You think I would be showered with accolades by my peers? Not likely! I should be looked upon with scorn, forfeiting what little respect the Linsley family name still has after the escapades of my two rackety parents.'' His hand raked through his locks. "No, until I have finished the large commission I am working on and am firmly established in my ancestral home, I cannot afford to have my real identity revealed.''

It was a moment before she spoke. "As you know, sir, I am very good at keeping secrets. You needn't fear that I will tell anyone—that is, on one condition.''

A stab of disappointment knifed into him at her last words. From her, such a mercenary proposal was somehow unexpected, and thus hurt all the more. "And what is that?'' he asked in a hard voice. What could she possibly want out of him?

She hesitated on seeing his grim expression. "I . . . I was hoping you might give me some further advice on how to deal with the walkway,'' she said in a small voice. "But if you are too busy to be bothered—''

The tight line of his lips had relaxed into a true smile. The idea of helping Miss Edwards with her project was infinitely appealing, and the prospect of what promised to be a lengthy time together nearly caused him to grin like some idiotic schoolboy. "No, really—I should be delighted to give you a more detailed opinion. Let me think on it for a bit so that I might give you more than just a passing impression.''

She nodded and her fingers toyed with the cover of her pad. "You may not be able to acknowledge in public the praise that is due you, but at least Miss Dunster must be very proud of your accomplishments.''

A harsh laugh sounded. "Neither she nor her parents would be in the least amused if they knew I was Chitley.''

"How can she not know?'' cried Derrien. "Surely when you talk about gardens she must sense the truth.''

He shook his head. "Honoria cannot tell a rhododendron from a rosebush. Nor does that fact trouble her in the least.'' Why was it that of late, it was troubling *him* more than he cared to admit?

She stared at him in disbelief. "That is awful—'' Her hand clapped over her mouth. "Oh dear,'' she mumbled through closed fingers. "There I go again, about to spout off on something that is none of my business.''

"No, indeed it is not," he replied, but there was no real sting to his words. "Perhaps it would be best if—"

For the second time, their conversation was interrupted by the appearance of others seeking a bit of respite from the music and dancing. It was Charles Ferguson who stepped into the room, Honoria close by his side. A rosy color had replaced the usual marble whiteness of her cheeks and a soft laugh sounded from her lips at something that the young professor had just whispered in her ear. Marquand blinked several times, but before he could speak, Derrien shot to her feet.

"Charles!" she squeaked in warning, afraid that her friend and his companion might fail to notice that the room was not deserted.

Ferguson's head jerked around and his face took on a deathly pallor. "Er, Derry—" he began, but Honoria's rather brittle voice overrode his own meek attempt to speak.

"Adrian! I had been wondering where I might find you, and then M—Mr. Ferguson suggested I might try the library and offered to show me the way."

The Viscount got to his feet as well, feeling a sudden stab of disappointment that his tête-à-tête with Miss Edwards was at an end. He drew in a deep breath. Lord, it made no sense! The lovely lady before him had all the attributes he could ever wish for in a wife—beauty, wealth, rank, and impeccable manners. Yet the prospect of escorting her back to the lilting music left him feeling decidedly flat. He gave a mental shake of his head, trying to banish such disquieting thoughts. It was the dratted wager that had his mind in a whirl, he assured himself. Once it was over, everything would return to normal.

"I'm sorry, my dear," he said, forcing a smile to his lips. "I hadn't realized I had been gone so long. Miss Edwards was, er, showing me Mr. Cheape's botanical prints."

"Yes," chirped in Derrien.

"Ah," murmured Ferguson.

"Mmmm." Honoria's eyes did not quite meet those of the Viscount.

The four of them shuffled and glanced rather awkwardly at each other for a moment before Marquand forced his steps forward and offered his arm to his intended. "I hope you have saved a place on your dance card for me?"

"Y—yes, of course." She moved away from Ferguson's side and placed her hand on Marquand's sleeve. He was surprised to find it felt cold as ice.

"My thanks, Ferguson, for escorting Miss Dunster to my side," he added, with a slight nod in the professor's direction. "Now, if you will excuse us . . ." He turned to Derrien as well and sketched a quick bow.

"Of course," chorused both of them at once. With another brief exchange of pleasantries, the Viscount and his intended bride left the room.

Ferguson made to follow, but Derrien's hand snaked out and grabbed his elbow. "Not so fast, Charlie. I want a word with you."

"Ahhhh . . ."

"No 'ahhhs' about it. Something very smoky is going on here and you're going to tell me what it is."

"I can't." He tried once again to move toward the door but she slid around to block his way.

"Er, maybe later."

She crossed her arms and her expression made it clear she wasn't going to be fobbed off quite so easily.

A harried sigh escaped his lips. "Can you keep a secret?"

"As if I would even dignify that question with an answer!"

Ferguson slumped onto the sofa and ran his hands through his ginger hair. "Lord, what a horrible tangle."

"What is?" Derrien sat down beside him. "Oh, no. Don't tell me you've developed a hopeless *tendre* for Miss Dunster."

He looked up, a bleak expression in his eyes. "Worse than that. I'm in love with her. Completely, irrevocably in love with her. But thankfully, her sentiments are much the same. We are going to elope as soon as I can make all the arrangements."

There was a heavy silence as she stared at him in disbelief. "You are foxed," she finally said.

His mouth twisted in a wry grimace. "I wish I were."

"Then you are mad."

"Perhaps." He shrugged. "But all I know is that I shall truly go out of my mind if I let her slip away again."

"I think you had better start from the beginning."

Ferguson sighed and leaned back against the plump down cushions. "When I finished my studies at Cambridge, I had little money and few real prospects for employment. When an offer was presented to me to tutor the young son of an English lord, I had little choice but to accept. Besides, it afforded me the chance to live in London for a time, something that I, as a raw youth, thought would be . . . exciting." He brushed at a wrinkle on his sleeve. "The position was decent enough. The lad was a trifle spoiled, but at least he was not a total dullard. My employer was not unkind, but as a penniless tutor, I was hardly important enough to engage his attention. As you can imagine, I saw very little of the family—that is, except for the daughter." His eyes pressed closed. "Nora—Honoria—was as starved for intelligent conversation as I was, I suppose. We began to exchange books, then to meet in the library to discuss our ideas. She had a sharp mind and was eager to learn . . ." Another sigh followed. "Well, you can image what developed between a lovely sixteen-year-old schoolgirl and a callow tutor of twenty-two."

It didn't require much imagination.

"Right out of the covers of a Minerva Press novel, isn't it?" he continued with a self-deprecating laugh. "Naturally, it was impossible for me to make an offer, given my rank and purse. So we decided, with the rashness of youth, to elope. However, her lady's maid raised the alarm not more than an hour after we had stolen away." His lips twitched in a near wince. "Her father caught up with us before we had gone too far—before we had . . . passed a night together on the road. I allowed myself to be convinced that a union with me would utterly ruin Nora's life. So I promised to keep silent about the whole affair, as well as to quit England. A position was arranged for me in Ireland." There was a slight pause as his hand came up to rub at his temple. "Just to be sure I understood the terms of the bargain, I was beaten to within an inch of my life before being tossed on board the ship in Liverpool."

"Oh, Charlie." Derrien's hand came to rest on his arm. She opened her mouth to say more, but held up. Mere words seemed woefully inadequate.

He smiled. "Don't look so stricken. In some ways, it was very good for me—it forced me to develop a certain strength of character if I wished to survive. After a year or two, I found I had been left a tidy inheritance by a distant uncle, so I returned to Scotland, determined to establish myself at a university. Well, you know much of the rest." He tugged at the end of his cravat. "Though not a day passed that I didn't think of Nora, I would never have thought to contact her. I naturally assumed she had long ago forgotten her rash, youthful infatuation and was happily married to some man of her own rank. But then she arrived in St. Andrews, a proof that the bones of our town's patron saint do indeed work miracles." A beatific smile spread across his face. "I'll not give her up this time."

Derrien swallowed hard. "But, Charlie, she is engaged to Lord Marquand."

He looked rather uncomfortable. "Would you have her marry a man she does not love?"

No, she realized with a sudden start. She did not care in the least for the notion of Miss Dunster marrying the Viscount.

Now why was that? Her fingers twisted the strings of her reticule into a series of knots. Perhaps because he deserved someone who would appreciate his magnificent talents, someone who would share his interests. She tried to push such thoughts from her mind, along with the less noble sentiment that if Miss Dunster were not around, Marquand would have that much more time to spend discussing gardens with her. After all, it was, as Marquand had clearly pointed out, none of her business.

"No," she answered out loud. "Of course I should not wish for anyone to be forced to marry where there is no love. But what of Lord Marquand's feelings? Won't he be terribly hurt and humiliated by such a public jilting?"

Ferguson's expression was a mixture of guilt and defiance. "We both wish there were some way to avoid it, but . . ." He seemed to be searching for some excuse. "Nora is not even sure how strongly his feelings are attached," he added lamely.

"And what of the consequences to you, Charlie? Have you given a thought to how such a scandal will affect your standing at the University? Despite a certain aura of intellectual give and take, the people here—including your colleagues—are extremely straitlaced when it comes to matters of morality."

"I know that, Derry." His jaw set. "But I am willing to accept the consequences, no matter what they are."

Derrien heaved a sigh. "Oh dear," she said under her breath. "It is going to take some very skillful play to get out of this rough."

Chapter Twelve

Marquand finished the sketch and put it aside, along with several others. That should give Miss Edwards a number of possibilities to consider, he thought with some satisfaction. This last one he particularly liked, what with the way he had worked in the addition of several discreet groupings of rhododendrons in subtle salute to the laird's preferences.

He tapped his pencil in some impatience against the polished oak of his desk. If only there had been a chance the previous evening to arrange a rendezvous with the young lady for this morning, he would have been able to show her his ideas without delay. Instead, he would simply have to hope she would make an appearance at Playfair's musicale so that they would be able to set up a meeting to discuss the plans. Or perhaps he would simply bring them along and try to steal some time alone with her.

As his eyes strayed to the clock on the mantel, he even toyed with the idea of taking a stroll. A stroll that might take him past the Edwards residence, so that he might—

The pencil paused in midair.

Something inside him warned that this was not exactly a direction in which he ought to allow his thoughts to stray. And yet, the prospect of another encounter with the outspoken Miss Edwards, of watching the passion of ideas set fire to her expressive eyes, of seeing the way the sunlight danced across the errant ringlets that always seemed to escape from the confining hairpins, made his pulse quicken. Not only that, it made the blood pool in his groin.

He tossed the pencil down and pushed away from his desk. *Good Lord, this was madness!* He was the envy of half the men in London, what with his engagement to a reigning Diamond of the First Water. Reason said that he should be thanking the Fates for his good fortune, rather than allowing himself to dwell on the image of a feisty country miss, no matter how intriguing the face. Yes, it was totally unreasonable that he should be sitting here wondering what it might be like to press his lips upon the alluring curves of her mouth.

With a muttered oath, he rose and stalked to the mullioned window, feeling distinctly uncomfortable, and not merely because of his physical state. Outside, the gusting winds and scudding storm clouds looked as unsettled as his own emotions. It promised to be a wet time out on the links, but perhaps a good dousing would help dampen the strange heat coursing through him.

This wouldn't do, he admonished himself, putting aside all thoughts of an early visit to the young lady in question. Through his own choice, he was bound to Miss Dunster and his honor as a gentleman demanded that he not stray from his commitment. Not even in thought. It was too late for regrets, if that was what he was feeling, and so he must simply cease thinking of Miss Edwards as aught but a talented designer of gardens. He would allow himself to look at her sketches, but he must not let his eyes—or imagination—stray to her pert nose or sensuous lips. . . .

His brow suddenly furrowed. *Those lips.* Something about them was nagging at the back of his mind. There was a familiarity about them, as if he had seen those exact curves somewhere else. Yet that was, of course, impossible. It was simply another sign of how addled his brain had become since leaving London. He let out a harried sigh and went off in search of an extra muffler.

If the squall didn't blow through, it was going to be a stormy afternoon on the golf course.

* * *

"Come now, you can do better than that, sir," said Derrien sharply as she slanted another quick glance at the Viscount and wondered what was prompting such a look of preoccupation on his lean face. If it was worry over the coming match, he would do well to pay more attention to the matter at hand, she thought. But perhaps it was concern over other, more personal things that had his mind wandering. . . . She tugged the large tweed cap down a bit more firmly over her curls and ordered her own thoughts to keep from straying too far afield. "Try to concentrate! A lapse like that against Lord Hertford and you shall find yourself in a deep hole before the match has really begun."

Marquand tried to make out through the spitting rain just where his ball had landed. "I don't think it ended up too far to the right."

She gave a snort of impatience. "On this hole, anything to the right of the fairway is grave trouble, remember?"

"Right."

"Those are the sorts of things you must keep in your head, sir," she went on as they started to walk toward the edge of the strand.

"Along with keeping my head down, my shoulders pointed at the target, my arms relaxed, my knees flexed, and the clubface square on contact," he muttered under his breath.

She tried to repress a grin. "Aye, those things as well—although sometimes it's best not to think of anything at all when you go to hit the ball."

Marquand shot her a dark look before ducking his head to avoid another shower of raindrops. "Ah, that's really quite helpful, Master Derry," he replied with undisguised sarcasm. "Any other words of wisdom you have been holding back, seeing as the match is only four days away?"

So perhaps it was, after all, merely tension over the approaching wager that had him looking rather distracted. She sought to help him relax. "I'm not entirely joking. It's all very well to think between shots, but when you step up to the ball, it *is* better to clear your thoughts of anything specific. Just . . . well, just trust yourself and swing."

"Hmmph."

They located his ball hard by a cart rut, resting on a patch of gravel with a large stone less than a foot behind it. The Viscount stared at it for several moments, his lips pursed in consternation.

"What are you going to try?" demanded Derrien.

His eyes went from the ball to the fairway, then back again. "Well, it's possible that with the long spoon I could knock it over that bunker and end up in a good position on the fairway, with a chance to make par."

"It's possible—that is, if you managed to avoid breaking your wrist on that rock and then were able to hit the best shot of your life off the graveled lie. What do you think the odds are of that?"

He kicked at a loose stone. "Ahhh, not great, I suppose."

"Aye, not great. The more likely result would be that you would need a seagull to retrieve your ball from the Bay or that it would be buried so deeply in that tall grass up ahead that you would need a scythe to extract it. In either case, it would result in a wasted stroke and a penalty, and your troubles would still not be over." She put one hand on her hip. "Come now, sir. Imagine that we are playing for real. What is the best decision?"

Marquand studied the lie of his ball once more, then heaved a sigh. "I suppose I should take a lofted iron and knock it sideways rather than trying to advance it straight ahead. That way, I should avoid the chance of injury, as well as of ending up in the water or the tangle of rough, and be certain of regaining the fairway."

With a brisk nod of approval, Derrien thrust the bespoke club into his hands and signaled for him to hit away. The results were as anticipated, eliciting another nod, this one betraying just the tiniest bit of smugness. "There, you see! At most you have lost one stroke and if you hit a good third shot you might still make par. There was no need to take a risky gamble, especially on the third hole."

The Viscount's jaw set. "Ah, but you are forgetting that I'm said to be a reckless fellow."

Though it was said half in jest, she didn't fail to note the rough edge to his voice and couldn't help but wonder again what thoughts were causing such an odd mood. Rather than reply with her customary bite, she gave a ghost of a smile. "That's why you have me here. For a hardened gambler, you seem uncommonly willing to listen to advice."

Her comment finally caused some of the grimness to ebb from his face and he gave a reluctant chuckle. "Usually it should work the other way around—the recklessness of youth tempered by the wisdom of age."

"It may not make much sense, but somehow we seem to make a good team, sir."

"Yes," he said rather thoughtfully. "We do at that."

For some reason, Derrien felt an unaccountable flutter inside her chest.

He stepped up, and after waiting for a moment for a gust of wind to die down, hit his next shot. It landed a bit short of the flag, but even Derrien had to admit that it was not a bad effort. And though his putt did not find the hole, he finished up, as she had predicted, with only a bogey rather than the disastrous score that might have resulted from his errant shot.

As though in charity with his efforts, the weather began to clear a bit during the short stroll to where Marquand was to hit his next drive. The blustery wind died down to a gentle breeze and the thick clouds thinned enough to allow a faint wash of sunlight to wink over the rain-soaked grass. The ball sailed straight through the rising mist, coming to earth in the middle of the fairway, a fair distance from where it had been struck.

It appeared the Viscount's thoughts were finally focused on the task at hand, so they played the next few holes with little conversation other than an occasional exchange over distance and choice of clubs. The lengthy silences had none of the overt tension of their previous outings but were of a much more companionable sort, the result of a certain hard-won comraderie winning out over the initial combativeness. Her experience as a caddie told Derrien to do nothing to break such a mood, but as they turned to play the inward nine she couldn't help but blurt out a question that had been dogging her thoughts for longer than she cared to admit. "It's, er, said you are engaged to a . . . beautiful lady, sir. You must be—well, you must like her very much."

Marquand's head came up with a jerk, and he nearly stumbled over a twist of ragwort that spilled out over the edge of the fairway. For an instant he appeared taken aback, then his expression changed into one of unholy amusement. "So, lad," he said with a slow smile, "you have an interest in the opposite sex after all? I was beginning to fear that your thoughts never strayed beyond the links."

Derrien felt her cheeks go very crimson.

"No need to look embarrassed, Master Derry. At your age, it would be most unnatural of you not to show a healthy curiosity. Is there something specific you wish to ask?"

The sound she made came out as a strangled squeak.

He chuckled. "I imagine that a well-favored lad like you has no need for explanations as to what takes place between a man and a woman who have a certain attraction for each other?" He paused in his steps, his brow raising slightly. "Or are you Scots really as impervious to normal desires as your flinty hills are to the elements?"

She was most grateful that he didn't demand a translation of her initial confused mumblings, but his look made it clear he expected something more to follow.

"N—no. That is, I imagine we are no different than most in that regard. What I was wondering was . . . what it is like to be in . . . l—love."

It was the Viscount's turn to stutter. "Er, well as to that . . ." He cleared his throat, but it was several more moments before he made a reply. "Marriage is a good deal more complex than mere emotion, Master Derry. Especially for one in my position."

Her mouth went a bit dry at the carefully worded answer. Suddenly it was very important for her to know the truth as to his feelings for Miss Dunster. "But surely you must feel some sort of . . . regard for the lady, to think of tying yourself to her for the rest of your life?"

His lips twisted in a strange sort of smile. "Of course I feel a regard for Miss Dunster. She is possessed of beauty, intelligence, poise, and charm. All the qualities that a man could wish for in a wife."

Derrien felt a sudden flood of relief! His words expressed the highest praise for his intended—but surely no more. It seemed that for whatever reasons the Viscount had made his declaration, one of them was not because his heart was irrevocably attached.

Viscount Marquand does not love Miss Dunster, she repeated to herself.

Why was it that the words flowed as sweet as wild heather honey over her tongue?

She swallowed hard, trying to find some rational explanation for the sudden pounding in her chest. She was simply relieved, she told herself, because she didn't wish to see him hurt. Yes, that was it. She had come to see him as a sensitive, caring individual rather than a cold, unfeeling aristocrat—in short, she had come to see him as a friend.

A slight cough interrupted her thoughts. "Does that answer your question, Master Derry?"

She didn't dare look at him. "Yes, sir. I think I understand what you mean." She fumbled with the hickory shafts resting on her shoulders. "Uh, it's the baffing spoon you'll be wanting next, sir. See that steep bunker you must clear? Well, it is wider than it appears and behind it . . ."

Marquand did not look at all unhappy to be leaving the questions of his personal affairs behind. With a tad more eagerness than usual, he took the club and executed the shot she suggested. "Now, I imagine I should take my heavy iron and chip the ball toward that crest on the right. The slope of the green will then cause it to roll close to the hole."

Derrien nodded.

He finished his play and made a note of his score with

the pencil and paper he kept tucked in his pocket. "Not bad," he murmured.

"Don't start thinking of your score, sir," she cautioned. "There is plenty of time to tally up the strokes once we are finished. It's best to keep your mind well away from such thoughts while still out on the course."

She was soon ruing such sage words of advice when, after knocking a decent drive at the start of the sixteenth hole, he handed back the long spoon and started to follow her down the fairway. "So, Master Derry," he began, "you've asked of my lady. What of you? Have you someone who has set your heart aflutter?" He grinned. "Someone whose sweet lips you dream of tasting?"

She nearly choked. "I . . . No!"

"No?" His grin widened. "Come now, don't be shy, lad. Surely you Scots are as wont to discuss the ladies among yourselves as we Englishmen. And as I have a bit more experience in that field than I do at golf, I might even be able to offer you some advice on how to coax a kiss from the object of your affection." He reached out and took playful hold of her chin, tilting her head up toward him. "Though I would think, lad, you would have no trouble stealing whatever you wanted from the opposite sex. Have you yet enjoyed a grope or a tumble in the hay?"

She twisted out of his grasp. "Sir!" Her voice very nearly slipped into a squeak. "This was not exactly the sort of topic I had in mind when I said to think of something other than the score."

Marquand let his arm fall to his side. "Since such teasing appears to make you uncomfortable, Master Derry, I shall—" His words cut off abruptly as Derrien's hand came up to rub at her chin and his gray-green eyes suddenly focused on her lips with an intensity that caused her to take a step back.

"W—what is it?"

It was a moment before he spoke. "Nothing," he muttered, letting out a harried sigh. "It's just that at times, you remind me of someone, but I can't for the life of me figure out who." Then he shrugged. "Well, it's of no importance, I suppose."

They had come up to his ball and Derrien was grateful for the excuse to look away into the distance. "Take the middle spoon, and aim for the church spire."

He did as he was told and the shot landed on a slight rise, just left of the sloping bunker on the left.

"Excellent placement, Lord Marquand!" came a voice from behind a thicket of tall gorse.

Both of them started as Philip stepped out from the flickering shadows. "I thought I might come out and check on what sort of progress you have been making, sir," he continued after taking several puffs on his briar pipe. It might have been Derrien's imagination, but it seemed the older man's gaze lingered first on the Viscount and then on herself for a touch longer than necessary. "But I see there is nothing to worry about. You are making great headway."

"Due in no small part to my caddie."

Derrien felt her face growing quite warm at the Viscount's praise. Good Lord, she must be more careful! The man was beginning to have entirely too much effect on her person, that a few simple words could cause her blood to heat.

"I have to admit that your Master Derry has taught me a thing or two," continued Marquand. "Though honesty compels me to confess that when we started, I would not have thought it possible. The lad has turned out to be quite a diamond in the rough."

A decided twinkle came to Philp's eyes. "Yes, Derry has quite a number of hidden facets."

She restrained the urge to kick him in the shins. "We had best start play if we are to finish the eighteenth hole before the rain returns."

"Yes, it was, shall we say, a rather amusing performance." Hertford tapped the ash from his cigar and a smug smile formed on his lips. "Perhaps, as Lord Marquand appears to have a fondness for sand, he should consider taking himself off to Jamaica, where the beaches are said to be quite extensive." As he paused to take another glass of champagne from a passing waiter, a harsh chuckle bubbled up from the depths of his throat. "And after I add Woolsey Hall to what I've won from his father, the poor fellow may have no choice but to seek his fortune in the New World, for there will be precious little of the Linsley inheritance that will not be in my possession."

Derrien couldn't help but overhear the last of the marquess's words as her steps brought her close to the far end of the terrace, where a group of gentlemen had gathered to blow a cloud without disturbing the ladies. She came to a halt in the shadows of the pergola spanning the graveled path and drew in a sharp breath to keep from making an angry retort. Several of Hertford's cronies who had come up with him from London laughed at the barbed quip, but the locals, having no fondness for their English neighbor, remained silent.

The unseemly bragging appeared to set particularly ill with Sir Twining, who gave a grunt and raised his shaggy brows a fraction. "You seem quite sure of victory, my lord."

A trail of smoke rings drifted out toward a row of espaliered pear trees, followed by a mocking chuckle. "As you said yourself, golf takes years to master."

"Indeed." The Baronet exhaled slowly. "But Lord Marquand does not have to master the game, merely acquire enough skill to be able to post a credible score for one round. From what I have heard, his efforts are beginning to add up."

The number that he mentioned caused the Marquess to choke on a lungful of smoke.

"Not bad for a neophyte," continued Twining with a nonchalant shrug of his shoulders. "Not bad at all. It seems that this contest may prove to be more interesting than anyone imagined." He paused to quaff a bit of his ale. "But naturally, as a keen sportsman, you must welcome the challenge of meeting an opponent who can test your skills."

More than one flinty smile appeared among the Scotsmen.

Derrien, too, found her scowl replaced by a look of grim satisfaction as she watched Hertford drop the stub of his cigar and grind it out under his heel with a show of unconcern.

"Any beginner may manage to put together a few lucky shots in practice," he drawled. "It would take a player of far greater expertise than the Viscount to give me cause to doubt the outcome of the real match." The smirk, however, had disappeared from his face, replaced by a certain tautness around the mouth. With an exaggerated shrug, he turned abruptly and stalked off down the steps leading to the gardens.

Trapped by his sudden approach, Derrien had no choice but to shrink farther into the shadows and hope that he might pass without noticing her presence. His gaze, however, seemed to catch on the gently swaying climbing roses entwined around the weathered wood. To her dismay, he halted, then drew closer to the fragrant blooms.

"Why, Miss Edwards, out for a stroll by yourself? Your interest in gardens must be great indeed." He lounged up against one of the thick posts and raked his eyes over her rigid features. "I, too, am fond of pretty blossoms, especially ones that have a show of color to them. They are far more interesting than some bland, fragile thing that loses its life the moment it is picked."

She gave a low snort of disgust. "I told you, sir, your likes and dislikes are of no earthly interest to me."

"No?" His brow rose in mock surprise. "But I was so looking forward to cultivating an acquaintance. Of all the local flora, you are quite the most intriguing."

"And of all the local fauna, you are quite the most despicable." Derrien made a move to go around him, but he shifted to block her path.

"A prickly little thing, aren't you," he continued in a low voice. "But I have a great deal of experience and skill at plucking—"

"Surely you would not be thinking of disturbing even a petal in Playfair's garden? I don't imagine he would look kindly on that sort of thing."

Hertford spun around. "Marquand, you are becoming a—"

"Thorn in your side?" suggested the Viscount. "No doubt I am proving a good deal more troublesome than the drunken fools you are used to fleecing."

"Just what are you implying?" snarled the other man.

"Why, only that this time, the cards you have dealt to yourself may not prove as lucky as usual." He stepped around to the other side of the pergola and offered his arm to Derrien. "Miss Edwards, perhaps I might escort you to a part of the garden that would be more to your liking?"

She flashed him a grateful smile. "Yes, I find this spot is not at all to my taste."

Eyes narrowed in anger, the marquess watched them walk away. "Ha! You haven't a prayer's chance in hell of coming up aces," he muttered to himself. But the unconscious furrowing of his brow showed that a seed of doubt had been planted.

"Are you quite sure, Nora?" Ferguson's eyes flooded with worry. "If he tells your mother, there is no telling what extreme measures she might take in order to keep you away from me."

"Oh, I have no doubts that she would be well capable of ordering me trussed up and carted back to London in a locked carriage if it would do any good, but like you, Charles, I am no longer a green adolescent, afraid to stand up for myself. I am of age and I cannot be forced into wedlock, no matter what my parents may desire. This time I shall inform them in no uncertain terms that my mind is made up—that is, if it comes to that." She drew in a deep breath. "But I believe Lord Marquand is too much of a gentleman to betray us."

Ferguson looked unconvinced. "A lover scorned is not going to be inclined to be overly magnanimous, my dear. Especially as he is losing not only a lovely bride, but a rather large dowry. And word has it that he could well use the blunt."

"I . . . I hadn't thought of that." She bit her lip, "Still,

I have made up my mind, Charles. For the sake of my own honor, I cannot leave in such a cowardly fashion, without telling him to his face."

He sighed. "You must do what your conscience dictates, Nora, but—" The rest of his words turned into a warning cough as another couple approached near to where the young professor was ostensibly explaining the history of the Roman sculpture on display on the outdoor terrace to the English visitor.

"A splendid evening, is it not, Ferguson?" Indeed, the unsettled weather had been blown out to sea, leaving in its wake a certain clarity to the fresh air and slanting light that most of the other guests were taking full advantage of by enjoying a stroll in their host's extensive garden.

"Yes. Splendid."

"And you, Miss Dunster. You are enjoying your visit to Scotland?"

She fixed the local magistrate and his wife with a brilliant smile. "I couldn't be more pleased with how things have turned out." Her lips twitched slightly as she stole a glance at Ferguson. "Not at all what I expected."

"Yes." The man looked a trifle confused by her words but gave a knowing nod. "Of course. Scotland is, er, like that."

Ferguson coughed again, this time to hide a smile. "I believe I have kept you away from Lord Marquand far too long, Miss Dunster." He began to scan the graveled walkways for some sign of the Viscount. "Shall we look for him . . ."

"Oh, as to that, I saw his lordship not five minutes ago, sitting by Cupid's fountain with Miss Edwards."

"Ah, thank you." Ferguson offered his arm to Honoria and led her toward a path bordered by a low hedge of clipped yews. As soon as they were out of earshot, he added, "I see I owe my friend Miss Edwards a debt of gratitude. Though I asked her help just that once at the picnic, she has since taken it upon herself to keep Marquand occupied, even though she cannot abide the fellow, so that I might have an easier time finding some private moments with you." Before Honoria could answer, they turned a corner and the circular marble fountain, topped by a statue of the impish archer, came into view. "Here is your opportunity, my dear. I hope you are not making a terrible mistake."

Her hand tightened on his sleeve. "So do I, Charles," she whispered. "But it must be done."

The Viscount was so intent on showing the sketches to Derrien that he was unmindful of the crunch of gravel until it was nearly upon him. He shot to his feet on seeing his intended bride and the young professor standing close by, spilling the papers in his lap onto the ground in the process. An audible oath nearly slipped from his lips as well. Hell's teeth, he growled to himself, surprised at the stab of disappointment that cut through him on realizing that his private chat with the young lady was at an end. Why, he was not nearly finished with pointing out all the nuances of the plan. Still, he carefully masked his feelings with a tight smile as he bent to retrieve the papers. "Ah, there you are, Honoria."

"I was wondering where you had gone off to, sir," she said softly. Her eyes went from Derrien's barely disguised scowl to the drawings in his hands before turning back to Marquand's rigid face. "But perhaps I am interrupting—"

Ferguson kept her from retreating a step.

"No, no. That is, I was merely showing Miss Edwards an . . . an idea or two. For a garden." He shifted uncomfortably from one foot to another, then gave himself a mental kick for behaving like a guilty schoolboy. "Forgive me, my dear," he went on, though his eyes unaccountably strayed to one of the golden ringlets that had escaped the silk ribbon binding Derrien's curls. "I must have lost track of the time."

"Adrian . . ."

His head jerked up.

"Might Miss Edwards allow me to steal you away for a moment?"

Derrien reached up and plucked the plans from his

fingers. "Of course. Lord Marquand had already been more than kind in taking the time to scribble a few pointers for me."

The Viscount had to restrain the urge to tuck the errant wisp of hair behind her ear. "Ahhh . . ."

"Derrien, perhaps you would care to walk down to the lake before it becomes too dark," offered Ferguson quickly. "The marble folly is particularly pretty at this time of the evening."

She stuffed the sketches into her reticule and got to her feet. "By all means, Charlie."

Charlie, thought Marquand with some irritation. Were they on such easy terms that she always called him Charlie? And who had given the impertinent fellow the right to use her given name? Or take her arm in such an intimate way, he added to himself, on seeing the other man's hand tuck around her elbow as they strolled away. It was a moment or two before he remembered he was not alone. "Er, would you care to be taken inside, my dear? The breeze appears to be freshening."

"No. Actually I prefer to stay here, my lo—Adrian. There is a matter of some importance that I wish to discuss with you."

He forced his eyes away from the receding figures. "Why, of course," he said, trying to sound as if she had his full attention.

She hesitated.

"Yes?" he encouraged.

"This . . . is very difficult, my lord."

He couldn't help but notice how her eyes were shuttered, and sought to avoid his own, unlike those of another young lady, which made no attempt to hide their feelings behind a heavy screen of proper manners. Good Lord, had he really wished for such a bride, he thought with a surge of regret, one who was so wooden that she couldn't unbend enough to say his given name. His jaw tightened as he recalled that Miss Edwards called her friend Charlie.

His intended bride's head was bent, her blond tresses knotted in an artful arrangement that called to mind a comment by Ellington. *Not a hair out of place*—that was what Tony had said. Suddenly, all he could picture was an unruly wheaten curl, dancing free of any hairpin or other constraint, and all his simmering frustrations finally boiled over. "Oh, for God's sake, Honoria, tell me what's wrong! We used to be able to talk to each other with a modicum of honesty, at least, even if there was little . . . passion between us."

The young lady's eyes flew up. "But Mama has always said that gentlemen do not want—"

"The devil take it! Your mama has no clue as to what a man might want from a lady! She is a bitter, withered stick, with not an ounce of sap left in her. Don't let her drain the life from you as well. Now out with it!" He tried to temper the heat of his words with a grim smile. "After all, how bad can it be?"

She tried to smile as well, though her lips were quivering. "Actually, I doubt it can be any worse." It took several moments for her to go on. "I feel you have a right to be told to your face, for you are an honorable, n—nice man, your—Adrian." A tear spilled down her cheek, however her chin held firm. "But I . . . I don't love you. I love Ch—Charles Ferguson. We are going to elope tomorrow and be married by nightfall. I should like to ask that you don't alert my mother as to our plans, but even if you do, I shall contrive to break away."

"Ferguson?" Stunned, he could only stare at her in blank disbelief. Of all the possible reasons for the subtle changes in her behavior, this was certainly not one that had ever crossed his mind. He supposed he ought to be experiencing some sense of outrage or betrayal, but instead he found himself wondering whether Miss Edwards knew, and whether she would be . . . disappointed in her friend Charlie's sudden change of heart.

Honoria's shoulders had stiffened, as if in expectation of an onslaught of anger. When he said nothing more, she relaxed slightly and ventured a nod.

"Ferguson," he repeated softly. "Well, I see I have been quite a fool about a number of things—most especially in thinking that there was little passion burning inside that lovely bosom of yours, my dear." His mouth pursed in a grimace of self-mockery. "I must admit, the man looks to be a rather ordinary fellow, but to have captured your heart in so short a time—"

"My heart has been his since I was sixteen," she whispered.

Marquand fell silent, his brow knitting in some confusion. "But—"

"You have a right to hear the whole story, sir. After all, you were very nearly sold damaged goods." She swallowed hard. "Charles was engaged as my brother's tutor after his studies were finished at Cambridge . . ."

A lengthy explanation followed, including all the unvarnished details of the first, failed flight to the north. "So you see, since you made your formal declaration I have been torn with guilt. I felt you had to be told the truth, and yet my father and mother had drummed it into to me that it was my duty to bring you up to scratch—especially as my earlier transgression had threatened to leave them with nothing to show for the effort and expense of grooming me to attract a lofty title."

He looked at her with real sympathy. "I know all too well what it is like to be at the mercy of your parents. I only wonder that your father didn't hold out for a Marquess or even a Duke?"

She choked back a sob. "He would have liked to, but I had already refused to consider several proposals and I suppose he was getting rather desperate to have me safely wed. You may think me naught but a scheming mercenary, yet I saw no choice but to obey my family's wishes." Her voice steadied. "I had at least vowed that I would never accept anyone for whom I could not feel a real regard. I thought with that as a basis, I could be a . . . good wife to you." She started to twist the end of her gown's sash between her fingers. "But then we came to Scotland. When I saw . . . Charles, whom I never thought to lay eyes on again, I realized that none of the things I had been taught to hold dear—money, fancy gowns, lavish balls, imposing homes, and armies of servants—were half so important as spending my life with someone I truly love."

Marquand continued to stare at her nervous fumblings for several seconds, then his lips began to quirk upward. "Bravo!"

"Y—you are not angry?" She looked up in some amazement. "I had thought that you might feel a blow to your pride, even though I sensed there would be no blow to your heart."

"No! I'm delighted for you." Indeed, he suddenly felt nearly giddy with emotion, though in all honesty, he had to admit to himself, it was more from relief than any nobler sentiment. "Truly I am. Lord, you have more courage and bottom than most men! You deserve to be happy. Really happy. I wish you all the best."

Honoria threw her arms around his neck. "Oh, Adrian, you are truly the most wonderful of men." She sobbed, the tears now flowing with abandon.

He gave a low chuckle. "Better have a care, my dear. I might lose my heart yet."

She smiled, dabbing at her cheek with the silk handkerchief he had thrust into her fingers. "You know, you might consider simply crying off," he continued. "Ladies are allowed to, you know. Perhaps I could help you convince your parents to accept Ferguson's suit, and you would be able to have a proper wedding, if that is what you would like."

Honoria shook her head resolutely. "It is most thoughtful of you, Adrian, but Father would never agree. No, Charles and I have no choice but to carry on with our plan. I am so sorry, for I know that it will cause you no little embarrassment." She lifted her tearstained face. "B—but I should like to think that we might remain friends."

Friend rather than bride—Marquand suddenly realized that was exactly how he would prefer to think of Miss Honoria Dunster. He gave her a quick hug, ending with a light kiss to her cheek. "You may count on it, my dear. Besides, after all the peccadilloes of my own parents, a touch more scandal attached to the Linsley name will hardly signify." He squeezed her hand. "Don't worry, I shall survive. I shall also have a little talk with your parents and convince them that a scandal will hardly reflect well on them in London. Together we should be able to scotch the worst of the rumors, so that you and Ferguson do not suffer unduly from your decision. You'll see—it will all work out for the best."

"Thank you, Adrian."

"Thank *you*," he murmured under his breath.

Tucking her hand in the crook of his arm, he turned their steps back toward the main house. "Er, I hope that Miss Edwards will not be, well, too hurt by your Mr. Ferguson's sudden defection. It appears they have a certain rapport that the young lady might see as something deeper than mere friendship."

Honoria gave him a rather odd look. "I don't think you need worry about that. I am quite sure Charles is not the gentleman for whom Miss Edwards has a developed a *tendre*."

"Oh." Marquand mulled over her words for the next few steps. He found himself strangely relieved that the young lady's heart did not appear in danger of being broken by the young professor, yet Honoria's words were not quite the complete reassurance he would have liked.

If Miss Edwards did not feel any romantic inclination for her friend Charlie, then who the devil was she interested in?

From their vantage point on the raised terrace, Derrien and Ferguson could just manage a glimpse of the shadowed couple by the fountain if they moved to the far corner of the railing.

"What's happening?" asked the young professor in a nervous whisper as he made a show of admiring the view out over the lake. "You don't think the Viscount is the sort of man to . . . strike her in a fit of rage, do you?"

Derrien ventured a peek through the tall rosebushes and caught sight of Honoria throwing her arms around Marquand's neck. "Ahhh, it does not appear that you have need to worry about *that* sort of physical contact."

She hesitated for a fraction. "In fact, neither of them seems angry in the least."

Her observation caused him to abandon all pretense of detachment, and he rushed over so that he might take a look as well.

"Ahhhem." He choked down a strangled cough. "Well, it looks as though Nora was right, and Marquand is not going to kick up a dust over the news."

Derrien bit back a tart retort as she watched the Viscount return the embrace of his intended bride—*former* intended bride, she reminded herself with some vehemence—then skim his lithe fingers across the flawless skin of Honoria's face. The gesture, though gentle and tender, made her feel as if she had been slapped.

What a fool she had been! To imagine that the Viscount was not in love with the beautiful young English lady, just because she wished it to be so, was absurd. More than absurd, it was hopelessly naïve. Hadn't Marquand himself remarked that relations between those of his social standing were . . . not something she would understand. She had clearly misunderstood his words on the golf course.

Why, look at what was right before her very eyes! She forced her gaze back to the two of them, feeling a sudden stab of jealousy at seeing Honoria still in his arms. At this moment, he was probably trying to change her mind with another gentle caress and a declaration of undying affection. And even if he did not convince her to give up Ferguson, his own heart would no doubt always be in thrall to such a paragon of perfection.

She blinked, surprised to feel the sting of tears against her lids. The state of Marquand's heart was really of no concern to her, she reminded herself. She need only worry about such things as the strength of his arms or the stamina of his legs.

"You are a lucky fellow, Charlie, to be so sure of your lady's feelings—and your own." She said in a tight voice, stepping back abruptly from the screen of roses. "Good luck on the morrow. I wish you all the happiness in the world." Giving a quick peck to his cheek, she turned and made to leave.

His head jerked around. "Wait! You aren't really abandoning me to face them by myself?"

"I'm certainly not needed here." Her eyes pressed closed once more, just for an instant. "And I'm afraid something in the night air has given rise to a nasty headache, so if you'll excuse me, I think I shall ask Aunt Claire to take me home."

"But—"

Leaving him no time to finish his pleading, she hurried off toward the open French doors.

Ferguson was still puzzling over her odd behavior when Honoria and Marquand appeared at the edge of the terrace and came up the steps. As the young professor shuffled in awkward embarrassment, the Viscount reached out and gave him a firm shake of the hand.

"Congratulations, Ferguson. I hope that you realize what a truly fortunate man you are."

Before he could answer, Honoria stepped around to his side and slid her hand in his. "Charles," she said, looking up at him with face aglow. "Adrian has been most noble about all of this, and wishes us nothing but happiness."

He stammered a suitable thanks while returning her rapturous smile.

"Is not Miss Edwards here with you?" inquired Marquand after a moment, searching among the potted roses for any sign of the young lady. "I thought I might offer to escort her in to supper so that you two might have a bit more privacy."

"You needn't bother, sir. Derry said the evening chill was making her feel a trifle ill, so she's gone home." Loath to admit that they had indulged in a bit of spying, Ferguson omitted any mention of what they both had observed down by the fountain.

The Viscount's brow creased slightly. "Ill? She didn't seem in the least ill—" His words suddenly cut off. "*What* did you call her?"

Ferguson looked confused. "You mean Derry?" he repeated. "Why, it's just an old childhood nickname that some of her good friends still use at times.

Marquand's mouth twisted in a wry smile. Lord, what a devilishly odd evening! The night air must be affecting his own head as well, to have him imagining, even for an instant, that there was any connection. . . .

No. It was impossible. Absolutely impossible.

He cleared his throat, hiding his disappointment at finding her gone by carefully straightening the folds of his cravat. "Well, it is a shame that Miss Edwards—or Derry, or whatever she prefers to be called—has succumbed to some malady. I have the feeling that it is not often that she allows *anything*, most especially a mere megrim, to get the better of her."

Chapter Thirteen

"Well, although you are not usually moved by adagios and crescendos, it appears last evening's musicale has served to help banish the recent flatness in your mood." Ellington picked up the newspaper and, with a small smile at the Viscount's bent head, signaled to the lone servant to bring him some tea.

Marquand ceased his cheerful humming and looked up from his sketchbook. "What? Oh, er, yes." He couldn't help but grin. "I suppose I am feeling a bit more in harmony with things, Tony."

Indeed, even though the streets outside their residence were enveloped in an oppressive gray fog so thick that its weight was nearly palpable, the Viscount felt as though some heavy mantle had been lifted from his own spirits, leaving him feeling more unfettered, more carefree than he had felt in ages. He nearly chuckled out loud. It made not a whit of sense—his carefully chosen bride was about to elope with another man, he was on the brink of losing his beloved Woolsey Hall, and the plans for the Duke's gardens were still mere scribbles of ideas. And yet, the coil of worry that had tied him in knots of late seemed to have unaccountably fallen away. Somehow, he found he was almost looking forward to the challenges ahead. His pencil hovered for a moment in midair as it suddenly occurred to him what else it was that he was looking forward to.

Another meeting with the deucedly distracting Miss Edwards. Her moods were nearly as quixotic as the Scottish weather, yet her intelligence and her passion overshadowed all her snappish words and hoydenish behavior. She was hardly the pattern card of predictability that he had thought was desirable in a young lady, and yet she intrigued him.

No, that was not entirely correct. He had to admit that what he was feeling was more than—

"I take it your work is progressing well, then?" His friend had leaned over to glance at the rough drawings on the open page of the sketchbook.

Marquand's thoughts were jerked away from his musings. "Er, well, I must admit I am rather pleased with how everything is turning out so far."

"I'm glad to hear it." There was a faint rustling as Ellington turned to an article on the latest news from the Continent. He read on for a bit, then slowly laid the newspaper aside when the humming began anew, this time louder and distinctly recognizable as Beethoven's "Ode to Joy." Ignoring the pot of tea whisked in from the kitchen, he fixed the Viscount with a quizzical look. "Adrian, if I didn't know you better I would be sorely tempted to think you had been indulging in a wee nip of the local spirits before breakfast. It seems you are in remarkably good humor, given that along with everything else, on the morrow you are set to finally match up with Hertford on the links."

The melody died away. "Well, now that the moment is at hand, there is precious little point in stewing over it. I shall just have to trust my newly acquired skills— and my caddie."

"How very sensible." With a slight shake of his head, Ellington made to pick up where he had left off reading, yet his expression clearly indicated that the sudden change in his friend's disposition was still a matter of puzzlement. He forbore further mention of the subject, however, deciding that whatever the reason, the odd cheerfulness was a distinct improvement over the moody scowls Marquand had been wearing since they had crossed the border.

Both gentlemen waved away all but the simplest offerings from the cook and a comfortable silence descended over the meal, each one turning his attention to the

paper in front of him. It was only when the servant returned a while later with fresh tea that the clink of china
and faint notes of the *Ninth Symphony* were interrupted
by a discreet cough.

"Yes, Rusher?" said Ellington, noticing that his friend
didn't even look up from his work. The man bent down
and whispered something that caused the English lord to
rise abruptly and follow him from the room. It was only
a matter of minutes before Ellington returned and took
his seat, though his expression betrayed the fact that the
breakfast room was perhaps the last place on earth he
wished to be at the moment.

"Ahem." He cleared his throat loudly enough that
Marquand stopped his sketching.

"Is something wrong, Tony?" asked the Viscount mildly,
on taking one look at his friend's rigid countenance.

Ellington sucked in his breath. "I'm afraid I have just
received some rather disturbing news."

"What do you mean, they are gone!" Philip lay his file
aside and hurried over to the crowded racks. "The Viscount's clubs are always put away in the same place,
Tommy."

The lad pulled at a lock of the carrot-colored hair that
spiked up from his brow. "I know werry well where
them's supposed to be, Mr. Philp, but have a look fer
yerself. I tell ye, they ain't here."

The master checked along the entire row, needing only
a quick glance at the myriad shafts and grips, all of his
own handiwork, to verify that Marquand's set of golf
clubs was indeed missing. He continued on into the back
room, and a deep frown slowly added another few wrin-
kles to his leathery face as he surveyed the small side
door standing slightly ajar. Closer inspection revealed
that the iron hasp had been pried away from the weathered wood, allowing someone to have entered the Argyle
Street shop during the night.

"Hmmmm." Philip reached into his pocket to pull out
his pipe.

"Why, the dastard!" Derrien had appeared at his

elbow and was now peering at the heavy padlock which hung useless from the damaged metal.

"It appears we have done our job a little too well." He blew out another ring of smoke. "Alexander Cheape mentioned that he had overheard one of Hertford's crones making inquiries of one of the lads as to the Viscount's recent scores." His eyes strayed to the splintered boards and a wisp of a smile played at his lips. "Apparently the numbers were not quite to his liking."

"This is nothing to make a joke of, Hugh," muttered Derrien. "How is Lord Marquand going to play without his clubs? There is no time for you to fashion another set—the match is to begin tomorrow at eight in the morning."

"I am well aware of the seriousness of the situation."

She bit her lip, feeling a sudden surge of outrage. All of them had worked too hard to let such a cowardly deed ruin everything. The Viscount simply couldn't be allowed to be beaten in this manner. Not only had her dear friend Philp promised Lord Bowmont that they would do their best, but she had given her word as well, that she would do all in her power to see the dastardly Hertford defeated.

But it was not merely anger that caused her chin to jut out in defiance of the odds. She understood perhaps better than anyone what Woolsey Hall meant to Marquand, and how important it was to him to restore it to its former glory with his own hands. It was no matter that he had chosen another young lady to reign over it with him, she was determined to see him free to fulfill his dream.

The thought of the Viscount bringing his bride to his ancestral estate caused a lump to form in her throat. Oh, it was not going to be Miss Honoria Dunster, but it would be someone equally beautiful and polished. How could it not be, given his title and his position in Society?

Still, she wanted more than anything to help him win back his home. Far from being the arrogant, jaded, selfish gentleman she had expected him to be, Marquand had proven himself to be kind, capable, and intelligent. More than that, he had also revealed himself as a remarkable talent, possessing a sensitivity and creativity far beyond any she had ever dreamed of discovering in any man, much less an English lord. She had come to see him as a kindred soul. A friend.

She bit her lip. Actually she had come to see him as much more than that, despite all her previous resolve, and the utter hopelessness of her true feelings.

"Hugh," she said in a steely voice. "I have an idea."

"And what news is that?" Marquand's eyes had already returned to the page before him.

"The devil take it, Adrian, this is deucedly hard to begin." Ellington ran a finger around his collar. "That was one of Hylton's servants at the door. He had an extremely urgent message regarding . . ." The words trailed off in some confusion. "Er, perhaps you should read the note that he brought." His fingers hastily pushed the folded paper across the polished pine table as if it were a hot coal.

Marquand took it up and, after a cursory look at the handwriting, dropped it by his cup. He began to add some shading around the outlines of a fountain.

"Good Lord, Adrian!" sputtered the other man. "I really think you had better read the damn thing. I doubt you will be bursting with song when you have learned its contents."

The Viscount looked up, a ghost of a smile on his lips. "On the contrary, Tony. I am delighted that Honoria and her Mr. Ferguson have found such happiness with each other. I imagine that by now, they are safely wed and finally free of all interference from her unbearable parents."

Ellington's jaw dropped in astonishment. "Y— you . . . know?"

"Yes. She told me last night."

"And you are not upset?" His voice revealed more than a tad of incredulity. "Or . . . angry at how all your carefully constructed plans have come crashing down like . . . like a house of cards?"

Marquand's smile became more pronounced. "Well, I suppose I have learned myself the foolishness of counting on cards to do one's bidding."

His friend shook his head. "Is there something bewitching in the Scottish air? Or has Hecate and her cronies added some special potion to your tea? You hardly sound like the same fellow I left London with."

"Perhaps I am not," he said softly, surprising himself as much as his friend.

Philp stroked a callused hand along his jaw. "You think it possible?"

Derrien gave a nod.

"Well, it's worth a try."

The two of them slipped out through the damaged door into the small alleyway behind the shop. Making their way through the swirling fog, they followed one of the narrow cobbled streets down to the harbor at the mouth of Kinness burn. The weather had caused a number of fishermen to delay their departure, so despite the early hour, the tavern next to the docks was far from empty.

"Wait here," ordered Philp as he turned to enter the place.

"But—" Derrien decided not to argue on seeing his expression, but it was with great impatience that she paced over the slick stones while he was inside. After what seemed like an age, Philp finally reemerged from the smoky confines of the public room, two hulking fellows trailing in his wake.

"Charlie Kidd, ye say, Hugh? Aye, I know where we're most likely ta find the scamp." One of the men flexed his bulging biceps as he spoke. "Ye think he's mixed up in sommink havey-cavey with Lord Hertford?" When Philp nodded, the man's broad mouth twisted in a ferocious frown. "Then Angus and me will have it out of him, see if we don't."

"It's the clubs we want, Jock, not just his deadlights darkened," piped up Derrien. "Remember to give them the purse, Mr. Philp." As the leather sack exchanged hands she went on. "You find that coins will work even better than threats with Charlie. Use both, and I'm sure he can be convinced to tell us where they are." She paused for a fraction. "Of course, they might have been tossed in the Bay, but I don't think so. Not yet."

"That's right smart of ye, Derry me lad," growled the one called Jock. "I'd wager as well that the clubs haven't been destroyed, even if that's wot the Marquess ordered. Charlie would figger they're too valuable not to stow away for some future profit."

"We appreciate your help, Jock. Somehow I think you and Angus will manage to be a tad more persuasive than myself and Master Derry."

Angus gave a short guffaw and shifted his prodigious weight from foot to foot. "Aye, don't ye worry. We members of the Society of St. Andrews Golfers must stick together, especially when someone dares go up against the likes of you, Hugh. Go on now, you and the lad head back te yer shop. Wee Charlie will turn over them sticks if he has 'em, or he'll at least tell us wot he knows. Count on it." A quick grin flickered over his meaty features. "What say ye ta owing us each one of those bonny long-nosed putters ye make if we find yer man's clubs?"

Philp returned the grin. "Auch, with pleasure."

"Now the scamp has no chance of wiggling out of trouble," said Jock. He turned to his companion. "Nor do ye, Angus, me friend. With such a magic wand as Hugh's club in my hand, you'll not best me again on the links."

"Ha! If you think . . ." The two men tramped off, their barbed teasing about each other's golf game soon muffled by the thick mists still blowing in from the North Sea.

"That was bonny thinking, lassie, to enlist the two of them to help out," said Philp as they started back up the hill toward the shop.

"You heard Angus—golfers stick together. And they are the biggest golfers I could think of, not to speak of being the toughest fellows around the docks. Why, the only men who dare getting in a fight with them are each other." Her nose crinkled in some satisfaction. "It would serve Charlie right if they wring his traitorous little neck."

"Let us simply hope that they return with Lord Marquand's clubs." After another few steps, he spoke again. "I have been thinking—Roxburghe is of a size and build with the Viscount. If the missing clubs do not turn up, we could send word to Floors Castle and I'm sure the Duke would gladly lend us the set I made for him."

"Don't worry, Hugh. I have a feeling we shall not have to resort to that."

Sure enough, not an hour had passed before Jock and Angus appeared at the shop door, a large bundle wrapped in oilcloth carried between them.

"Nary a scratch on them, Hugh," said Jock in a low voice as he handed the clubs over.

"You could almost say the same for Charlie," added his companion with a short chuckle. "He's taken off to pay a wee visit to his aunt in Dunfirmline. Decided the climate would be a bit better for his health, didn't he?"

"Aye, you could say that." He returned the purse to Philp. "We didn't need to make use of this."

"Well done, my friends." Philp began to unwrap the wet cloth and wipe the beads of moisture from the varnished hickory. "Come around in a week's time for your putters. However you both must promise me they won't end up knocking up against each other's skulls."

"Auch, no, Hugh. A club fashioned by your hand is far too valuable to risk damaging in that way," replied Jock with a grin. "Gud luck in besting Lord Hertford. We had best be getting down to the boats now that the weather looks to be breaking."

Derrien came over to help inspect the Viscount's clubs as the two men headed back down to the harbor. They were indeed undamaged, save for a slight tear in one of the sheepskin grips which could easily be repaired in the space of a quarter of an hour. Philp went to trim up a piece of new leather. When he returned to his bench, he found that she had already cut the old one away and was carefully rewrapping the underlisting.

"Don't wind yourself too tight, Derry," he cautioned, taking in the pinch of worry on her face. "There is really nothing more you can do now, save going out and helping him play a good round tomorrow."

"I know that, Hugh." She looked up, her blue eyes darkened by the crosscurrents of concern and some other, more unfathomable emotion. "But it . . . means so much to him."

"And to you, lassie. Does it mean so much to you, now?"

Derrien ducked her head without answering.

"Hold the shaft firm while I apply a layer of glue," he said after a moment's pause. Though he pressed here no further, his expression became quite grave, though he, too, bent low to hide his thoughts.

The work was nearly done when Marquand walked into the shop. His hair was damp from the lingering mist, drops clinging to the raven locks that curled over his brow and against the collar of his upturned jacket. Derrien had to force her eyes away from his chiseled profile, away from how the fine wool clung to his broad shoulders, and how his buckskin breeches molded to the contours of his muscled thighs.

Fool! she chastised herself. She must get a grip on such wayward thoughts. It wouldn't do to see the Viscount as aught but a golfer who needed her skill and expertise, unclouded by any sort of emotional distraction. No, she must never show that she . . . loved him.

Her fingers tightened around the tapered shaft with such force that her knuckles went white. There—she had finally admitted it, if only to herself. She had done the unthinkable and fallen in love with the English lord, despite all her resolve to the contrary. It made no sense at all, but suddenly the mere sight of him was enough to set her heart to pounding and her breath to coming in ragged gulps, no matter that her feelings would never be reciprocated. But somehow she must keep yet another secret hidden away, for one more day at least. That should not be so impossible—after all, she had a good deal of practice in the art of disguise.

"Is something amiss?" Marquand's gaze shifted from Philp's drawn features to Derrien's rigid shoulders.

"A slight accident, but nothing to be concerned about, my lord." Philp finished applying a wrapping at the butt of the shaft. He held the club out at arm's length and inspected his handiwork. "It's already fixed," he added with a curt nod of approval.

"Good, for I should like to get in one more round of practice before tomorrow." His lips curled into a faint smile. "That is, if it is agreeable to you, Master Derry?"

"Of course," she mumbled, turning to gather up the rest of his clubs from one of the other workbenches.

"Mr. Philp," continued the Viscount. "I wondered whether you might have the direction of Mrs. Edwards and her niece, as I have been given to understand that you are a friend of the family?"

A long spoon clattered to the floor.

"Er, yes, I am . . ." Philp took a moment to light his pipe.

On seeing the older man's furrowed brow, Marquand added an explanation. "Miss Edwards was taken ill last night, and I thought I might inquire as to how she is feeling when I am finished here."

"Oh, as to that, I happened to stop by their home on my way to the shop this morning so I can assure you that Miss Derrien is fully recovered," he replied in some haste. "Enough that she has . . . gone out for the day. I don't believe she is likely to return much before dusk."

"I see." He shrugged. "Well, I'm happy to hear it is nothing serious."

Nothing serious, thought Derrien as she opened the door. Perhaps it was true, and that as soon as the dratted man returned to London, her heart would indeed fully recover. But somehow she doubted that the image of his piercing eyes and lean face would be quite so easy to banish as a bout of sniffles.

As he lingered in conversation with Philp, she ventured another surreptitious look at his face, searching for some sign of his own bruised emotions. Ferguson had sent word that he and Miss Dunster had slipped away before dawn, so surely the Viscount would have heard of it by now. However, far from exhibiting any brooding sighs or mooning eyes, Marquand looked to be in excellent spirits as he traded one last quip with the master. Her brow furrowed. It was odd—he certainly was not acting like a gentleman whose heart had just been broken.

She shifted the clubs on her shoulder and resolved to keep her thoughts from straying off the fairway. Golf, for all its maddening nuances and frustrations, was at least a game whose rules she understood.

Marquand surveyed the terrain that lay between him and the distant flutter of cloth. "Ditch skirting the right side fairway, those two bunkers, The Spectacles, guarding either side of the far approach, and a tricky swale sloping off behind the flag," he muttered under his breath. After tossing up a few blades of grass in order to better gauge the direction of the breeze, he turned to Derrien with a furrowed brow. "I should think the best play is to lay up with the heavy iron and count on the baffing spoon to get me close on the next shot."

She handed over the club with a bob of her head. "Very good, sir. You are beginning to think like a true golfer."

He chuckled. "High praise indeed, Master Derry." Having finally elicited some reaction other than a curt yea or nay, he was now trying to pry a smile from the lad, but to no avail, it appeared. The young caddie merely lowered his head in the face of the gusting wind, the floppy tweed cap hiding even more of his smudged face than usual, and hurried off toward the ball. Marquand followed at a more leisurely pace, thinking not for the first time what an odd fellow the lad was. Well, it was of no great concern, he told himself, for at the moment his thoughts were not the lest inclined to dwell on a boy, odd or otherwise.

Quite the opposite.

Though he knew it was important to stay focused on his golf, it was deuced difficult not to let the image of an unruly profusion of golden curls come to mind. Or a pert freckled nose. Or a most interesting set of lips, no less expressive for all their softly rounded curves. The devil take it, he found his blood was beginning to heat, and not from the exertion of the game. This would never do—he must banish all thoughts of that intriguing face, at least until after tomorrow.

And then? With a harried sigh, he forced such a question out of his head as well. It was the state of his golf swing that should be of utmost concern at the moment, not the mysteries of his heart.

The ball lay just where he meant to place it, perfectly positioned for an easy chip over the bunker and a gentle roll down to the flag. His caddie was already holding out the baffing spoon. Taking a deep breath to steady his concentration, Marquand stepped up, studied the distance, and let fly with an easy stroke. The stitched featherie arced up over the hazard and came to earth on the fringe of the green, its spin pulling it to within a scant foot of the hole.

The Viscount repressed a wry grimace—perhaps he should let his mind wander after all!

"I hope you are saving a few of those for the morrow," Derrien said rather gruffly.

He strolled over to his ball and tapped in for his par. "Never fear, Master Derry, I am beginning to feel as if Lady Luck is not such a fickle harlot after all."

It seemed that a strange look flickered over the caddie's half-hidden features. "That's a strange sentiment, coming from a gentleman whose intended bride has just run off with another man," she blurted out.

There was dead silence for a moment, then his lips quirked upward. "Yes, I suppose it is." He handed the putter over and slowly took the scorecard from his pocket. "You seem to be as skilled at ferreting out information as you are in driving one of Mr. Robertson's featheries. But be that as it may, the subject is not one I intend to discuss with a mere child."

"I'm *not* a child—" she cried hotly, before her jaw clamped shut and she bent over to retrieve the ball.

"Come, let's keep our attention on golf and not brangle with each other," he said lightly. "We've only to endure each other's company for another day. Surely we can do that without the usual fireworks."

Derrien didn't answer. Shouldering the clubs with an exaggerated hitch, she turned and stalked off toward the next hole without so much as a glance in his direction.

Marquand deliberately finished filling in his score before following her. A low oath, chased by an exasperated sigh, sounded under his breath as he regarded the angry tilt of the shoulders up ahead and the peculiar sway of the slim hips— Hell's teeth, those hips! What was it about them that seemed so hauntingly familiar?

Suddenly he froze in his tracks. Some mad impulse made him call out the caddie's name, for the first time omitting the word "master" before it.

"Derry!"

The shout caused Derrien to stumble. The clubs spilled to the ground as she spun around, shock and confusion evident on the set of her lips.

Those lips!

Marquand covered the distance between them in a few quick strides. As his hand closed around the slender arm and his head bent closer to the dazed face, it occurred to him that if he was wrong, what he was about to do was quite likely illegal as well as insane.

It took only an instant to know he was not about to be committed to Newgate—or Bedlam. The lips parting under his were most definitely not those of a lad, nor did the rounded swell of curves pressing up against his chest resemble any part of the male anatomy. The mere touch of them against his own taut form drove him to deepen his kiss, his tongue stealing inside her mouth to taste the faint tang of salt air and an indescribable sweetness. For one long moment, she seemed unsure of how to react, but then her mouth softened in response to his embrace, a bit hesitantly but with an undercurrent of the same hot passion he felt flaring up inside him.

Her fingers came up to his shoulders and at first he thought she meant to shove him away. Then suddenly they were entwined in his long dark locks, pulling him into an even more intimate embrace. A muffled groan escaped his lips as her slim hips arched into his, and his hands tore away the tweed cap so that he, too, might revel in the sensuous silkiness of her curls. His lips broke away to trace the trail of freckles across her cheekbones, leaving her free to nibble at the lobe of his ear and utter the softest of whispers.

The sound of his name shattered whatever was left of his self-control. With a hoarse cry, he sunk to his knees, dragging her, unresisting, down with him. Her arms were still wrapped around his neck and as he leaned forward to cup her softly rounded bottom, his hard arousal rubbed up against her in such a way that he feared he might disgrace himself like the callowest of schoolboys.

He shifted slightly and his hands began roaming toward the inside of her legs. She gave a soft moan and through a haze of desire he realized that had she been wearing skirts they might well have been tossed up around her glorious thighs by now. Perhaps it was just as well that breeches on a woman were beyond his experience, for he was not quite sure that he could bank the flames of passion that her touch, her kisses, her very scent had ignited.

It was the damp chill of the rain-soaked ground that finally brought them both back to earth.

With a sudden squeak of embarrassment, Derrien slithered out from between his knees and scrambled none too steadily to her feet. Marquand rose as well, his own legs betraying a slight wobble. For several moments they stared at each other in awkward silence. It was Derrien who wrenched her eyes away first, and then kicked at the shaft of the long spoon that had fallen close by her feet.

"Damnation!"

Though the tension between them was nearly as thick as the low bank of fog rolling in from Eden Estuary, Marquand couldn't help but give a twitch of a smile. It was so utterly like her, to react in a way no female of his previous of acquaintance would ever dream of. A month ago he would have been shocked beyond words, he admitted. But now, he found himself wondering why all the perfectly behaved misses from the sparkling ballrooms seemed rather flat and faceless in comparison.

"You know, Miss Edwards, only men are supposed to swear like that, not proper young ladies."

"Well as you can clearly see, I am hardly a proper young lady," she replied rather acidly, slapping at a cluster of curls that had fallen over her cheek.

"The sporting of breeches and boots might raise a few eyebrows, I admit," he said in a low voice. "But let me assure you that other than that, every bit of you is most definitely a real lady."

Her face turned a dull scarlet as she bit at her lower lip, still swollen with the passion of his kisses. "Th—this wasn't supposed to happen," she whispered, struggling to hold back tears.

"But it did." He raked a hand through his own disheveled locks, hoping the gesture would help restrain the urge to pull her close to his chest once more and soothe the confusion from her pale face. "Lord, it is as if your Scottish witches of yore are making sport of us mere mortals, what with all the misunderstandings and masquerades that have been going on," he muttered. "The problem is, this little charade certainly changes—"

"No!" She forced her eyes back to meet his. For a moment he was awash in the tempest of emotions swirling in their blue depths. "Please, you must not tell! Why, it would ruin everything!"

"Miss Edwards, by all rights, I should be furious at your deception."

"Why?"

He hesitated and felt himself sinking, as if caught in the shifting sands of the deepest pot bunker. "Well, er—"

"Hugh asked me to do this because I'm the best caddie here." She bent to pick up her cap. "What does it matter that I'm not a male? Has my advice or guidance been any less valuable?"

It was the Viscount who was forced to contemplate the tips of his boots.

As if sensing that things were turning to her advantage, she pressed on. "Besides, you are hardly in a position to criticize me for disguising my true identity in order to engage in something I'm good at."

"Miss Edwards, that's playing dirty, to use my—"

She played her trump card. "Look, you want to win, don't you?"

He drew in a deep breath. "So you are suggesting we continue as if . . . none of this has happened?"

"As you said yourself, it's only for another day, then we can both forget about the entire thing. I've already agreed with Hugh that it is time for Master Derry to disappear from St. Andrews."

Marquand tried to fathom her expression, but once again her features were submerged in shadows due to the replacement of the damn cap. Would she really find it so easy to forget their time together? His jaw tightened as he shifted his gaze from the subtle contours of her face to the myriad nuances of the linksland, with its rolling fairways, sandy bunkers, tall grasses, and hearty gorse. Here they had traded taunts, shared laughter, endured frustration, made mistakes, and sweated through hard work in order to celebrate some small measure of progress. At times it hadn't been easy, but they had somehow managed to see it through together. He knew it would be no simple matter for him to simply excise these few weeks from his mind, as one would tear an unsatisfactory page out of a sketchbook, crumple it up, and toss it away.

But perhaps she did not care for the broad strokes and delicate shadings of their relationship. After all, he knew quite well what her sentiments were regarding titled English lords.

What he wished he knew more clearly were her sentiments regarding *him*.

"And anyway," she continued in a halting voice, "I . . . I imagine that what just happened was only due to the fact that you are overset over . . . Miss Dunster."

"You think I kissed you because I was thinking of Miss Dunster?"

Derrien swallowed hard. "W—why else? She is a perfect picture of a fine, highborn lady—beautiful, poised, and n—not a hair out of place." Her fingers fumbled to tuck another errant ringlet up under the wool brim. "While I am an outspoken country . . . brat in breeches."

Once again it took all of the Viscount's considerable self-discipline not to sweep her up into his arms and continue where he had left off until she could make no mistake about whom he was thinking. Instead, he took several steps closer so that he could reach out and cup her chin. "Miss Honoria Dunster may be beautiful, poised, and perfectly groomed, but she cannot swing a long spoon, loft an errant shot out of the briars, or knock the ball to within a foot of the flag on the eighteenth hole. Pick up the clubs, brat. We have work to do."

Chapter Fourteen

It was barely past dawn, and yet Derrien had already let herself into Philp's shop. By the dim light of a single oil lamp, she inspected each of the Viscount's clubs for any minute flaw which might affect play. Once assured that none of the grips were loose or cordings frayed, she ran a cloth dampened with a mixture of linseed oil and pine spirits over the hickory shafts and shaped hawthorn heads to remove any residue of salt or dried mud.

Having passed the scrutiny of both master and caddie, a dozen new featherie balls lay on the adjoining workbench, waiting to be pocketed for play. She tucked them in her jacket, along with a pouch of sand, then looked around. There was really nothing else that needed to be done, but to keep busy she began to polish the forged heads of the irons, even though there was not a trace of dirt to be seen on them. A soft sigh escaped her lips as she worked. It was not difficult to find something to occupy her fingers, but it was not nearly so easy to keep her mind engaged on any of the mundane tasks she tried to appoint for it.

Her thoughts kept straying to things she knew were best forgotten, like the feel of Marquand's lips on hers, a warm gentleness underlying the searing passion, or the intoxicating scent of him, a subtle mixture of woodsy spice with overnotes of bay rum and leather which even now, in mere memory, were doing strange things to her breathing. Her fingers tightened on the cold iron. After today, all she would have of the Viscount were memories. She would have to picture in her mind's eye the way the salty gusts ruffled his hair against the upturned collar of his shirt, the way damp linen clung to the corded muscles of his back.

No, that was not entirely true, she realized. There was one tangible remainder of his brief presence in her life in the carefully folded sheet of drawing paper that lay tucked away inside her sketchbook. The thought of it was nearly her undoing, and it took all of her self-control to keep from sobbing aloud. It was something she would always treasure. Those deft lines and shadings, so simple yet so eloquent, showed more than just a masterful talent for mixing color, texture, and shape. They revealed the toplofty English Viscount to be, in reality, a true artist, passionate and sensitive as well as boldly original in his thinking.

They also drew a picture of someone who was kind and generous. That he had taken the time to study her paltry efforts and offer such meaningful suggestions showed him to be far different from the cold, selfish aristocrat she had expected, just as his surprising personal revelations had shown him to be far more vulnerable than she had ever imagined. He was just the sort of man she had secretly given up hope of ever meeting—one whose intellect and imagination were matched by his compassion and his sensitivity. One for whom she could feel nothing but utmost respect and regard.

The club dropped into her lap. Who was she trying to fool? What she felt for Marquand was something much more than respect or regard. Her lip curled into a mocking grimace. Lord, she had really made a mull of things, for despite all her resolve to the contrary, she had fallen in love with an English lord. She supposed she deserved the dull ache that now settled in her breast for thinking, with all the hubris of youth, that she was immune to the intricacies of the human heart.

A sound nearby caused her head to come up. Philp took a seat at his workbench and slowly unfolded a heavy linen napkin on its scarred pine top. "You had best eat something, lassie. You are going to need your strength." He held out a hot scone, refraining from any comment on the faint trace of a tear or two on her pale cheek.

"Thank you, Hugh." Derrien managed a bite of the rich, raisin-studded pastry and found to her surprise that she was indeed hungry. The rest of it disappeared rather quickly.

A small smile played on his lips. "That's a good sign, you know, that you aren't so nervous as to have lost all appetite." He broke off a bit for himself. "So, have you confidence that you and your man have a chance?"

A part of the scone was reduced to crumbs between her fingers. "What Lord Marquand lacks in experience he makes up for in determination, Hugh. And this match is of the utmost importance to him. So, yes, I think we can win. We shall no doubt need a little luck as well as skill, but it can be done."

"I think his lordship is not the only one with pluck," murmured Philp. "Now best put on that cap of yours before he arrives—"

"He knows, Hugh."

"What?" Philp nearly choked on his last bite. "How?"

"He . . . guessed." She hoped her cheeks were not as flaming as they felt. "I think he said it had something to do with m—my lips. But it doesn't matter. I convinced him he had no choice but to keep me as his caddie for today." She essayed a note of humor. "At least Master Derry shall take his leave of St. Andrews with a grand flourish—and hopefully with a much plumper pocket."

The master carefully folded the napkin so as to keep the remaining scones warm. "Derry, I hope that—"

His words were interrupted by the arrival of the Viscount. He shook a few drops of rain from his jacket as he stepped inside and latched the door. "Good morning," he called, rubbing his hands together to ward off the early morning chill. "A bit of a squall has blown in, but it looks to be clearing off shortly." As he approached the workbench, he paused to sniff the air. "That smells delicious, Miss Edwards, I hope that you are going to share some of your treats with me . . ." A tinge of color rose to his cheeks as he realized how his easy banter might be interpreted. "Ahhh, that is, what I mean is—"

Philp saved him from further embarrassment. "I should

hope you've taken more than a bit of scone for your
breakfast, sir. It's going to be a long day."

"I have," he admitted with a sheepish grin. "My friend
Ellington threatened to tie me to my chair until I polished off Cook's porridge, several shirred eggs, and a
platter of gammon. Falling faint with hunger will not be
the worst of my worries."

"Still, you are welcome to the last of Mrs. Hamish's
creations. She is accorded to be the best baker in town,"
said Derrien, taking great care to match the Viscount's
light tone.

"I shall take your word for it." Marquand took a seat
next to her—much too close for her own peace of mind.
She quickly looked back down to the golf club in her
lap, in hopes that his perceptive gray-green eyes would
not see what she feared was so clearly written on her
face.

Philip picked up his pipe and stowed it in one of his
pockets. "I had best toddle along and fetch Duncan
Brewster from his table." He gave a curt nod to the
Viscount. "As captain of the Society of St. Andrews
Golfers, he shall serve as judge for the match. He's a
good man—an authority on the rules and scrupulously
fair."

"Above temptation as well?" asked Marquand in a
low voice. "The Marquess would no doubt be willing to
be quite generous."

"Aye, you may count on his honesty. Of that I'm
certain."

"Good. Now, I only hope I may count on my own
rather suspect skill as well."

"You have become a good golfer, sir. Stay focused and
relaxed. Remember to think of the shot at hand, rather
than the outcome and you shall do fine. Oh, and between
shots try to think of something other than golf." The
master looked slowly from the Viscount to his caddie. "I
have a feeling in these old bones that all is going to turn
out well, my lord." With that, he took his leave. "You
are expected at the first hole at eight," he added over
his shoulder before closing the door. "Don't be late."

Derrien's head was still bent, the iron in her hands fast becoming burnished to a silvery glow. Marquand began to toy with the grip of his putter. "All is in readiness?" he asked, more to break the silence than because he feared she might forget anything.

She nodded, still not daring to look up.

There was a slight stirring as he shifted his seat on the bench. "You know, with all the recent, er, events, I have not had a chance to properly thank you for all you have done. It cannot have been an easy task, putting up with my clumsy efforts and foul moods, not to speak of the sort of rough teasing I would not have dreamed of inflicting upon a female's ears." He cleared his throat. "I—I know you have soldiered through it out of loyalty to Mr. Philp and the young ladies who have suffered at the hands of Hertford, rather than out of any regard for me, but nonetheless, I am terribly grateful for your help. Without it I am well aware I wouldn't stand a chance." There was another fraction of a pause. "I would hope that in spite of all our differences and disagreements, we might cry friends."

Friends? Oh, how she wished they might be much more than that. However, she supposed she must be satisfied with it. After all, a hoydenish little hellion was hardly likely to inspire any more passionate response when the Viscount had the likes of Miss Dunster and other polished London belles to choose from.

"Of course." Her voice was carefully schooled to reveal none of her inner turmoil. "I have thought of us as a . . . a team for some time now, sir."

He gave a strange sort of smile. "Have you now? I am glad to hear it."

Despite a firm resolve to keep a cool demeanor, she couldn't help but ask, "I imagine that whatever the outcome, you will be leaving St. Andrews as soon as the match is over?"

"Yes, Tony and I must return to London as soon as possible. I'll be hard-pressed as it is to finish the preliminary sketches for the Duke's commission."

"I am sorry we have not had much of a chance to

discuss your work, sir. I—I hope that you might be kind enough to send me a copy of your essays when they are published."

"You shall be the first to see them, I promise." A flare of emotion lit in his eyes before they strayed to the club in her lap. "I think you may leave off working on that, unless you intend on using it for a mirror."

"Oh!" She gave a short laugh. "I guess I am more nervous than I care to admit." Laying it in the pile with the rest, she stood up and fumbled in the pocket of her breeches. "We had best be on our way. But first, sir, I wanted you to have this." A thin silver chain lay in the palm of the hand she thrust forward. Attached to it was a silver charm in the shape of a thistle, its design and detail wrought with exquisite craftsmanship. "It is the symbol of Scotland and it . . . well, it reminded me of you and your gift with gardens," she said with halting awkwardness, her voice barely above a whisper. "It has always brought me good luck, so perhaps it will do the same for you."

She looked away quickly after he took it up, wondering if he thought her ridiculous—or worse—for such a forward gesture. No doubt a proper young lady would never dream of acting in such an impulsive way, but then again, she thought with an inward sigh of resignation, the Viscount was well aware of her hoydenish ways.

But Marquand did not seem to be put off by the gift. He slowly undid the clasp and put it around his neck, carefully tucking the chain in beneath his shirt and Belcher neckerchief. "Why, thank you, Derry."

She drew in an involuntary breath at the sound of her name on his lips. The sound turned into a slight gasp as those same lips brushed against hers with a gossamer touch. Before she could react any further, the kiss—if that was what it was—was over and he had drawn back, a strange expression on his features.

"I have always thought of Lady Luck as someone I would not care to have an acquaintance with, but recently I find I have changed my mind about that." Under his breath he added, "Indeed, I have changed my mind about a great many things since arriving in Scotland."

The carved silver felt cool against his skin at first, then quickly took on a comforting warmth. It was a bit like the young lady before him, he mused. Her quixotic moods seemed to run just as hot and cold regarding himself. At times, he was sure she was, at best, indifferent to his presence, if not outright annoyed at being forced to endure his company. Yet once in while there was some hint of emotion on that lovely face that gave him cause for hope that her feelings were not altogether negative.

A team, she had called them. He suddenly realized he wanted nothing so much as to continue the partnership far beyond the coming few hours of the golf match. What a complete ninny he had been to imagine he desired nothing more than a prim, well-behaved young lady whose thoughts never strayed beyond the borders of propriety!

Good Lord, Tony had been right after all, sensing that as his own odd behavior bucked the rigid rules of the *ton*, a conventional match would never do. But it had taken a delightfully different sort of female to show him just how flat his life would have been, leg-shackled to someone who could not share his passions or his dreams.

He was tired of disguising his true self. He longed to share with Miss Edwards the full range of his ideas, to hear her opinions, to engage in spirited debate, even to argue. His mouth quirked in a grudging smile. That they would exchange heated words on occasion he did not doubt, as he recalled some of their run-ins on the golf course. She was not one to back down from what she thought was right, even when facing someone twice her size who wielded a wooden club! Rather than finding the notion disturbing, he found himself once again admiring her courage, her grit in challenging the overwhelming odds against her, from her birth to her love of the links, to her desire to excel in a world deemed closed to those of her sex. He understood her struggle, for he didn't accept Society's strictures any more than she did. They were, quite simply, oddities in their own worlds.

They were, quite simply, perfect for each other.

The trouble was, Marquand was not certain of how to convince her of such a thing. He stole a glance at her face as they hurried down Argyle Street. She wore so serious an expression that his hands tightened in his pockets. How the devil was he going to win her regard? Perhaps it was a start that she admired Mr. Chitley, but he wished for her to like Adrian Linsley as well!

The wash of the surf on the rocky strand warned that the golf course was just around the corner. With grudging reluctance he forced the conundrum of Miss Derrien Edwards to the back of his mind. Right now he had better start concentrating on winning something rather less ephemeral than a lady's heart.

The showers had already blown out to sea, and a faint hint of blue sky was showing at the horizon as they drew near the first hole. Lord Hertford had not yet appeared, but Philp and Brewster were standing with their backs to the gusting breeze, along with a small group of spectators that included Ellington and Lord Bowmont, who had arrived in town the night before.

Brewster graced Marquand with a barely perceptible nod. "I see you, for one, are prompt, sir." He pulled a large steel pocketwatch from his waistcoat, and after a deliberate wait of nearly thirty seconds, he continued with a loud announcement to the small gathering. "It is exactly eight o'clock. The Marquess has exactly five minutes before he will incur a penalty—"

"That won't be necessary," came a lazy voice from some distance off. Hertford sauntered over at a leisurely pace, followed by his caddie and several cronies. Handing his walking stick to one of them, he removed his cloak with a theatrical flourish and tossed it over as well. "It seems poor Marquand has trouble keeping a grip on his possessions—word around town is that he has just lost his intended wife to another man," he remarked to one of his friends in a voice clearly designed to be overheard by all present. "A shame that he is about to lose his ancestral estate as well."

A slight twitch of his jaw was the only reaction from Marquand.

"Gentlemen, let us not waste time," interposed Brewster in a trice, seeking to keep things from heating up too quickly. "A sporting wager is to be decided by a round of golf between the Marquess of Hertford and Viscount Marquand," he went on to inform the spectators. "It will be scored as match play—each hole shall be won by the man shooting the fewest strokes. If the scores are the same, the hole will be deemed a tie. After eighteen holes, he who has won the greater number of holes shall be the winner. If there is a tie at that point, we shall play on until someone emerges victorious on a hole. Any questions as to rules or procedure shall be decided by me. Is that clear?"

Both gentlemen nodded their assent.

"Very well. Who shall hit first?"

A mocking smile spread over Hertford's lips. "As the nominal host, I cede the honors to Viscount Marquand," he replied smoothly, taking advantage of the opportunity to put the pressure on the other man right from the start.

Marquand ignored the other man's sneering tone and gave a nonchalant shrug. "Whatever you wish."

As Derrien brushed by him in order to construct the mound of sand for his ball, she managed to murmur a bit of advice. "The best way to wipe that smirk off his face, sir, is to smack it right down the middle of the fairway. Forget there is an audience and let it fly as I know you can."

After a moment's wait, he stepped up to the new featherie she had set upon the small pyramid. His stomach gave a nervous lurch as he set his feet and waggled his wrists, but then he closed his eyes for a second and took a deep breath, determined not to play into the Marquess's expectation of seeing the ball slice out onto the rocky stand. All was still as the club drew back, swinging up in a wide arc that brought the shaft nearly parallel to the ground. With barely a pause, it began its descent, gathering speed until it was almost a blur as it made contact with the small orb of stitched leather. A low

murmur ran through the crowd as the ball lofted high
and straight into the air, finally coming to ground a tad
shy of one hundred eighty yards from where it had
been struck.

"That should give the dastard something to think
about." Derrien reached for the long spoon and clapped
it over her shoulder, flashing a big grin in his direction.

The Viscount couldn't help but grin back, and the
twinkle in her eye caused him to add a quick wink.

A team, indeed. Suddenly all the tightness seemed to
ebb away, numbing fear replaced by calm confidence. He
stepped aside to allow the Marquess to hit, further
buoyed by the barest flicker of doubt that passed over
the other man's features.

Hertford's drive landed not far from his own, on the
left fringe of the fairway but well out of trouble. The
two caddies exchanged scowls, then hefted their full com-
plement of clubs and started off.

The match had begun in earnest.

The first few holes were a seesaw affair, with Hertford's experience balanced by Marquand's raw athleticism and Derrien's sage advice. Neither man could gain
a clear advantage, and they reached the sixth hole tied
at two, with two draws.

It was there that the first dispute arose. Marquand's
drive hooked into the light rough, but Hertford, anxious
to take advantage of his opponent's mistake, made a big-
ger one of his own. Overeager, the Marquess jerked his
arms through a fraction too fast, sending his ball much
farther left than that of the Viscount's, right to the edge
of a thick tangle of gorse. With a muttered curse, he
threw the club to the ground and motioned his caddie
to be quick about mounting a search for the errant shot.

"The hole is yours, sir," said Derrien with some satisfaction as she and Marquand started down the fairway.
"I saw where it landed—not even a ferret would manage
to find a ball in there, even with considerably more time
than the allotted five minutes."

It was with great surprise, therefore, that several moments later they heard a cry ring out from the other

caddie. "Here, my lord, I've found it!" He waved to Hertford and pointed to a spot at his feet, several yards to the right of the hazard, where sure enough, the stitched featherie sat, not only free from any entanglement in the bushes but in a perfect lie, atop a short clump of grass.

Derrien said a particular word that would have caused the Viscount to choke with laughter had the situation been different. "If that is the Marquess's original ball, I shall eat it for supper, along with a side of haggis," she added with barely contained rage. Her hand went to her hip as she waited for Brewster and the others to draw near. "Sir, I tell you I saw quite clearly where Lord Hertford's shot landed and it was *nowhere* near that spot," she protested.

Brewster's slight frown indicated he was thinking much the same thing. He hurried over to the ball and bent down to check the marking.

"Ah 'H' with a dot below the crossbar—that's our mark," said Hertford's caddie, shooting a sly smirk in Derrien's direction. "You may see for yourself, sir."

The judge straightened after a moment. "Yes, it appears it is," he said grudgingly. His eyes narrowed with the suspicion that he had just been played for a fool, but since no one had witnessed any transgression, he was forced to allow the fortuitous discovery to stand. "In the future, both lads will wait for the rest of us to help with any search."

The caddie bobbed his head in mock contrition. "Yes, sir."

Marquand brushed a bit of sand from the sleeve of his jacket. "How extraordinarily lucky, Hertford," he remarked dryly as the Marquess made his way toward the spot. "But then again, luck seems to have a way of appearing around you at the most opportune times."

Several voices in the small crowd sounded in muted agreement with the not-so subtle implications of the taunt. Hertford's face darkened but he made no reply. His next shot landed close to the green, and as Marquand also recovered from his spot of trouble, the hole ended in a draw.

"Luck my arse," muttered Derrien when play was finished, this time drawing a strangled cough from the Viscount. It took a considerable amount of self-control not to let his thoughts—and eyes—shift to that interesting spot of her anatomy rather than remain focused on the task at hand. "It is no coincidence that Jimmy wears long trousers rather than breeches," she added.

"Ah, is that how he did it?"

"Aye, I should have kept a closer watch, knowing what a weasel he is, but from now on, he'll get away with no other tricks." Her jaw set. "You've lost a hole because I didn't do my duty well enough."

Marquand wished he could hug her to his chest and tell her, in both words and action, how much her plucky loyalty meant to him, but all he dared was a quick pat on the shoulder. "Don't fret on it, Derry," he said rather gruffly. "I have seen that look in a man's eye on enough occasions, both in the ring at Jackson's and facing the targets at Manton's, to know what it means." His lip curled upward. "Trust me, Hertford is beginning to get a little nervous."

The match moved on to the seventh hole, where the Marquess edged ahead by sinking a long, snaking putt of over twelve feet. Marquand squared it on the next with a wonderful chip to within a foot of the hole, allowing him an easy tap in for par while his opponent needed an extra stroke to finish up. No blood was drawn on the ninth, and both the players and the spectators sensed the tension mount as the turn was made for home.

"Your friend is giving a good account of himself," murmured Lord Bowmount as both Marquand and Hertford paused for some refreshment at a wooden crate set out with several earthenware jugs.

"Aye," replied Ellington, noting with some interest that the Viscount sipped water while the Marquess took a long swig of ale. "But I don't trust Hertford by half, Jamie. He has already cheated Adrian out of one hole and no doubt he has more tricks up his sleeve—or trouser leg."

"We will have to hope that his caddie is a sharp lad, then, for—"

"You need not worry about Derry." Philp took a moment to fill the bowl of his pipe and strike a flint. "You asked me to give Lord Marquand my best, and so I have." He sucked in a mouthful of the fragrant smoke and let it out slowly. "Between the two of them, I have every confidence they'll sort out the wheat from the chaff." With that enigmatic statement, he moved off to answer a query on strategy from one of the other spectators.

Neither gentleman had much time to dwell on the master's meaning, for Brewster called in a loud voice for play to begin on the inward nine.

Chapter Fifteen

It soon became evident that the Viscount's observation had more than a grain of truth to it. Beneath the cocky sneers and smug grins for the benefit of his cronies, Hertford's face began to take on a certain tautness around the mouth, and his step lost a bit of its swagger. The clever comments began to die away, replaced by a fierce silence between shots. And when he stepped up to his ball, there was none of the earlier casual nonchalance in his posture. On more than one occasion, when faced with a tricky shot, his knuckles went nearly white from gripping the club with such force.

Marquand repressed a smile. So the pressure, more acute for its unexpectedness, was getting to the man. That was good. Very good. It was clear his opponent had expected this to be no more taxing than a stroll in the park, but what he had thought was firm ground had quickly turned into a quagmire beneath his feet. A bar of *Beethoven's Ninth* nearly escaped from the Viscount's lips. If he could keep up his level of play, he was sure the Marquess would soon be sunk.

Derrien seemed to sense his thoughts. "Just stay relaxed, sir," she counseled, dropping back to walk by his side on the way to the next hole. "And don't think overly on the score, or the next holes. You have only to play steady and avoid any mistakes."

She ventured a look up at him and flashed a tentative smile, but it was the expression in her eyes that was worth untold words of encouragement. He could see she truly understood that this wager was about so much more than mere assets changing hands between two gamesters.

How he was fighting to save not merely a fortune but something that resonated so much deeper in his soul— the chance to fulfill a lifetime dream.

Then in a rush, it came to him that he no longer wanted Woolsey Hall just for himself anymore. He had been blindly, idiotically wrong to have thought that his life had room for only one passion. Just as he had been a fool to think the power of such emotion was in any way diminished by its being shared. In truth, divided it only grew stronger.

His breath caught in his throat as he realized it was love he was thinking about.

He had carefully drafted plans for his future with all his usual attention to detail, determined to leave nothing to luck or chance, and love had made a mockery of such hubris. He had drawn a perfect model of his intended countess, but all the straight lines and precise angles had been knocked askew by a brat in breeches, with unruly golden curls and an exuberant smattering of freckles across her cheeks.

Luck? Why, right now he counted himself the luckiest man in the world—

"Sir . . . Sir!"

His head jerked up.

"I said, remember there is that large bunker, the Principal's Nose, hidden by the swale on the right," she said in a low whisper. "Make sure to aim well to the left." Her words trailed off as she fixed him with an odd look. "Are you feeling all right?"

"Er, yes. Couldn't be better, actually."

Her brows tweaked up in some skepticism, but she forbore making her usual tart rejoinder and simply reminded him once again to keep his mind on the next shot, nothing more.

Hah! Easier said than done. But as he stepped up to hit his drive, a strange sort of calm came over him. The stitched featherie looked as big as a cricket ball, and before he drew the club back, he knew for certain that the shot would fly true. All at once he knew that he was going to win, not because of his superior skill but because he was feeling, well, inordinately lucky.

After all, the ace of diamonds had already turned up in his hands.

Both drives had been well struck, as had the second shots. The two balls lay close to each other, well within range of the fluttering flag. Marquand was determined to be a tad farther from the hole, so he stepped up to hit first. His club swept back with perfect timing, but just as it started down, a sharp jangle broke the silence. The Viscount flinched slightly, not much, but enough to pull the clubface off-line. The ball popped up weakly, dribbling barely past the fringe of the green.

"Terribly sorry," smirked Hertford. "Don't know how I was so clumsy as to drop my coin purse."

A low buzz of protest rumbled through the small crowd. Brewster scowled as well, but there was nothing he could do about the bit of gamesmanship other than to issue a pointed warning. "May I remind both of you gentlemen that golf is a game based on honor and sportsmanship. It is meant to be played within the spirit as well as the letter of the rules."

The Marquess bowed his head, more to hide a nasty grin than from any true contrition. His shot landed within easy range of the hole. If he were to make what looked to be an easy putt, he would go up by one with only two holes left to play.

Marquand marched up to his ball and took his time in studying the slope of the ground and the grain of the grass, knowing that his only chance for a tie was to make what looked to be an impossible putt.

"A moment, sir, while I go pull the flag for you." Derrien started out in a straight line, then suddenly swerved to the left, so as to approach the hole in a roundabout fashion. The change in direction caused her steps to cross directly in the line between Hertford's ball and the hole. A slight trip caused her heel to dig deeply into the soft turf.

A howl of protest escaped from the Marquess as he realized what she had done. "Look," he cried, pointing to the visible gouge. "The damn brat has ruined my shot! I demand to move my ball."

"Just one moment, my lord," said Brewster firmly as Hertford's caddie made to bend down. "It is an unfortunate accident, sir, but you know quite well that the rules do not allow you to take relief from such a thing. You will have to play it as it lies." Then, trying mightily to wipe the look of suppressed amusement off his features, he turned to Derrien and waggled a stern finger under her nose. "As for you, lad, you should know better than to tread in the line of a putt. See that it doesn't happen again."

"Yes, sir."

When the titter of the spectators had died away, Marquand took his putt, rolling the ball close enough that he had no trouble finishing out in two. Grabbing up his own putter with a muttered oath, the Marquess stepped up for his attempt to take the lead in the match. The alignment was dead-on, the speed was perfect and the ball started off straight toward the center of the hole. Then, as it hit the heel mark, it gave a little jig to the left and Hertford could only stare in white-faced fury as it missed the lip by a scant two inches.

"Terribly sorry, Hertford," murmured the Viscount on brushing past the other man. "Don't know how my caddie was so clumsy as to interfere with your shot." He let out a mournful sigh. "Bad luck."

Behind him, the dull thwock of the putter head caused the heel mark to become a good deal deeper.

The Marquess was not the only one venting his anger. The spectators had already moved ahead with Brewster to the next hole, leaving the players and their caddies to follow along, so when Marquand rounded a tall stand of prickly whin, there was no one to witness that the much larger Jimmy had the collar of Derrien's jacket wrapped in his fist.

"Try sommink like that agin, an' I'll pound yer gob so deep in the mud, ye'll be picking sand outter yer eyeballs fer weeks, Dirty Derry," he growled. He had dropped all of his clubs but one, which cut through the air in threatening swipes, coming closer and closer to Derrien's head.

Marquand started forward at a run, but before he could interfere, Derry's knee came up with lightning quickness, catching the other caddie flush in the groin. With a high-pitched squeak, he dropped to the ground as if struck by a bolt from the heavens.

"If you are trying to keep my thoughts from dwelling too heavily on my game, you are doing an excellent job," quipped the Viscount as his own hand took hold of her and hurried them past the whimpering lad. "Where on earth did you learn that?"

"Ahhh, Charles thought it might be a useful thing for me to know, seeing as I have occasion to wander the moors alone."

Marquand found his estimation of Ferguson rose another notch. "Very useful indeed. But pray, stay close to me for the rest of the match. My physical prowess is being tested quite enough without having to excavate you from a bunker or fish you out of the sea."

"I can take care of myself," she snapped defensively.

He stifled a chuckle. "Yes, I can see that, but still, let us not chance it. You see, I would really hate to have to lug around my own clubs."

A grin chased away the lines of tension pulling at her mouth. "It's only two more holes," she teased back. "I'm sure you could manage by yourself."

His hand gave her arm a quick squeeze. "Go it alone? No, I don't think I care to try. For whatever it's worth, we are in this together. Until the very end."

It was worth a great deal. More than he would ever realize. She made a show of shifting the clubs from one shoulder to the other so that he would not notice the spasm of emotion his casual words had elicited. He could not know how much it meant to her that he, too, saw the two of them as a team, at least for next little while. Her throat suddenly tightened. And after that?

It didn't bear thinking on.

She set her jaw, determined to heed her own advice

about concentrating on the task at hand rather than thinking on the past or the future. There would be time enough for long reflection when he was gone from her life. But now, they had a match to win.

Marquand had already hit and Brewster had begun to stomp in some impatience by the time Hertford appeared, followed by his whey-faced caddie, who was moving in such a gingerly fashion that every few steps drew a bark of rebuke from the Marquess. The long spoon already in his hand, he took a practice swing, casting a murderous look at Derrien as the club cut a swath through the low stubble, before stepping up to make his drive. The ball bounced off into the low rough, but the Viscount's effort had not been one of his better shots so neither man had the advantage.

It remained that way over the course of play. Marquand's second shot found a pot bunker on the left, but Hertford failed to capitalize on the error by putting his own ball in a cart rut near the edge of the road. Both gentlemen took a shot to recover, so they reached the green all square. Two putts later, it remained that way, so the hole was halved.

And so they marched on to the eighteenth hole, the match tied.

Though it was the Viscount who should have shown signs of unraveling, given the magnitude of the stakes, it was Hertford whose nerves had begun to show signs of fraying. Over the inward nine, his play had steadily deteriorated, his once-smooth swing turning jerky, his choice of shots questionable. His experience, which should have allowed him to pull away from a less-seasoned player, was proving no advantage. Indeed it was Marquand who appeared the cooler, calmer of the two.

As they crossed the ancient Roman footbridge over Swilkan Burn, the Marquess was muttering to himself when not snarling at his caddie, and a sheen of sweat had appeared on his forehead although the chill gusts had not abated. Both gentlemen took an extra moment to swing their clubs through the air before Brewster, as

was his wont before each hole, announced the score and
called for play to begin.

Marquand hit first, his drive nothing spectacular but
one that stayed safely out of any hazard. Hertford followed with one of his better shots of the day, and for
the first time in a long while, the sneer came back to
his lips as his ball landed a good distance past that of
his opponent.

Catching sight of the grim set of Marquand's mouth,
Derrien gave him a not-too gentle nudge in the ribs on
her way up the fairway. "It is the next shot you must be
thinking on, not the last one. Remember, you do not
have to play perfectly, just one stroke better than your
opponent," she reminded him in a low whisper. Her
brows drew together in mock anger. "Now hit a good
one, will you? I don't want to have carried these sticks
around all morning for naught."

The quick rebuke coaxed a reluctant chuckle from
him. "Ahh, now that is the Derry I have come to know
and love."

Her heart gave a little lurch. Her words had proved a
distraction, as she had hoped. But so had his! She knew
his quip was meant to be as teasing as her own, so there
was no reason for her feet to suddenly feel tangled or
her pulse to race.

"The middle spoon, don't you think."

It took her a moment or two to recover her wits. She
squinted at the distant flag, then gauged the wind by
tossing a bit of grass in the air. "Take the scraper."

He hesitated. "But—"

She silenced him with a withering look.

"The scraper it is," he said with a twitch of his lips.

For an instant after the ball left the club, it looked to
be flying too far, not only clearing the near hazard with
ease but threatening to carry all the way into the far
bunker. Then a gust of wind kicked up to alter its trajec-
tory and it fell to earth perfectly positioned for the next
shot into the green.

Without comment, Derrien reached for the club and
put it back on her shoulder.

Up ahead, Hertford demanded a club and, ignoring a squeak of dissent from his caddie, let fly. The same swirling wind quickly caught his shot, toying with its progress before causing it to land a bit short of where the Viscount's ball lay. Seeing he had lost his initial advantage in distance by the wrong choice of club, the Marquess flung it aside, nearly dealing the unfortunate lad another blow to his anatomy.

Nerves seemed to be affecting both men. Neither hit a particularly good third shot, and a tense murmur ran through the assorted followers as they took up position to watch the next shot, speculation mounting with each moment on who would manage to eke out victory.

It was Marquand's turn to hit first, since he was farthest from the flag. A tricky swale, the Valley of Sin, made his the far more difficult shot, but on Derrien's advice, he took the baffing spoon and knocked a nicely lofted shot up onto the green.

A chorus of muted whistles greeted the result, and from the number of barely suppressed smiles that appeared throughout the small crowd, it was clear with whom their sympathies lay. Face white with suppressed fury, Hertford stalked forward to hit his own shot. Despite his glowering expression, he still held a big edge, with a lie and angle that allowed him to take dead aim at the hole. But whether from anger or tension, his wrists remained too stiff, causing him to hack at the ball, rather than swing through with a clean stroke. The featherie popped up, and instead of heading toward the flag it hooked left in a wobbly arc before dropping to earth and rolling weakly for several feet.

Derrien stared with disbelief as the ball finally came to rest. "Stymied!" she exclaimed softly. "Of all the cursed bad luck!"

A collective groan sounded as the muderous expression on the Marquess's face turned to one of unmitigated glee. Though Marquand didn't understand the term she had just used, it took no more than a few seconds to see that the situation was not good.

Hertford's botched shot had stopped within eight

inches of his own, but it lay directly in his path to the hole.

Brewster hurried over and hunched down to examine the position of each ball. "Since the balls cannot be judged to be touching, Lord Marquand is not allowed to move his opponent's shot," he announced, with what sounded like some regret.

"Shouldn't we fetch a ruler, to be sure?" demanded Derrien, though without much conviction. At Marquand's questioning glance, she added in a low voice, "If the distance between the balls were less than six inches, the rules would deem them to be touching, and you would be able to move Lord Hertford's shot."

The judge shook his head. "The span of my hand fits between them and it is well more than six inches, lad." He stepped back. "I'm afraid you must play it as it lies, sir."

As the Viscount was required to go first, because he was farther away from the hole, there was little choice but to comply. He took his time circling the balls, careful to study every angle, then returned to where Derrien was standing.

"Hell's teeth, I see no alternative but to give my ball a tap sideways, even though it means losing a stroke, and quite likely the match," he whispered.

Her nose wrinkled in concentration. After a moment, she motioned for him to follow her back to the far edge of the green, where she turned around and crouched down.

The Viscount did the same.

The only sounds were the rustlings of the tall grass and the whoosh of the wind blowing in from the North Sea.

"What are we looking at?" asked Marquand softly, his cheek inches from hers as they both leaned forward on their hands and knees.

"The slope of the ground, the height of the grass and the grain—remember, the ball always tends to roll toward water."

"But, Derry, how can it matter? I cannot go *through* his ball."

"No, you cannot go through it, sir. You are going to go *over* it."

"The deuce take it, Brewster, make him play," demanded Hertford in a petulant voice. "He's taking entirely too long over this." A malicious smile stole over his features. "In any case, it's clear that he is only putting off the inevitable defeat for an extra few minutes."

The judge waved off the whining. "Quiet, sir. That may be so, however the Viscount is well within his rights to take a reasonable amount of time to decide what shot he wishes to attempt."

The sharp rebuke wiped some of the smugness from the Marquess's face, but nearly all of the lines of doubt were gone as well, smoothed away by the assurance that victory was his at last. Turning to several of his cronies standing nearby, he began to make plans for a celebratory ale at one of the nearby taverns.

"*Over* it," repeated Marquand. "How the devil—"

She put a hand on his chest, and he could feel both the softness of her fingers and the hard edge of the silver charm. "You take the short iron, lay the face open to add loft and hit down on the ball."

A spark of rare intensity had kindled in her eyes, reminding him of the glow that came over her features when she studied his sketches or explained her own concepts. He drew in his breath, struck again by the depth of her character, the boldness of her imagination, the courage of her spirit when faced by adversity. Never had he met another person, let alone a female, who not only seemed able to understand his own hopes and fears but whose passion and determination matched his own. He nearly laughed aloud realizing that for all the time he had spent amid silk and spendor searching for the perfect Countess for Woolsey Hall, she had magically walked into his life sporting a floppy tweed cap and baggy breeches.

"It's simple, really. Just land the ball there"—she pointed to a spot four feet away where a slight undulation rolled away toward the flag—"and the slope will carry it right into the hole."

He looked at the ball, then the ground, then her face. "Do you know, I think you would like Woolsey Hall very much. The land behind the gardens also slopes down—"

"My lord!" Her elbow caught him smack in the ribs. "What on earth are you babbling about? You are supposed to be thinking on the shot. And only the shot."

His mouth quirked upward. "Yes, yes. The chip. Up and over you say? Can it truly be done?"

She gave him a smile that caused his heart to skip a beat. "Come now, surely the man with the vision to create the plans for Highleigh Manor has the imagination to see how easily such a thing can be done."

A good number of the spectators craned their necks to see what was going on at the sound of Marquand's amused laugh.

"Easy you say? Precious little has proved easy around you, my dear Derry, but I suppose that is what has made it so interesting—" he murmured.

"My lord!"

"I know, I know, the shot. Well, I should hate to think of disappointing my caddie, so I guess there is nothing to do for it but try." He paused for a moment. "You know, there is something I should like to tell you—"

"Good Heavens, whatever it is, it can wait!" She went over to where she had laid the clubs and picked up the short iron. "Here," she said in a fierce whisper when she had returned. "Now will you kindly shut up and make the plaguey shot so we can all go home? I have no desire to traipse another hole with your sticks on my shoulder."

Several gasps of surprise punctuated the buzz of excitement that ran through the crowd as they realized what Marquand intended to do. The noise quickly died away as he stepped up to his ball and made a practice swing, taking care to lay the face open just as Derrien had advised. The club came back for real, in a short, steep backswing, then he brought it through with just the right touch, soft, but still firm. The ball hopped into the air, sailing over the other featherie with ease and coming to land within inches of where Derrien had indicated. The slope and spin caused it to gather speed when it hit the short grass. Off it rolled, turning left, then right, then at the last moment left again. For an instant it hung on the lip of the hole before dropping in.

A cheer erupted from the small crowd and they surged forward a step or two before Marquand waved them back. With an impassive countenance, he turned to his opponent. "You can still tie if you make your putt, Hertford." His hand came up to rub at his jaw. "But I must say, *I* wouldn't want to be faced with such a devilishly tricky shot. Can't for the life of me decide whether it breaks left or right." It was only when he turned to face Derrien that he gave a quick wink and a grin.

The Marquess could only gape in stunned disbelief. "Of all the bloody luck, you poxy son of a dog," he snarled under his breath. "That was an impossible . . ." His words trailed off in a flurry of impotent curses. Hands shaking, he attempted to study his line, but effort proved to no avail. As soon as he struck the ball it was clear he had pulled it badly. It rolled well left of the hole.

"Goddamn it, I—I've been cheated!" Hertford whirled, the club clenched in his hand, and glared at Brewster. "Marquand's shot was not a fair one! I demand the match be forfeit—"

"As Captain of the St. Andrews Society of Golfers, may I remind you that I am well acquainted with the rules of golf." The other man stood his ground, his expression as stony as Scottish granite. "And there is nothing in them that prohibits such a play." A crack of a smile appeared. "Indeed, it was one of the bonniest bits of shotmaking I've seen in all my years on the links."

"I swear, it was only foul play that allowed—"

"Have a care how you go on, Hertford," interrupted Marquand softly. "Or do you wish to meet on a different patch of grass tomorrow morning? I have a good deal more practice with executing *that* type of shot, so it would prove an even more interesting match of skills."

The Marquess's mouth hung open for a moment, then shut with a near audible gnashing of teeth.

"Don't care for that sort of challenge?" Marquand's lips curled up. "Didn't think so, as it is well known that you don't play any game unless the odds are thoroughly stacked in your favor. Today, however, was not your lucky day." He held out his hand. "I believe you have in your possession a number of things that now rightly belong to me."

Defeated on all counts, Hertford wrenched out a fistful of crumpled vowels from his coat pocket and threw them to the ground. In the same motion, he turned and with a vicious heave sent his putter flying in a high arc out toward the rocky strand. A string of curses trailing after it, he stalked from the field amid a chorus of low whistles and jeers.

"My God, Adrian, you did it!" cried Ellington, pounding his friend on the back as well-wishers flooded onto the green. "Against all odds, you really did it!"

"You showed grit, Marquand. And heart. My congratulations," added Bowmont.

Philp sucked at his pipe and merely smiled.

"What a relief! It's hard to believe it is finally over and we may finally think of taking ourselves home," continued Ellington. "Lord, I am looking forward to the comforts of London, despite the rather quirky charms of Scotland. And you must be even more eager to be gone from here, Adrian, now that you have accomplished all you set out to do." He took a moment to consult his pocketwatch. "Why, it's only noon. With dusk not falling until well into the night, we could have a number of hours on the road if we choose to leave this very afternoon."

Marquand's eyes were glued on a lone figure, fast disappearing along the edge of the first fairway. "Actually, there is one thing still unsettled, Tony." His lips twitched into a wry expression. "Would that I knew the score on that account . . ." He cleared his throat. "I shall see all of you back at the house shortly and we will crack a bottle of champagne to celebrate. But right now, I'm afraid you must excuse me."

*   *   *

He caught up to her along the rocky shore. The gusting wind had freed several golden curls from the confines of the tweed cap and they danced across her freckled cheek, obscuring the expression on her face.

"Just where do you think you are going?"

She didn't turn around. "As you no longer need a caddie, sir, I am free to return to my own concerns. Just as you are finally free to return to London. And Woolsey Hall."

"Yes, I'm . . . free. Quite free."

She swallowed hard, seemingly confused by his odd words. "I—I didn't have a chance to offer my congratulations back there, sir. You showed great courage and determination on the course today, and I'm very happy for you. I know how much this victory means to you." Her voice seemed to be ebbing away. "I—I should like to see what you have in mind for the improvements you mentioned," she added in a near whisper. "Perhaps one day, you might have time to send me a sketch."

"A sketch? Is that all you would like?"

Not trusting her voice, Derrien looked out to sea.

"You know, I have been thinking . . ." He reached out and gently turned her chin toward him. "It seems a great shame to break up such a successful partnership." There was a wetness on her cheeks that could have been flecks of salty spray, or perhaps tears. "I could use a hand if I am to finish the designs for the Duke on time."

"But . . . that's utterly impossible!"

"Why?"

"You can't really mean that you would consider hiring a female to help on one of the most important commissions in all of England. It would cause an uproar if it were to be known."

"By now you should realize I pay little heed to the strictures of convention. What matters is that you have a rare talent and imagination. I should very much like you to consider . . . the position."

"B—but I've never seen the Duke's estate in person, so I could hardly be of much help. Besides, you must return to London right away and I—I have the plans for

Rossdhu House to think about and must arrange a visit there. So you see, it is quite out of the question."

"Ah, a logistical problem?"

She nodded.

Marquand paused. "Well, then it is a good thing we are in Scotland and have no need of reading the banns or even of a special license. If we marry tonight, we could pass by Loch Lomond on our honeymoon before journeying South."

Derrien blinked. "But you can't possibly think of marrying me!"

"Why ever not?" There was a warmth to his expression that belied the chill wind blowing in from the sea. "Is the position of wife so very less appealing than that of caddie or assistant designer? I promise you, the recompense would be a good deal more . . . satisfying."

Her gaze dropped to the toes of her scuffed boots and when she answered, her voice was barely audible. "You know quite well the reason."

"You think you don't fit into my world? Well, neither do I, and thank God for it! I engage in trade, which is no doubt a worse sin than yours in the eyes of my peers!" He hesitated. "But perhaps what you meant was that the idea of a titled English lord for a husband is still repugnant to you. I had hoped you wouldn't hold that against me."

She dared raise her eyes. "You mean . . ."

"I mean that we make a smashing team, my dear Derry. What say you to continuing the partnership?"

She threw her arms around him, trying not to cry. "You mean it? You are sure you don't prefer a lovely lady in silks rather than a brat in breeches?"

"I have never been more sure of anything in my life. London may glitter with all manner of polished ladies, but I have found my true Diamond here in the rough of St. Andrews." He hugged her close and his mouth came down to capture hers in a kiss that left no room for question as to how deeply his passion ran. His hands twined in the silky splendor of her curls, knocking the cap to the ground for the last time, then trailed down the arch of her spine to the rounded curves below. "In fact, you must be sure to wear breeches often in the privacy of our home," he murmured, pulling her hard up against his muscled thighs. "Though I shall insist that they be cut a good deal snugger than these." Then he kissed her again with a searing urgency, his mouth drinking in the heady taste of her. To his elation, she responded with an equal ardor.

As their embrace became more intimate, their hands roaming beneath the folds of damp linen shirts, it couldn't help but occur to him that only a short time ago the idea of behaving in such a mad, impetuous manner would have been unthinkable. What an utter fool he had been to imagine that a conventional bride would be any more right for him than the role of a conventional gentleman in Society! Fortune had indeed smiled on him the day his carriage had headed north. By taking the biggest gamble of his life, he had won something infinitely more precious than any tangible treasure.

"D—does Woolsey Hall have a golf course nearby?" she asked after his lips had finally come away from hers.

Marquand's eyes danced with laugher. "Actually there is a splendid tract of pasture land along the river that I have been eyeing." His boot began to draw a few lines in the sand. "If we move some earth, carve out a series of pot bunkers and plant a few trees to create . . ."

Her mouth came up to stifle any further words. "I should love to see a sketch of it, Adrian," she said between torrid kisses. "But perhaps it could wait until later."

Author's Note

For those readers unfamiliar with the sublimely delightful and infuriating game of golf, a few short short historical notes and explanations may serve to clarify some of the terms and scenes that appear within the story.

St. Andrews is recognized as the birthplace of golf, with references made to the game as far back as the fifteenth century. (Proclamations were issued banning golf on the Sabbath because it was interfering with archery practice, a requisite for defending the realm. A modern day law announcing such strictures might well foment revolution!) The Old Course at St. Andrews is perhaps the most revered spot in golf, a magical tract of flat linksland with a storied history and tradition unmatched by any other golf course in the world. Its bunkers, or sand traps, do indeed all bear names, with "The Beardies," "The Spectacles," "Hell," and "The Principal's Nose" being just a few of the wonderful monikers. All manner of legendary matches have been contested on its fairways and greens, from the feats of Old Tom Morris, the first real superstar in golf, to the play of modern hero Tiger Woods. While there is no account of the match played within these pages, such a sporting wager would not have been impossible.

The equipment used during the early 1800's was a far cry from the high-tech gear available today. Clubheads were fashioned from hawthorn, pear, and apple wood rather than titanium or other high-tech metallurgy. Shafts were made of hickory instead of graphite or steel. The ball was made of bull's hide cured with alum and then stuffed with feathers. Hence it was called a "featherie." Featheries were replaced during the 1850's by balls made of gutta-percha, a gum derived from certain Malaysian trees. Today, technology allows all manner of two piece, wound, double cover, balata, surlyn, etcetera. (Don't ask.) There was no such thing as tees during the early 1800's. The caddie—who carried the player's clubs under his arm rather than in a bag over his shoulder—simply built a small mound out of sand on which the ball was placed. The terms "long spoon," "short spoon," and "baffing spoon" refer to clubs that are are roughly equivalent to the driver and woods of today. Irons were not used as much, and the sand wedge did not come into existence until well into the twentieth century.

The original thirteen rules of golf were drawn up in 1744 by the Company of Gentlemen Golfers in Edinburgh. They were adopted by the Society of St. Andrews Golfers in 1754. The Society has since become the Royal and Ancient Golf Club. Its imposing clubhouse, built in the 1850's, stands at the eighteenth green of the Old Course, and it is still the arbiter of the rules of golf for the world except the United States (where the PGA calls the shots). The list has become considerably longer over the ensuing years.

Some of the characters mentioned in the book are real. Hugh Philp worked in St. Andrews during the time period and his graceful, beautifully crafted clubs were highly sought after even then. Today he is considered the Stradivarius of clubmakers and an example of his work would bring a fortune at auction. The Robertsons were the leading makers of featherie balls for generations. Lastly, I have taken liberty with ascribing a passion for golf to the Duke of Roxburghe and his son, the Marquess of Bowmont. But the present Duke is a fine player with a single-digit handicap. He has recently built one of the finest new courses in Scotland, aptly named The Roxburghe Golf Course, and its signature hole does run along the Teviot and an old Roman viaduct.

As for my own game—well, as more than one of the characters says in the story, golf takes a lifetime to master. If you are lucky. So does writing, so I shall be rather busy for the foreseeable future.